HE WASN'T THER

The doors rolled apart, and Gil Houghton, minister of fisheries and oceans, froze.

Mistress Kali stood, hands on hips, arms akimbo, her domino-masked face lowered so that her eyes regarded his with a blazing up-from-under glare. They were like blue diamonds now, icy and fiery, and they made the pit of his stomach clench.

"I trust I am not late for the meeting," he remarked.

"You are early."

"Good."

"I despise earliness."

Houghton swallowed. His tongue turned to dry rubber.

"I—I can come back, if you'd rather."

At that moment he noticed the long-stemmed scarlet rose tucked into the loop of chain draping her lyrelike hips. With a quick gesture, she plucked it into the air.

Turning so that her body showed in full profile, the uplifted breasts and the stunning ice-princess profile, she lifted the rose to the light. Red mouth compressing, she began snapping off the thorns one by one.

"Approach," she invited.

Created by
WARREN MURPHY
and RICHARD SAPIR

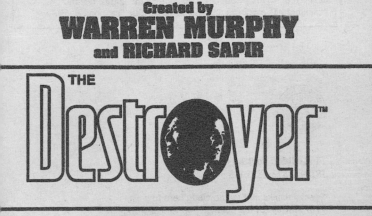

THE

Destroyer™

WHITE WATER

A GOLD EAGLE BOOK FROM
WORLDWIDE.

TORONTO • NEW YORK • LONDON
AMSTERDAM • PARIS • SYDNEY • HAMBURG
STOCKHOLM • ATHENS • TOKYO • MILAN
MADRID • WARSAW • BUDAPEST • AUCKLAND

First edition February 1997
ISBN 0-373-63221-5

Special thanks and acknowledgment to
Will Murray for his contribution to this work.

WHITE WATER

For Carole*, the Scheherazade of La Jolla.

And for the Glorious House of Sinanju,
P.O. Box 2505, Quincy, MA 02269

PROLOGUE

Since Man first stepped out of the seas to breathe open air and walk on mud, he has reached back into the cold soup that spawned him for sustenance, first with his naked hands, then with rude clubs, baskets, baited hooks and netting.

As many species of fish as there were to tempt him with their cold, delicate meat, Man discovered even more ways to capture them. The more he fished, the farther from the safe shores of his dry new habitat he needed to venture to fill his eternally hungry belly. Logs became rafts, and rafts acquired sails. Sails gave way to gigantic floating factories that caught, gutted and processed the multitudinous fish into fillets and steaks to feed the upright multitudes.

Soon no edible denizen of the deep, from the lowliest urchin to the mightiest whale, from the most delicious finfish to the most repellent scavenger, was safe from the species that had claimed the apex of the food chain for its own.

For centuries Man thought the oceans he plundered of bounty to be inexhaustible reservoirs of protein. And so he fished farther and farther away from his safe shores and home ports, on greater and more-efficient sailing craft. Even when the mighty whales became scarce, he paid no heed and continued his unrelenting pursuit of the cod and tuna, the lobster and the mackerel, until their vast numbers began to dwindle. Even when the warning signs became alarm bells, Man's response was to redouble his efforts. For by this time Man was no longer a small, sustainable population, but six billion strong. Six billion mouths clamoring for food. Six billion perpetually hungry bellies of a species who possessed the skills and technology to consume all other species with whom they shared the Earth.

Man, having climbed to the top of the food chain, found himself a prisoner of his adaptive success. Like the sharks he now consumed in greater numbers than had consumed him in the past, Man had to keep moving to eat, keep hunting the lesser species if he was not to sink back into the cold soup that gave rise to him.

But the more fish he caught, the fewer fish remained for his next meal.

1

It was supposed to be the last haul.

One last tow. It was all Roberto Rezendez desired. One last good landing before he let the federal government buy his boat, the *Santo Fado*, out of Innsmouth, Massachusetts, and he took up cabinet making, turning his back of the livelihood that had fed seven generations of Rezendez going back to the days when Innsmouth was the whaling capital of the New World.

The morning sky was the color of oyster shells lying discarded on the beach. The heaving swells were masked by sea smoke generated by the midwinter cold. That the waters of the Atlantic were choppy and heaving Rezendez knew from the way his bow pounded through them, making a relentless thudding that was like a drumbeat to the forlorn melody of his rust-colored trawler engine's noisy *ta-poketa ta-poketa* stuttering.

In more plentiful times, the Rezendez family hauled active nets brimming with kicking cod and halibut and haddock from Georges Bank, 125 miles out from Cape Cod. It was the cod that was best. King cod, the fish that had sustained the Pilgrims. That had been long before the first Rezendez left

Portugal for a new life doing what Portuguese men had done for centuries to sustain life: fish from boats.

From his grandfather, Jorge, Roberto had heard how Georges Bank had teemed with cod in those days of wonder. How in 1895 the Patriarch cod, six feet long and weighing 211 pounds, had been pulled up from the deep. No fisherman had landed a Patriarch cod since those days of plenty. Cod did not live so long in the new century. And as the new century began to dwindle, the cod had dwindled, too.

Now that the new century was old and almost done with, the trawler nets brought up plenty of trawler trash—starfish and sea stars, skate and rusty beer cans—but few of the white-bellied cod. So damn few that even the men who lived off them had begun to understand they had dredged up almost all there were left.

Men like Roberto Rezendez had been barred from taking cod from Georges Bank. The yellowtail and the haddock were also scarce. If men of the seas respected the bans, the Commerce Department promised, the depleted groundfish stocks would replenish themselves. In ten years, they said. Some species in five. But what was a fisherman to do with himself during those five years?

Other draggers turned to scallops, but the scallop beds were being taxed by the new boats. And it cost money to refit a boat for scalloping. Some Innsmouth men went after lobster, but it was too labor-intensive. Lobstermen still caught lobster the way lobster was caught a century ago, in traps and pots that had to be laid down in the morning and taken up at night. Poachers were a problem for the lobster-men. Roberto Rezendez would have nothing to do with lobsters, which his great grandfather would grind up for fertilizer, he thought so little of the rust red ocean crawlers.

So he fished on, farther and farther out, taking as his primary catch the junk fish he used to toss back into the water dead. Instead of tender cod or delicate flounder, he harvested chewy pout, or cusk or but-terfish or froglike monkfish and lumpfish. People ate them now. They cost as much per pound today as had cod or yellowtail two decades ago.

But it was a living. And as the *Santo Fado* mut-tered around the protected areas of Georges Bank, Roberto engaged the sonar scope that made finding fish such a pleasure.

His two older sons took tricks and the wheel while Roberto, now forty-nine and bent of back if not of spirit, hovered over the greenish fish-finder scope as it pinged and pinged forlornly.

They were cruising at a mere dozen knots now. Salt spray, whipped by the steady wind, deposited a rime of ice on the radar mast and gallows and net-drum reels. From time to time Roberto knocked it off with a boat hook. Too much ice could capsize a trawler like the *Santo Fado* if allowed to build up.

It was while seeing to the ice encrusting one of the matched cable-drum reels that Roberto heard the sonar scope begin pinging wildly. Giving the huge steel drum a final ringing crack, Roberto rushed to the scope, boat hook in hand.

"Madre!" he muttered, reverting to the tradi-tional curse of his ancestors.

"What is it, Father?" asked Carlos, the eldest.

"Come look. Come look at what your forefathers lived for, but never saw with their own eyes."

Carlos bustled back while Manuel remained at the wheel. He was a good boy, was Manuel. Steady. Light on his feet on the pitching deck. He had fishing in his blood. His blood was fated to be thwarted, Roberto knew. He would not fish past his thirtieth birthday. That was how sad the state of the family-operated fishing enterprise had become.

The screen showed a vast mass shaped like a saucer. Over a mile long, it was composed of close-packed synchronized blips.

Roberto lay a finger against the screen and whispered, "Cod."

"So many?"

Roberto nodded fervently. His finger shifted. "See these large blips forward? These are the mature ones, the scouts. The others maintain a constant body width between them. This way they are always in sight of one another, should danger threaten."

"Amazing." There was respect in the boy's voice. Then he asked a question. "What do we do?"

"We will follow them. Perhaps they will lead us to a place where they can be legally taken."

"Is there such a place?"

"This is to be our last haul. There are places that are legal and there are places that are not so legal. Perhaps Our Lady of Fatima will smile upon us, on this our last haul."

They followed the bottom-swimming school, using only their sonar. From time to time, columns of cod would make for the surface to spawn. As the day lengthened and the cool sun burned off the sea smoke, they could see the cod break the surface all around them. It was a vision.

"I wish Esteban could be here to see this," Roberto lamented.

Esteban was his youngest boy. Just in junior high, he would probably never fish, never own a boat except a pleasure craft. He played shortstop for the Innsmouth Crustaceans and often spoke of baseball as a career. But that was a young boy's dream, nothing more.

Roberto was back attacking the ice when Manny—now taking his turn at the sonar scope—called out, "Father, something is happening down there."

Back at the scope, Roberto saw that the school of cod was spreading out. He nodded.

"They are beating the sea floor for prey. Probably capelin." He called up to the pilot house, "Carlos, where are we?"

Carlos consulted a marine chart. "We are approaching the Nose."

Roberto frowned, his sun-weathered face a mask of beef jerky. The Nose was the easternmost portion of the Grand Banks fishery that Canada lay claim to. Technically the Nose was beyond the two-hundred-nautical-mile limit claimed by Canada. But the Canadians had chased the Spanish, and before them the French, from these waters as if the Nose legally belonged to them. They said the free-ranging cod were Canadian. As if any fish could possess a nationality. They existed to be taken. Nothing more.

Taking up his binoculars, Roberto scanned the

skies for Canadian Coast Guard aircraft. These skies were empty of all that—and of all promise.

"Stay the course," Roberto said, throwing his luck in with the cod as his ancestors had.

The trawler muttered on, its ice-encrusted bow smashing the ten-foot swells like a stubborn bulldog with a foamy bone in its teeth.

The school did not swim in a straight line, of course. It veered this way and that. With every veer, Roberto signaled the *Santo Fado* to veer.

Inexorably the cod were taking them into the Nose.

"I don't like this," said Carlos.

"Slow," said Roberto, who did not like it either.

They were not in legal waters. There could be a fine just for suspicion of the intent to take fish from these waters if they crossed the invisible two-hundred-mile limit into Canadian waters.

Still, the temptation was very great. This was their last haul, and the teeming cod moving beneath their aging hull were oh so very tempting.

The trawler reduced speed. The waist of the great saucer of cod, like a gigantic living thing composed of green spots of light, moved on. The trailing edge came into view.

Carlos made a noise of surprise in his throat.

"What is it?" Roberto demanded.

In answer, Carlos laid his finger against the large, elongated blip swimming directly behind the school.

Roberto stared at it in disbelief.

"I have never seen this," he breathed.

"What is it, Father?" Manuel called from the faded white pilothouse.

"It cannot be a codfish. It is too long."

"How long would you say?" asked Manuel.

"As long as a man," Roberto said. "Weighing as much as a man." And his voice trailed off. "A Patriarch," he said under his breath, not daring to believe it himself.

"What?"

Roberto's deep voice shook with a growing excitement. "It swims with the cod. It must be a cod. But it is not a scout. Yet it is larger than the scouts."

"A porpoise?"

"No, a Patriarch cod. A fish not seen in over one hundred years." Drawing a breath that burned with sea cold, Roberto Rezendez spoke the words that doomed himself, his sons, and sealed the fates of many fishermen in the days to come.

"I must have it. I must. This is the dream of my forefathers to catch that magnificent monster. We will bring it back living, as proof that the cod stocks are rebounding. The industry may yet be saved."

Rushing to the wheel, Roberto ordered Carlos back to the sonar scope.

"Both of you guide me. We will follow until the cod stop to feed. Then we will lower our net."

"Where are we?" Carlos asked.

"It does not matter. This is a miracle. It is bigger than one boat or one family or even which nations lay claim to what patch of cold, gray water."

They followed the school deep into the Nose. Here cod fishermen from Nova Scotia and Newfoundland were forbidden to practice their livelihoods while boats from other waters were not constrained. Over forty thousand men had been thrown out of work by the edicts of the Canadian Department of Fisheries. Men who watched their nets dry on their docks while other men took what they could not. Roberto knew them to be honest, hardworking men. He understood their plight. He had suffered since the closing of Georges Bank. It was sad.

Until they lowered their net, it would only be a fine. Perhaps not even that. And if the seas were clear when the cod struck their prey, there would be time enough to drag the net twice. And with luck, the great cod would be hauled up from the deep. That one, Roberto and his family would personally consume once the authorities laid their incredulous eyes upon it.

Deep in the Nose, the cod struck a school of capelin. The capelin were lurking on the bottom. Sensing the approaching school, the smeltlike little fish came off the ocean floor like a rising cloud. Predatory arrows, the cod fell upon them, and the gray-green water churned.

"Slow the engines. Drop the net!" Roberto shouted.

They fell to the netting with a grim will. The square-meshed orange otter net—required by the new regulations so they would not catch immature fishes—went over the stern and into the cold water below. They took up the five-hundred-pound steel-framed oak doors and affixed them to the great U-shaped stanchions called gallows. These were dropped into the water, where they sank.

"Full throttle!" Roberto called.

The boat shook and rumbled along.

The great reels paid out cable as the forward motion of the dragger caused the net to bell and open like a great, all-catching spiderweb. The huge net vanished from sight.

Down below, the doors would be forced part, keeping the net wide for the unsuspecting fish.

Ahead a little blood was already rising. And fish flecks. Soon the sea would be alive with churning and consuming. It was the law of the sea. The big fish ate the little fish. And mankind ate the big fish and the little fish both.

Like a meshy mouth, the net was approaching the school when, out of nowhere, a great factory ship appeared.

It was gray. Against the soupy gray of the sea and the dull gray of the sky, it had lain there like stealthy winter's ghost.

A foghorn blew, bringing Roberto's head jerking ahead.

"Madre!" he whispered. Grabbing up his binoculars, he spied the name on the bow.

"Hareng Saur."

"Quebecers!" he muttered. They were not much for high-seas fishing, preferring to crab the familiar waters of the St. Lawrence River. And they were at odds with Ottawa. Perhaps they would leave well enough alone.

But soon the ship-to-shore UHF radio was crackling with an urgent voice.

The call was in French. Only French. The only part Roberto understood was the name of his own boat, which they mispronounced atrociously.

Nervously Roberto grabbed up the mike and said,

"*Hareng Saur,* I do not speak French. Do any of you speak English?"

More excited French garbled out of the radio speaker.

"I repeat, *Hareng Saur,* I do not speak French. Who among you speaks English?"

It seemed no one did.

The big factory ship came bearing down upon them.

Leaping to the stern, Roberto rejoined his sons.

"Do we cut the net cables?" asked Manny.

Roberto hesitated. This was to be the last haul. But otter nets were expensive. And he was loath to relinquish the Patriarch.

"Wait. There is still time." He rushed back to the sonar scope. Hovering over it, he scanned the blips.

The fish were feeding ferociously. The screen was a frenzy of greenish blips. It was impossible to distinguish cod from capelin. But there was no doubt who were the predators and who the prey.

The big otter bag was slowly sweeping them before it, the cod end filling up with living cod and capelin both. As it should be.

Roberto scanned the area for the Patriarch cod. He did not see it at first, increasing his hope that it had already been swept up by the net.

Then it darted into view. These was no mistaking the blip. Curiously it was moving through the frenzy of fish with a detached purpose. Was it not hungry? It struck out on an undeviating line through the school, and zoomed off the screen.

Roberto looked up. The unerring direction would

take it toward the big factory ship. But, of course, cod do not swim unerringly, except after prey.

With a sigh, he realized he had lost the opportunity of a lifetime.

"Cut the net!" The words choked in his thickening throat.

His two sons threw themselves on the brake levers controlling the matched cable reels. They jerked them hard, angrily. The reels let go. Cable whizzed out and spilled off the stern.

And as the last strands dropped into the cold, inhospitable Atlantic, a great sadness overcame Roberto Rezendez. This was how the final haul of the *Santo Fado* was to end. Ignominiously.

AFTER THAT, things happened with bewildering rapidity.

The factory boat lowered two dull gray dories. They beat toward the *Santo Fado*. It was possible to escape, but Roberto decided it would be unwise to attempt to flee. There was no proof any of wrongdoing. Suspicion, yes. But no proof. Not with his otter net lying on the ocean floor.

As the dories drew closer, they could spy the faces of the approaching ones. They were strangely white. And there were weird blue vertical spotches covering the faces centered on their noses.

Roberto recalled that the fisherman of Nova Scotia were known as "bluenoses" because the dye of their blue mittens came off when they rubbed their cold noses. But Nova Scotia dory men did not paint their faces white or call their ships by French names.

Only when they were surrounded on both sides

by the two dories could the true nature of the white-faced ones be discerned.

White greasepaint coated their faces. The blue splotches were greasepaint, too. They formed a crisp design. At first Roberto thought of a fish. But, of course, he would. Fish were his life. The designs were not fish. They were too ornate. Coats of arms are sometimes filled with similar designs. In this case, Roberto did not know the name or significance of this design. Only that it was hauntingly familiar.

"Why are their faces painted that way?" muttered Carlos.

"To protect against the cold," said Roberto, who thought it must be true. What other reason could there be?

The dories bumped the old dragger's hull and were made fast. Roberto ordered his sons to help. He himself stood on the heaving deck, shivering in his orange waders and rubber boots, the hood of his grimy gray sweatshirt protecting his head. He was still thinking of the father of codfish that had almost been his.

"Who speaks English?" he asked as the first of the white-faced ones clambered aboard.

No one, it seemed. For when they were on board, pistols were displayed.

"Are you Canadian fisheries inspectors?" Roberto asked nervously, knowing that fisheries officers operated undercover at times.

No answer. Not even in French. It was strange. Their faces were strange with their blue clown mouths and bold blue noses spreading angular wings over their gleaming white cheeks.

"We are a U.S. vessel," said Roberto, thinking that perhaps with the Spanish name on their stern they were being mistaken for a Spanish vessel. Relations between Canada and Spain were very strained even now, two years after the so-called Turbot War.

They were urged into the boats. Not a word was spoken. It was all grunting. Perhaps some of the grunts were French grunts. Roberto could not say. He knew little enough of French.

Nodding to his sons, he led them to the dory that awaited them.

"We will obey these men, for we are in their lawful waters," Roberto said simply.

Soon they were being conveyed to the immense factory ship. One man remained with the *Santo Fado.* If their boat was seized, there would be very great trouble. It had happened before, during the trouble over turbot. Scallop poachers had lost their trawlers for illegal fishing. They never got them back.

As they muttered toward the *Hareng Saur,* something in the water caught Roberto's eye. It looked like a shark making its way. Or a porpoise. But the waters were too cold for a harbor porpoise.

With a stab in his heart, he thought, Torpedo!

The wake was arrowing unerringly toward the big gray sea behemoth.

Roberto started to speak up. To point. He was shushed with a hard look and a wave of a pistol. It was very eerie the way the white-faced ones operated in utter silence.

Roberto counted the long seconds to impact.

The thing had to be a torpedo. It was closing very fast. Glimpses of gunmetal gray showed in the gray water. It looked to be as long as a man. Or the Patriarch cod, he thought. But that was impossible. Cod were silvery of skin. And this thing moved like a machine.

Three seconds, Roberto counted. Two. One...

The wake ran into the gray hull, just below the waterline.

No explosion sounded. No impact came. No nothing. The wake simply ran into the side of the ship and was no more.

Perhaps it was a porpoise after all, diving playfully under the great gray hulk, Roberto thought.

Roberto turned his thoughts to his predicament. When the dory eased to the hull of the big ship, lines were lowered from davits and the dory was hoisted to open cargo holds in the side of the ship, then swung in.

They were escorted through the stinking hold, where fresh-caught fish were processed and frozen as quickly as they were disgorged from nets.

Even for a lifelong fisherman like Roberto Rezendez, it was an ugly sight. This was a gigantic processing plant. This was why there were no cod. Ships such as this devoured and reduced to cat food and fish sticks entire fish schools in a day's time.

A corporation owned such a vessel, he knew. No hardworking family fisherman could afford it.

"This," he whispered to his sons, "is why we have no future."

Fish were being ripped—gutted and halved—at

conveyor belts in cold rooms. The stench of gurry in the malodorous hold was nauseating.

Passing a porthole, Roberto chanced to look out. There, out in the cold gray-green Atlantic, he saw the rusty bow of the *Santo Fado* slip beneath the waves. Just like that. He froze but was prodded on.

Glancing out through the next porthole he came to, Roberto saw no sign of his trawler. Only a lone dory cutting the water from the place he had left his livelihood.

Could it be? Had they scuttled her? Was it possible? Roberto said nothing. But all over his body the sweat was cold and clammy, and his stomach began to heave not from the dismal stench but in fear for his life—and the lives of his sons.

They were taken to a steel room whose floor was choked with fish entrails and other leavings. Roberto knew what this was. The fish paste called *susumi* would be made from such offal. Probably in this very room. It would be used in cat food.

The door valved shut. It was a very bad omen. Interrogations were not conducted in such quarters.

"I would like to explain myself," Roberto began.

He was ignored. Workers in bright orange waders and black rubber boots used long forks to pitch fish offal into a vat. There were blades or something whirling in the vat. They whirled and spun, chewing up the bony fish so that the bones would be small and soft and digestible.

"We were not taking cod. We were tracking the Patriarch. Do you understand?" Roberto repeated the word *cod* and made the time-honored gesture to show the fish's span. Of course, his arms were too short to truly encompass the size of the cod he had tracked with his fish-finding sonar.

The men with the blotchy blue-and-white faces laughed at him. A fish story. They thought he was telling them a fish story. It was understandable.

Roberto was searching his memory of Portuguese for common words that a Frenchman might understand. The languages had many similar roots. It was possible to communicate with these men before something strange transpired. He remembered the French word for *cod*, amazed that he possessed this knowledge.

"Morue," he said, stumbling over the syllables.

One of the men pointed to the vat of pureeing fish. *"Poisson chat,"* he said in response. His blue smile was rimmed in pink, like a cut mackerel.

"Eh?"

"Poisson chat." The smile widened so the red of his gums and inner lips was grotesque against the blue greasepaint surrounding them.

"Catfish!" Roberto exclaimed. "Yes. Catfish. I understand." But he didn't understand. Why were they speaking of catfish? Catfish were not caught out here in the cold Atlantic. Catfish were freshwater fish. What did they mean by catfish?

Then it hit him. Not catfish. Fish cat. Fish for cats. They were processing cat food. That was what they meant.

A kind of relief settled over Roberto Rezendez's weathered features, and he smiled sheepishly.

That was when two men stepped up and ripped Carlos. Just like that. It happened with stunning suddenness.

Two white-faced men. They strode up, swinging long tuna knives. Both stepped in, and one thrust his blade into Carlos's unsuspecting right side while the other pierced his left. In the belly. Low in the belly. The blades touched one another with a rasping sound—touched deep in the bowels of Roberto Rezendez's eldest son, and he screamed as Carlos screamed. It was a stereo scream.

Manuel joined in, too. A whisking blade separated Manny from his nose. It fell to his feet, perfectly intact. He ran. Or tried to.

Someone gaffed him like a fish. They used a pole with a hook at the end of it, plunging it into his back. Like a fish, Manny fell to the scummy floor and flopped as the harpoon was driven deeper into his helpless body. The point made an awful rasping sound as it scraped living bone.

Roberto Rezendez had both of his case-hardened fists up and was rushing to the defense of his sons, when the two with the long tuna knives drew them out and turned to confront their attacker.

The blades were red with the blood of Carlos. Roberto stared at them in numb disbelief. It was the blood of his son on the blades. His blood. The blood that had flowed through the veins of the Rezendez family for many generations. And here these—these crazed Frenchmen were spilling it as casually as they gutted fish.

Face atwist, Roberto made to seize those blades. They were sharp, but his anger was sharper still. He swore foul oaths his grandfather seldom used. He cursed these butchers when his hard fingers closed over the bloody blades and the white-faced ones whipped them back, leaving blood on Roberto's palms that might have been his sons' or his own. It didn't matter. It was the same blood, and he would shed all of it to avenge his family.

The blades danced and cut the air, shedding scarlet droplets with each twist. The blood spattered Roberto's face. It got in his eyes. They stung. He tasted blood through his set teeth and he grunted out the low Portuguese curses his foes did not understand, could not understand, because all they spoke was doggerel French.

The blades whacked and chipped at Roberto Rezendez as if he were a totem pole being whittled. Except that he bled. As his sons writhed on the floor in their death torments, their lives irredeemably lost, Roberto threw punches and kicks at the white-faced tormentors, who danced in and out of range, claiming pieces of his own flesh.

The end came for Roberto Rezendez as one man feinted, while the other slipped around and, with two expert slices, whacked off a collop of biceps.

The man danced back with the piece of meat that Roberto knew was his flesh balanced on the tip of his red blade. He flicked it back over his shoulder. It landed in the vat, where it made a raspberry blotch that was soon swallowed by the churning puree.

Roberto knew his fate then. He was to be cat food. No one would ever find him. No one would ever know his fate. Nor the fate of his sons. Not Esmerelda, not Esteban. Not the grandchildren who had yet to be born to carry on the Rezendez name.

"Why are you doing this?" Roberto screamed.

The blades found his belly and his throat, and in

that last memory, Roberto Rezendez knew how it felt to be a fish taken from its natural environment to be flayed and boned by strange creatures for an alien purpose.

That last knowledge was a very bitter one. He was a man. He stood at the pinnacle of the food chain. It was absurd to be killed to feed the idle cats of the world. Let the cats fish for their own food. Let them eat fish, not Portuguese.

In his last moments of life, they gutted him. He was too weak to resist. The ripping sounds of his parting abdominal muscles were like sailcloth tearing in a gale.

Roberto watched the gray, slippery loops that were his own entrails as they were deposited into the vat of fish offal.

Santa Maria, he prayed. *I call upon you to send to earth an avenger. For I have done nothing to deserve this. Nothing but fish.*

In his last moment, he wept. Then he was one with the fishes who were, and had always been, his destiny.

2

His name was Remo, and he didn't understand the mission.

It was not the usual mission. The usual mission generally came in one of two flavors. Hit a known target. Or infiltrate and discover an unknown target's identity. Then hit him.

Nothing was said about hitting anyone this time out.

That was strange thing number one.

Strange thing number two was the tractor trailer.

Remo was not licensed to drive tractor trailers. Not that he would let that stop him. After all, a tractor trailer was nothing more than an overgrown truck. Remo had driven trucks before. This one was longer and it had a lot more wheels, but it was still just a truck.

The instructions were simple enough. Pick up truck at rendezvous point A, drive it to point B and wait.

"Wait for what?" Remo had asked the lemony voice on the telephone.

"You don't need to know at this time."

"Do I need to know ever?"

"You'll know what to do when the time comes."

"How's that?" asked Remo of Harold Smith, his boss.

"Everything has been arranged. The loading will be done for you. Just drive the shipment."

"Drive it where?"

"Call me en route."

"En route where? North, south, east or west?"

"You cannot drive east of Lubec. You will drive into the Bay of Fundy."

"I feel like driving into the ocean right now," Remo complained.

"Just obey instructions. You cannot go wrong."

"If you say so," said Remo. "Anything else I should know?"

"Yes. How to double clutch."

"I'll ask someone," said Remo, who then went in search of the Master of Sinanju.

Chiun was not at home.

"Must have gone for a walk," muttered Remo. He was going to leave a note, but the single Western style pen in the house was out of ink. The goose quill and ink stone Chiun used were locked up tight, so Remo simply dropped down to the corner market and called his own house from a pay phone, leaving a message on the machine. It cost him a dime, but he figured it was worth it.

The drive to Maine had one good thing about it. The part of New Hampshire he passed through was very short. Of all the states of the union, Remo liked New Hampshire the least. He had heard about New England Yankees. His boss, Harold Smith, was one. Remo once thought Harold Smith was just a tight-ass until he visited New Hampshire and realized that

Harold Smith was a typical product of New Hampshire—bloodless about everything except money. Smith would rather swallow a nickel than see it roll down a sewer grate.

Once in Maine, Remo began to relax. Maybe it was the fact that trees outnumbered people in Maine. It wasn't that Remo didn't like people. It was that he had to be particular about whom he associated with. Since he was a sanctioned assassin for a supersecret government agency, this was important. It wasn't that Remo had a cover to protect. He had once been Remo Williams, a Newark cop, until his existence had been erased. Now he was just Remo, last name optional. According to his truck driver's license, he was Remo Burton. But that was just in case he was pulled over. He lived simply, did no work except take on missions and tried to lead an ordinary life within those narrow constraints.

For many years, it had been simple. Remo had no social life to speak of. But now he was dating again. Really dating. They way normal people normally did. And it was an education.

For one thing, Remo had to relearn that women liked to know a lot about their dates. Otherwise there were no more dates.

They particularly wanted to know what their date did for a living.

Normally all Remo had to do was pull out a fake identity card and he was whoever the card said he was. That was fine for missions. But what about a second date? Or a third? He was stuck being Remo Bogart, FBI special agent. Or Remo MacIlwraith, with the Massachusetts State Police.

Then there were the dietary differences. On one memorable date he sat across a restaurant table from a woman who calmly poured milk into her iced tea, explaining that the milk bound the cancer-causing tannins, then confessed to having been a former substance abuser.

"What substance?" Remo had asked guardedly.

"Sugar."

Remo's feeling of relief lasted only as long as it took to wonder what kind of person could turn common table sugar into a abusable substance.

When she started salting her iced tea, Remo decided there would be no second date.

Then there were the ones who were pretending to be single when they weren't. After a while Remo learned to ask Smith for a husband sweep via computer. Two times out of three, a husband would pop up on Smith's monitor. Once, thanks to Harold Smith's diligence, Remo discovered he was dating a female bigamist.

It was all very discouraging.

"Where are all the sane single women?" Remo had shouted into the phone one disappointing day.

"Married," said Smith over the wire.

"Avoiding you," said Chiun calmly from the next room.

And everybody, but everybody, wanted to go to bed on the first date. There was no chase involved. Remo liked the chase. Instead, he was the chasee. It was a problem he'd had for years. Women reacted to him the way cats react to catnip. One sniff and they were rolling on their backs, purring.

The way things were going, Remo felt he was going to have to retire from dating again.

But first he had to get the eighteen-wheeler he picked up in the Lawrence, Massachusetts truck stop to Lubec, Maine, located at the easternmost point of the U.S. according to the map. It was tucked up there on the Bay of Fundy, under New Brunswick.

Why he had to drive the freaking truck all the way up to Lubec still eluded Remo. He hadn't figured out how to double clutch yet. He had gotten on the cab CB and hailed various truckers who came into view.

They patiently explained it to him, but every time Remo tried, he managed to miss a step and found himself crawling along in first gear.

Finally Remo decided to speed shift through the sixteen or so gears and let the transmission watch out for itself. He had a run to make.

JUST SOUTH OF ELLSWORTH, barreling along in eleventh gear, Remo ran out of luck. He was ramming it through the gears, and the transmission soon began grinding like a coffee machine trying to turn lugnuts into espresso.

"Uh-oh," he muttered.

The eighteen-wheeler slipped into the low-ratio gears, and Remo urged it along with all his strength, which was considerable.

In third gear he crawled along another two miles while traffic blared and veered around him. Then he pulled over.

From the soft shoulder of I-95, Remo called Dr.

Harold W. Smith, the director of CURE, the agency he worked for.

"Bad news. I lost the transmission."

Smith said, "It is imperative that you make the drop zone."

"This is a drop?" Remo said.

"The *Ingo Pungo* is due in three hours."

"Is that a ship?"

"Yes."

"I'm meeting a ship?"

"Yes," Smith repeated.

"*Ingo Pungo* sounds Korean," said Remo. "Why am I meeting a Korean ship?"

"It is connected to the last contract I negotiated with the Master of Sinanju," explained Smith.

"Oh, yeah? Usually you ship the yearly gold tribute to the village by submarine. Why is a Korean ship coming here?"

"That is not as important as your making the drop zone on schedule. Can you get to Lubec?"

"Probably. But don't I need a semi?"

"Make the drop point. I will arrange for another truck."

"Okay." Then Remo had a thought and he groaned. "I hope Chiun isn't bringing a bunch of his relatives to come live with us."

But Harold Smith had already terminated the call.

Abandoning the truck, Remo used his thumb. No one offered him a ride, so he waited until the next eighteen-wheeler came barreling down the highway.

Climbing atop the cab of his own semi, Remo crouched there, waiting. His eyes tracked the approaching rig. He calculated instinctively—and not by numbers—variables such as speed, wind velocity and timing.

When the semi roared past, emitting diesel exhaust, Remo launched himself from his crouch, landed on the semi with his arms and legs spread and became a human suction cup.

Slipstream tried to tear him off, but his body adhered to the stainless-steel top as if Super Glued there.

Squeezing his eyes shut to protect them, Remo climbed down the blind side of the truck and slipped under the chassis where the spare tire sat flat in a tubular rack. There was enough room for Remo to stretch out if he deflated the tire. Which he proceeded to do with kneading motions of his long thin fingers.

There Remo sat like a frog on an inner tube on a pond, protected from view, wind and discovery.

He just hoped the truck was going where he was going.

EVENTUALLY, THE TRUCK pulled into a truck stop, and the driver got out to chow down in a diner. Remo slipped from his perch and called Harold Smith from a pay phone.

"How are we doing?" he asked.

"You have an hour," returned Smith.

"I'm in Machias."

"Hire a cab. Have the driver drop you off a quarter mile from the zone. Walk the rest of the way. You will find a power boat moored to a blue buoy."

"Power boat?"

"Take the boat fifteen nautical miles due east."

"You might as well say fifteen furlongs. I don't know nautical miles from kilometers."

"Rendezvous with the *Ingo Pungo*. Tell them to hold their position until you have secured a new truck. Then return to shore and find the truck."

"Okay, got it. So what's this all about?"

"It is all about punctuality," said Harold Smith. "Now hurry."

"Damn that Smith!" said Remo, hanging up.

He was walking back to the highway when the truck driver caught his eye. A tall, rangy blonde with a pleasant but lined face, she was on the scruffy side in torn jeans and flannels. But Remo decided she had an honest face. He needed someone like that now.

She beat him to the punch.

"You look like a guy who could use a lift," she said.

Remo said, "I need to get to Lubec fast."

"I'm running a load of sea urchin to the cannery there. I could use the company."

Remo climbed aboard. He watched as the woman double clutched the big rig onto the highway and laid down rubber for Lubec, hoping to pick up a few pointers.

"Name's Ethel."

"Remo."

"What's your business in Lubec?" Ethel asked.

"Gotta meet a boat," Remo told her.

"Say no more." She fell silent. It was a very thick uncomfortable silence.

Remo decided it didn't matter what she thought, as long as he got the ride.

Dusk was falling, but the interval between the sun dropping from sight and night seizing the world was brief.

After a while, Ethel started talking again. "I'm from Nashua. New Hampshire, that is. You?"

"Boston."

"Beantown," she snorted. "Where they drive like they learned how in bumper cars, and the rules of the road are—there ain't none."

"No argument there," said Remo.

"But it's home, right? I know. Once I finish this run, I go back to four walls full of boredom. But it's home."

The unspoken invitation hung in the noisy cabin for a full mile.

Normally Remo's tastes didn't run to truck drivers, but this was a special situation. He took the opening. "Can I hire your rig to haul some stuff back to Boston?"

Her smile was tentative. "Could be. If there's money in it. What stuff?"

"I don't know."

She looked at him sideways, her nostrils flaring. "You can't expect me to swallow that line."

"I'll know when I meet the boat, not before."

"You must be in a fascinating line of work."

"If you're not interested, I'll make other arrangements," Remo said.

"Hold on, now. Believe me, I'm interested." Her voice got low. "You ain't married, are you?"

"No," said Remo.

"Good, because I don't care to have my ass shot off by law or lovers. If you catch my drift."

"Been there, too," said Remo.

"I'm making a good living hauling urchin now. Don't want to mess it all up to do the midnight cha-cha."

"Urchin?"

"Yeah. Used to haul sardines, but the industry's in decline. Would have died, but the Japanese have a yen for sea-urchin roe. They pay big. I make good money taking it to the processing plant. Wouldn't touch the stuff otherwise. I'm a steak-and-potatoes kind of gal. The kind you can take home to mother."

She threw Remo a wink. Remo threw it back. That seemed to satisfy her, and the cabin fell quiet, which was how Remo liked it. In her Red Sox ball cap and raggedy work clothes, she was too tomboy for Remo's taste.

It was after sundown by the time they pulled into Lubec. Remo didn't see much of the town except it was old and on the hardscrabble side.

Within sight of the water, Ethel braked the truck. "I'll let you off here and go on and unload my cargo," she told him. "Meet you by the water as soon as I can. Deal?"

"Deal," said Remo, getting out. He hated to trust a stranger, but she had such an honest face.

REMO FOUND THE BOAT moored to a blue buoy. It was a long, sleek, ivory white cigarette boat. The kind drug smugglers use down in the Florida Keys.

The Lubec coast was very rocky, and the boat bobbed in the water a quarter mile out. There was no sign of a rowboat to take him out to it, so Remo simply started out along a long finger of rockweed-covered granite and kept on running when he hit the water.

It was a short sprint to the boat, and the tops of Remo's Italian loafers were dry when he hopped into the cockpit.

Running on water was one of the most difficult techniques Remo had mastered, but he made it look easy.

Venting the gas tank so it wouldn't explode when he fired up the inboard-outboard, Remo waited impatiently.

By the moon's position in the night sky, he was running ten minutes late. Maybe it wouldn't matter on this run.

The boat aired, Remo started the engine, threw off the spring line and backed the craft away from the buoy. When he had good draft, he turned it around and let out the throttle.

He hoped the *Ingo Pungo* was big enough to spot by moonlight. Otherwise there was a real good chance he was going to miss it completely....

3

Captain Sanho Rhee knew his cargo. He understood his destination. What he did not understand was the *why* of the long voyage from Pusan, South Korea, through the Panama Canal to the North Atlantic.

Was this somehow illegal?

He didn't think so. There was nothing illegal about his cargo. Such cargo was routinely transported from port to port.

Of course, he'd left his home port empty. The cargo was picked up along the way, some here, some there. That was normal. That was the kind of ship the *Ingo Pungo* was. That was what it did.

Normally the perishable cargo was off-loaded in a commercial port. Not this time. This time they were to lower the cargo over the side to a waiting craft. No port duties. No inspections. No nothing.

This clearly wasn't legal. But arrangements had been made. It was all taken care of.

So the *Ingo Pungo,* her full holds displacing four hundred tons of the cold Atlantic, steamed through the waters off Nova Scotia.

These were dangerous waters these days, with the Canadians so protective of their exhausted fisheries. But the *Ingo Pungo* had done nothing to disturb Canadian waters. There would be no trouble from Canada.

Captain Rhee was in the wheelhouse watching the scaly effect of moonlight on the cold water when the sea before them turned green and luminous.

A whale, he thought.

Right Whales sometimes surfaced in these waters, an impressive sight. Their great, hulking bodies would churn the naturally phosphorescent phytoplankton of the sea. This would account for the greenish phenomenon.

But the black nose slamming up from the deep was no whale's snout. It was metal. Made by man.

A lookout spoke the word before Rhee's brain framed the startled thought.

"Submarine! Submarine off port bow!"

"All engines, stop. All stop!" Rhee screeched.

And belowdecks the laboring diesels ground to a halt.

The submarine finished crashing down from its sudden surfacing breach. Rhee could not recall the name of the maneuver, but understood that it involved rising bow first until the sub's nose broke the surface, poised like a missile, only to smash down, throwing up brine, and wallow in the unsettled seas.

The submarine wallowed now. It blocked their way, then inched ahead slowly as if to let the *Ingo Pungo* pass.

"Raise this submarine," Rhee ordered.

The *Ingo Pungo*'s radioman got busy. He spoke in the international language, English, for five excited minutes, then turned his confused face Rhee's way.

"The vessel does not respond."

"Searchlight! See what flag they fly."

Deckhands sprang to action. Searchlights were energized and brought into play. They roved the choppy water, then converged on the black submarine hull.

There was no readable name on the bow. Faint white letters showed just below the waterline, but the water distorted them into unreadability. On the conning tower was a swatch of white with a blue mark sprawled in the white field. It was very ornate.

"I don't know that flag," Rhee muttered.

They were sliding past the sub now. Soon it fell behind their stern, making no move to follow or intercept.

"Maneuvers. They are on maneuvers," Rhee decided.

But still they kept their lights and their eyes on the silent black submarine.

As they put distance between the submarine and their stern, Captain Rhee noticed the sub began to submerge. It was a very slow but also sinister maneuver. The steel cigar bubbled slowly from sight, and the conning tower slipped down like a dull predator returning to its watery lair.

"Maneuvers," muttered Rhee, returning to his course. The searchlights were doused and covered again with canvas protectors.

Moonglade mixing with the fading phosphorescent wake was their only warning of approaching trouble.

Something cut through the moonglade on the black water, roiling it noticeably. Then the long, lazy, bioluminescent tail their screws were bringing to life went crazy.

A lookout announced it. "Torpedo! Astern and closing!"

Rhee's mind went blank. Then he heard the impossible word again.

"Torpedo!"

"Hard a-port full!" Rhee screamed. It was a blind order. It might save the ship. It might not. His was a commercial vessel. It had no experience in wartime. He didn't even know that there was a war on.

The great ship lurched in response to the wheel. It heeled left, sliding into the beginning of a long turn it never completed.

The torpedo struck the stern with a dull thunk that immediately flowered into a thunderous boom. The *Ingo Pungo* lurched ahead, shuddered deep within— and so rapidly that it was like an ugly miracle, it began to list to the stern.

The ruptured stern was drinking bitter ocean, engulfed by a thirst that filled the rear holds with heavy, draggy brine.

Terrified seamen started pouring up from below. Rhee met them at the top of a companionway.

"How bad?" he demanded, his voice a rip of sound.

"We are sinking!" one moaned.

"We cannot sink."

"We are sinking. We have no stern."

On the verge of nervously pushing past the uprushing seamen, Rhee knew he had only time to accept the word of his crew if he was to save their lives.

He turned and cupped both hands around his mouth to give his orders volume. *"Abandon ship! Abandon ship!"*

Alarms rang the length of the *Ingo Pungo*. Confusion overtook all decks. Boats were put over the side. Anxious crew ran them down off davits, and they made splashes in the water.

Rhee ranged the deck stem to stern, calling out the abandon-ship order. He wouldn't lose a man if he could help it. He wouldn't lose a single seaman, no matter how lazy and unworthy of life.

Leaning over the side, he called to the large boats below. "Row away! Row as fast as you can! Lest the sinking ship suck you all down to your doom."

His men fell to rowing. There was time yet, he hoped.

More lifeboats splashed into the water—until only one remained.

Satisfied that he had done all he could, Captain Rhee helped his remaining crewmen swing the last lifeboat out on its davits. When it was poised over the heaving ocean, they urged him to climb aboard.

He saw the second torpedo charge toward the starboard. The wake was like a furious, foaming arrow. It ran between two lifeboats, nearly upsetting them. Men clung to the gunwales in fear.

With a sudden drying of his mouth, Captain Rhee saw that the torpedo was going to strike the *Ingo Pungo* amidships. Strike at the waterline directly beneath the spot where he intended to deposit the last lifeboat.

And he knew all was lost for himself and his remaining crewmen.

The ship shuddered alarmingly upon impact. Cold salt brine was thrown up. It streamed down Rhee's openmouthed face, freezing instantly, stilling his tongue and sealing one eye shut to the elements.

Rhee grabbed for the rail but it slipped from his grasp. The deck was already pitching. It pitched its brave captain overboard, which was a kind of mercy.

The *Ingo Pungo* slipped beneath the waves as if dragged to its doom by something inimical. From the moment the first torpedo demolished the stern, ten minutes had transpired. But only two more after the starboard hull had been breached.

The sucking of water drew three of the lifeboats down into a brutally cold vortex, carrying its crew to a violent death.

But not as violent as those in the surviving lifeboats.

They were bobbing in the water in sheer disbelief of the calamity that had overtaken them, when the heaving sea around them flattened strangely, belled, then heaved up again as if from some subsea earthquake.

In their midst a black steel snout surfaced, hung poised for a heart-stopping moment, then came crashing down to dash every last lifeboat into kindling.

A hatch popped up in the top of the gleaming conning tower.

A man whose face was as white as the flag on the sail stepped out and looked around. His face mirrored the blue heraldic design in the flag.

He called out. Not words. Just a questioning shout.

He got a return shout from the water. Frightened and disoriented.

A sweeping searchlight rakcd the disturbed Atlantic. It fell on a bobbing human head.

The bobbing survivor of the *Ingo Pungo* called out for rescue, his shivering arms lifted imploringly.

The man with the blue device marking his death white face lifted a short-barreled machine gun and chopped the lone survivor into fresh chum.

Then the searchlight began picking out other bobbing heads. And the machine gunner began picking them off with methodical precision. A few ducked when the hot lights swept toward them. They never resurfaced.

The rest screamed or prayed or did both in their last, terrible moments before the searchlight blazed a pathway for the merciful bullets. Merciful because a ripping bullet was preferable to drowning or hypothermia.

The black submarine slipped beneath the waves soon after that.

Other than scattered slicks of blood in the water, no trace of the *Ingo Pungo* remained.

4

Remo Williams held the thundering cigarette boat on a dead eastern heading, his dark eyes raking the tossing seas before him.

It was bitterly cold, but the bare skin of his forearms showed no gooseflesh. The wind whipping through his short dark hair seemed to not bother him at all. It pressed his black T-shirt to his chest, and made his black chinos flap and chatter off his legs.

In the moonlight Remo's face had the aspect of a death mask. Old plastic surgeries had brought out his skull-like cheekbones under the tight, pale skin. His eyes were set so deep in their sockets they looked empty, like skull hollows. Long ago Remo had been electrocuted by the state of New Jersey so that his past could be erased. He might have been the old Remo Williams come back from the grave to avenge his own death. But he had never died. The chair had been rigged, his execution faked.

Remo's body temperature was slightly elevated to compensate for the cold. It was a small technique in the greater repertoire of Sinanju, the Korean martial art from which all succeeding martial arts were descended. Sinanju placed Remo in full control of his body and at one with the universe. Conquering deadly cold or running as if weightless across open water were things he had mastered long ago and would never forget.

Somewhere beyond the drop point, Remo smelled blood in the water. Remo knew death more intimately than most men know their wives, so he knew human blood from ape blood. Chicken blood from beef. He could even sometimes distinguish male blood from female, though he couldn't put the difference into words.

The blood he smelled was human male. And there was a lot of it.

He let his nose guide him toward the metallic scent.

Moonlight on the water didn't show up the blood. It was his nose that told him when he was in the middle of it. He chopped the engine and sent the power boat gliding around in a long arc that brought it back to where the blood scent was.

Reaching over the side, Remo dipped his fingers. They came back mercurochrome red. He could see the red clearly now. It blended with the black of the night sea. There was a lot of it.

Standing up, Remo looked all around. Other smells came to his nostrils. Human smells again. He smelled fear-sweat. There was no mistaking that odor, either. Machine smells. Machine oil. Diesel fuel. Other things that he could not identify by scent but that he associated with ships.

A big ship with a big crew had been on this spot not long before Remo arrived. But a ship that big should be visible on the water. There was plenty of moonlight.

As Remo scanned the horizon all around, something went *bloop* behind him. Turning, he saw nothing but heaving swells.

Then the blended stink of oil and diesel filled the air.

He saw it then. A rainbow slick. Something far below had vomited up diesel fuel.

Stripping off his T-shirt, Remo stood in his chinos as he toed off his shoes.

Without hesitation he jumped into the frigid Atlantic. It enveloped him like a cold vise. A biological sensor in his nose caused his body temperature to elevate ten degrees. The same natural reflex had been discovered in children who fell into icy ponds and survived because it threw the body into a kind of limited suspended animation, preserving the brain from oxygen starvation.

Remo's body temperature was now in the danger zone, but the cold of the North Atlantic would counteract the effects of the self-induced fever. Sinanju again.

Remo's eyes quickly adjusted to the changing light conditions. The red end of the spectrum was filtered out thirty feet down. At sixty, orange vanished.

At one hundred feet Remo began picking out shapes in the predominantly blue-gray realm. His skin was slick with oil. He hated the sensation, but the coating helped insulate his skin.

Five hundred feet down in shoal water, he found the *Ingo Pungo* lying on her side. He read it as a long, dark, night blue hulk, the stern broken open.

Releasing a solitary carbon dioxide bubble once

every thirty seconds, Remo reconnoitered the sunken wreck. There was a hole in its side, he discovered—more by feel than sight. Something had knocked the hole in the thick black hull plates. There were jagged edges pointing inward around a human-sized hole. Other holes had edges that pointed outward. No boiler explosion sank this ship.

There were bodies floating in the water, some still trailing cloudy, dark filaments. Blood. Already fish were pecking at them.

There had been no survivors. A finger floated by but Remo ignored it.

Then, reaching out, he momentarily arrested a body slowly drifting by. The dead face looked back with sightless, oblique eyes. A Korean. Remo let go.

Holding his position with lazy stabilizing sweeps of his arms, Remo noticed a strange thing. There were a lot of fish. Maybe it was the bodies that drew them. But they seemed to be coming out of the wreck as if it had been their home a long time.

One swam close, and Remo reached out to catch it. It fought for its freedom and Remo let the fish have it, but not before he had identified it as a coho salmon. A fish native to the Pacific Ocean. What the hell was it doing in the Atlantic? he wondered.

Moving closer, Remo discovered other Pacific species. In fact, they were almost all Pacific fish. To Remo, who knew fish very well, it was as weird as discovering a Pekinese perched atop a candelabra cactus.

Returning to the surface, Remo recharged his lungs with air.

Except for his own lonely craft, the seas were empty.

Back on board the cigarette boat, Remo rubbed his oily arms dry and diverted body heat to the top of his head. His wet hair began to steam. It was soon merely damp, and before long it would be dry.

He threw on his dry T-shirt and, as he kicked the engine back into life, he redirected his body heat to his legs, where his pants were sticking to his flesh like a cold, clammy shroud.

The power boat dug in its stern as it heeled about. Remo lined the nose up with land and let the throttle out.

Something was very wrong here. And the worst part was he didn't know how much trouble it meant.

DR. HAROLD W. SMITH was working late. It was one of the occupational hazards of being the head of CURE, the supersecret government agency that had no official existence. The cover for CURE was Folcroft Sanitarium, a three-story redbrick building perched on the lip of Long Island Sound. Smith's Folcroft duties were no less demanding than his higher responsibility. So he often worked deep into the night.

The Sound was a bejeweled carpet of anthracite at Smith's back as he trolled the Internet from his desk. The desk was as black as the Sound. Its wide glass top was like obsidian. Set under the glass so that its luminous amber screen canted up to face him, was the monitor that connected to the Folcroft Four—a set of powerful mainframes hidden in the sleepy sanitarium's basement.

Smith was a spare man whose color might have been bleached out of him by virtue of the tedium of his job. There was nothing glamorous about running CURE. Smith did it from his Spartan office unsuspected by his employees, who thought of him as a hard-nosed, tight-fisted, anally retentive bureaucratic paper shuffler—which he was. And stubbornly proud of it.

Smith was tracking the progress of the *Ingo Pungo* on his screen. The ship was equipped with the global positioning system transponder beacon carried by many modern vessels. It beamed a constant signal up to orbiting satellites, which sent its position back to earth stations. Smith had accessed the network and was looking at a real-time schematic of the *Ingo Pungo*'s current position.

The blipping green light was fifteen nautical miles off Lubec, Maine, in the Bay of Fundy. It had stopped dead in the water precisely where it should. This was good.

If Remo held up his end, he should rendezvous shortly, and Harold Smith could go home to his bed and his understanding wife, Maude.

Time passed, and the *Ingo Pungo* remained in place. The off-loading was probably going slowly. Or perhaps there was weather. Smith punched up a real-time feed from the National Weather Service.

There were no storms in that part of the Bay of Fundy. He frowned, his grayish face like that of a corpse wearing rimless glasses in a failed attempt to look natural. Smith resembled nothing more than a third-generation New England banker teetering on the creaky edge of retirement. In fact, Smith was well past retirement age, but as long as America had a need for CURE, he could not retire. Except in death.

Smith was monitoring news feeds on a window on one corner of his screen when the blue contact desk telephone rang, startling him into action.

Smith scooped it up.

"Hail, O Emperor! What word?" cried a high, squeaky voice.

"None."

"The hour has come and gone," said the voice of Chiun, the Reigning Master of Sinanju.

"Remo ran into difficulties. But the ship is on station."

"Of course. It is manned by Koreans. They would not dare be tardy. Unlike my adopted son, who would sink to any low embarrassment."

"I expect the cargo transfer is going on right now," Smith said.

"I should have overseen it myself. But if I cannot trust Remo to accomplish a simple exchange, how can I place the future of my House in his clumsy, thumb-fingered hands?"

"I will let you know when I hear from him, Master Chiun," said Harold Smith, terminating the call.

The blue phone rang again so fast Smith thought the Master of Sinanju had hit Redial.

It was Remo this time. He sounded cold. And Remo never sounded cold.

"Smith. Bad news."

"You failed to make the rendezvous?"

"I made it. The ship made it, too."

Smith squeezed the blue handset. "Then what is wrong?"

"I found it on the bottom of the ocean. It sunk with all hands," Remo told him somberly.

"How can you be certain it sunk?"

"I found blood in the water and an oil slick. I can add two and two, so I went down and found a ship. *Ingo Pungo* was on the stern—what was left of it."

"You are certain that the ship was the *Ingo Pungo?*"

"I can read. I can also tell a Korean from a Japanese at ten paces. There were Korean bodies floating around the wreck. Looks like no survivors."

"It had just reached the rendezvous point. What could have befallen the ship in that short a time?" Smith said in a deeply disturbed voice.

"I'm no expert, but I'd say it was torpedoed. There was a hole in the starboard side as big as a Buick. The metal was punched inward."

"Who would torpedo a cargo ship?"

"Who would know about it?" countered Remo.

"No one other than you, Chiun and I."

"And the crew," Remo corrected.

"Yes, of course, the crew."

"Loose lips sink ships. Could be somebody talked."

"That is unlikely," Smith said testily. "This particular cargo would not attract pirates."

"Who said anything about pirates? And just what was the cargo?"

"Unsalvageable," said Smith. "We must start over. Stand by. I must speak with Master Chiun."

"But you don't know where—"

Hanging up, Smith dialed Master Chiun's Massachusetts number.

The Master of Sinanju picked up the phone immediately.

"What news?" he squeaked.

"There has been an accident."

"If Remo has failed me, I will have his ears!" Chiun screamed.

"It is not Remo's fault. He reached the rendezvous zone only to find the *Ingo Pungo* had gone to the bottom. He believes it was torpedoed."

"What lunatic would torpedo such a worthy vessel as the *Ingo Pungo?*"

"That is what I am wondering. Who knew of the vessel's mission?"

"You. I. But not Remo."

"This is not random," Smith said firmly.

"And the consequences of this act of piracy will not be random, either," Chiun said in a thin voice. "I will have satisfaction."

"I will make new arrangements, Master Chiun."

"That goes without saying. The satisfaction I seek is in the form of heads. Many heads. Staring sightlessly at eternity."

"This matter bears looking into, I agree. But we must not call attention to ourselves."

"I will leave the details to you, O Emperor. Just so long as I have my cargo and my heads."

Smith depressed the switch hook, shifted the receiver to his other ear and keyed a few strokes on the capacity keyboard on his desktop.

Instantly the line began ringing. Remo's unhappy voice came on.

"How'd you get back to me? I'm at a pay phone."

"It is a simple computer program."

"But this pay phone doesn't accept incoming calls."

"Override program."

"If AT&T ever finds out about this, you're looking at hard time in Leavenworth," Remo muttered.

"Master Chiun is very unhappy with the way this has turned out."

"I'll bet. You told him it wasn't my fault?"

"Of course," said Smith.

"Good. So, what was lost?"

"That is no longer important. I am making other arrangements. But in the meantime I need answers to the *Ingo Pungo*'s fate."

"It sunk. What more do you need to know?"

"Who sunk it and why," said Smith crisply.

"Beats me."

"Take the boat out again. See what you can find."

"It's a big ocean."

"And the longer you delay, the farther away the attacking vessel will get."

"Okay, but only if you put in a good word with Chiun for me. I don't want any of the blame for this. I made the drop point on time. More or less."

"Of course," said Smith, hanging up.

He returned to his screen. The blinking green light that was the *Ingo Pungo* continued relaying its position to orbiting navigation satellites. Before long the batteries would go dead or seawater would get into the electronics and the signal would die.

In the meanwhile it was like a ghost calling out to the world of the living from its watery grave.

5

Anwar Anwar-Sadat was enjoying his insomnia.

As Secretary-General of the United Nations, Anwar Anwar-Sadat had been experiencing more than his share of sleepless nights of late. Things were not going well for his grand scheme to subsume sovereign nations under UN control. It was very distressing. He had expected backlashes. All manner of backlashes. This was why he had tread so very carefully in the early phases.

Not many months ago his office polar-projection map of the globe was checkerboarded in blue. Blue for UN blue. Blue for nations enjoying UN oversight and occupations. It was the golden age for United Nations influence upon the nations of the world. Or a blue age.

Anwar-Sadat much preferred to think of it as a blue age.

But now the blue tide was receding. UNPROFOR—the United Nations Protection Force—had been discredited in the former Yugoslavia. Now the uneasy truces were under NATO control. His loyal blue berets had been replaced by the so-called Implementation Force, or IFOR. True, UN forces currently occupied Haiti, but Haiti was a nothing in geopolitical terms. Not even a factor. In fact, when painted blue on the UN maps, it tended to disappear into the blue of the Caribbean Sea, itself a watery nothing.

Haiti was a useless beachhead. It would not advance the cause of the global supernation that Anwar Anwar-Sadat envisioned in his One World of the future.

It was after the debacle in the former Yugoslavia, now a jigsaw comprised of shattered Bosnia, Serbia and Croatia, that the sleepless nights began to steal Anwar Anwar-Sadat's all-important sleep.

No pills would help. Not Sominex. Not Nytol. Not Excedrin PM. Not the new thing called melatonin. Nothing.

So Anwar Anwar-Sadat had had a computer terminal installed in his Manhattan high-rise apartment and taught himself to turn it on and manipulate its complex commands, whereas before, various functionaries performed that duty during working hours.

Anwar-Sadat was too private a man to allow a staff functionary to remain on call during his leisure hours. So he learned to use the mouse and a simple program called Bob and in time became quite proficient in manipulating them both.

In time he became truly glad to have expended the effort to master the computer.

Thanks to Mistress Kali.

The Secretary-General had never met Mistress Kali, but that day was approaching. She had promised him so. Promised many times. Twice they had agreed to rendezvous. But the first time Mistress

Kali had canceled. The second time it was UN business that had interfered.

The delays only made Anwar Anwar-Sadat itch with a mighty itching for the golden day he would at last meet his golden goddess.

He knew she was a goddess because she had told him so.

"Please describe yourself to me," Anwar had written those many weeks ago.

"I am golden of hair, and my eyes are as green as the Nile. When I walk, I am like a desert wind sighing through date palms. I am the wind and the palms both. My breath is warm, and my hips are supple and sway lyrically when I move."

"You sound...enticing," Anwar had typed, feeling a strange warmth he had not felt since he was a young man back in Cairo.

"I am a goddess in womanly form," Mistress Kali had replied.

And Anwar had believed. For who would lie about such a thing?

"Are you...voluptuous?" he typed.

"My shape is very pleasing. My features are delectable. My skin, flawless."

In those few words, Anwar wove a mental image that had yet to be modified by photographs or videotape. Left to his own imagination, he took the vague description of a blond-haired green-eyed enchantress and filled in the blanks with the woman of his dreams.

Since he had created most of the mental image, of course he fell in love with it. Mistress Kali was the personification of his deepest longings, the embodiment of his most denied desires.

"I worship you, Mistress Kali."

"I exist to be worshiped."

"Am I your only worshiper?" he typed, fear in his heart.

"You have the opportunity to earn that distinction, my Anwar."

"Command me," Anwar found himself typing.

"You must prove yourself worthy of my commands, my Anwar."

With that, Mistress Kali had signed off for three days. Three tedious, hateful days in which his e-mail address and his real-time computer-chat calls were haughtily ignored. Three endlessly sleepless nights in which he tossed and turned, thinking the worst. She had died. She had fallen in love with another. She was married and her husband had discovered her infidelity. For three nights he could not tear his eyes from the always-running blue computer screen with its burning white letters.

When on the fourth day an e-mail message popped up on the screen, Anwar leaped for the terminal.

The letter was brief, to the point, but pregnant with meaning: "Did you miss me?"

His reply was even briefer. "Damnably so."

"We should chat."

Eagerly Anwar Anwar-Sadat logged on to the chat line they used when their difficult schedules coincided.

"Where have you been?" he demanded.

"Away. But I am back."

"I thought the worst."

"Never fear. There will always be a place for you in my life, my darling."

Anwar's heart thumped. It was the first time she had used an endearment.

"My Pharaohess…" he replied, his eyes misting over.

"So how has been your life, Anwar?"

"Difficult. Things do not go well."

And he poured out his woes and ambitions and frustrations, divulging more about his schemes and goals than even his most trusted Coptic aides were told.

To his utter dumbfoundment, her replies were intelligent, insightful and very much on target.

"What is it you do that gives you such a mind?" Anwar Anwar-Sadat demanded.

"I am Everywoman. You need know no more."

"I ache to know all about you."

"Woman is mystery. Once you know all, I will cease to attract you."

Anwar Anwar-Sadat had to be satisfied with riddles. And he was. For a time. Nightly he told her of his day. And each night she advised him on the day to come.

One day he lamented the receding blue tide that was the seven continents.

"I cannot control the nations of the world. They are like mischievous children. If only they would cede some control to me. I could solve many of the world's problems. But the blue nations are reverting to green. In Bosnia my UNPROFOR has given way to a NATO thing called IFOR. If the tides continue to ebb, the only blue that will remain will be the seven seas.''

To that, Mistress Kali made a reply that Anwar Anwar-Sadat at first dismissed as childish.

''Why not seek control of the seven seas?''

Anwar Anwar-Sadat was weighing a judicious reply, calculated not to offend, when Mistress Kali followed up with another thought.

''The oceans of the world cover three quarters of the face of the globe. It is the source of food, life and is the oldest medium for intercontinental travel. It keeps nations apart, yet connects them by commerce. He who controls the ocean controls the landmasses. Control of landmass equals control of the world.''

''This is an astute observation. But oceans are international. No one political body controls them.''

''The oceans are controlled for two hundred miles out by nations that have encroached on waters that for centuries were free of man's domination.''

''Yes, yes, that last round of treaties expanded them. This was to protect fishing rights. This was twenty years ago. Before my tenure, you understand.''

''From where I view the world, two hundred miles is insufficient for the needs of most nations.''

''This may be true,'' Anwar Anwar-Sadat admitted. ''But to extend it any farther would invite disastrous conflicts.''

''Exactly why the two-hundred-mile limit should be rolled back, and control over coastal waters and deep-sea oceans should fall where it rightfully belongs—under United Nations control.''

"This is an intriguing idea. We already speak to this issue in many respects. There is a UN-sponsored international treaty that will allow signatory nations to board and detain violators of recognized fishing regulations. But it will be years before nations sign in sufficient numbers to give it teeth."

"Is it not clear that the extension of the two-hundred-mile limit has only worsened the pillage of the oceans?" Mistress Kali continued. "Today there is virtually no coastal fishery that has not been fished out. This could have been avoided had only your forces taken control of the situation."

"You are unusually well-informed. May I ask where you were educated?"

"I am a student of human nature."

"You are the most brilliant woman I have never met," Anwar Anwar-Sadat typed, ending that bit of admiring whimsy with a smiley: :-)

He only wished there were some way to type out a heart, for he was utterly smitten by this creature who possessed the brain of a shrewd diplomat and the statuesque body of a goddess.

After that bewitching night, Anwar Anwar-Sadat had studied the situation and decided it was feasible.

He gave a speech warning of a global water crisis if the world's precious resources were not husbanded quickly. It was carefully calculated not to offend world governments. It said nothing of control of the seas or fishing rights.

And it sank like a lead balloon. Those newspapers that carried the story buried it on the obituary pages. This infuriated Anwar Anwar-Sadat. These days he found himself buried more and more in the obituaries. It gave him a very ugly feeling. Newscasts reported his remarks as a one-sentence summary just before the car commercials.

By the next day it was completely forgotten.

Except by Anwar Anwar-Sadat.

"There has been no interest expressed in my ideas, Pharaonic One," Anwar Anwar-Sadat informed Mistress Kali that evening.

"You are not a man to give up easily. All you need is an incident to draw attention to your cause," she replied crisply. He could almost hear her dulcet tones, though they had never actually spoken.

"I am not in the business of manufacturing incidents. Only in taking advantage of them," Anwar Anwar-Sadat replied unhappily, adding a frownie face: :-(

"Perhaps there is something I can do up here," replied Mistress Kali.

"What, my sweet?"

"Be patient, my Anwar. And if you do not hear from me for some time, understand I think of you hourly and work to fulfil all of your brave dreams."

After she had logged off, Anwar Anwar-Sadat did an impulsive thing. He was not given to impulsive gestures, but this one welled up from deep within him.

He kissed the cold blue computer-screen glass.

6

Remo sent the cigarette boat skimming through the oil slick that had now spread an eighth of a mile over the site where the *Ingo Pungo* went down.

There was a sonar set on board. Remo had figured out how to turn it on, which was pretty good for him. He sometimes had trouble with the VCR.

Passing over the *Ingo Pungo,* he got a big dead blip. That was his first clue that he had it turned on correctly. Mostly it pinged and binged pointlessly.

Running past the site, he kept the boat on an easterly course. He figured he was looking for a submarine. Maybe the sonar would find it, maybe it wouldn't. Couldn't hurt to try, he figured. Perhaps he'd get lucky.

An hour passed and he watched his gas gauge. He wasn't much of a boater. Fortunately boats were simple. You just had to point the bow where you wanted to go and follow it. The hard part was making landfall. Remo preferred to just run them up on shore and hop out while the hull and propeller chewed themselves up on sand and rocks. Someday they'd build a boat with brakes.

In the end Remo didn't find the submarine so much as the submarine found him.

He got a string of noisy pings. The boat took him past the point of contact before he could check out the screen. Before the pinging stopped abruptly, the last ping sounded like a very big ping, so Remo brought the power boat around for another sweep.

The gleaming black submarine surfaced directly in his path.

It came up with the sail showing first. It lifted out of the water, a slab of blackness with a square of white on its side. Seawater cascaded and drooled from various places on the hull.

Then the long flat deck broke the surface.

Remo cut the power and let the boat glide toward the sub.

The sail loomed closer and closer. It dwarfed the power boat into insignificance.

At the last moment before collision, Remo turned the wheel, and the side of the boat bumped against the hull. He flung out a looped line, snagged a steel cleat and pulled the boat snug to the submarine.

Stepping off casually, Remo walked up to the imposing black sail. He knocked on it once, hard with his knuckles.

The sail rang like a bell. It was a very satisfactory sound. So Remo knocked again.

"Submarine inspector. Anybody home?"

A hatch popped atop the sail. Remo looked up. At his back another hatch popped. It fell down with a clang.

One eye on the sail, Remo glanced over his shoulder.

Two men in white sailor suits were climbing up from the hatch. They carried Uzis. With their faces painted white, they looked like mimes. The white blankness of their expressions was broken by a dark, flowery tattoo in the middle.

Remo recognized the symbol instantly. It was the Boy Scout crest. No, that was gold. This was blue. It still looked familiar.

"You clowns have caused me a lot of trouble," Remo said casually.

The two creeping closer failed to answer. Remo couldn't read their faces, but their weapons were pointed at him with professional intent.

"I surrender. Don't shoot me," he said, hoping they stepped right up to him. But they approached carefully. They weren't fools.

Remo raised his hands to encourage them. That worked. They moved up on quick sneakered feet.

A man appeared up on the sail and pointed a rifle down at Remo, complicating things. But only a little.

Remo offered a weak smile as the two seamen took positions on either side of him. They looked up. Remo looked up, too.

The man on the sail had a white face, too. He gave a hand signal while keeping the rifle trained on Remo.

The two on the deck took comfort in that, and one holstered his Uzi while the other stood back and trained his weapon on Remo with businesslike intent. His eyes were two dark squints.

Remo realized he was about to be frisked for weapons and decided he really didn't want to be frisked.

When one sailor put his hands to Remo's sides,

Remo broke both forearms with his elbows. He dug them into his sides. Crunch. Bones splintered. The seaman let out a high, frightened howl.

Pivoting, Remo spun the screaming sailor in a half circle and let go. The flying body slammed into the other sailor, and they went tumbling down the steep side of the sub.

Remo backpedaled in place ahead of the rifle bullet that punched a hole in the deck where he had stood a second before.

Arcing into the water, he made almost no sound, his lean body cleaving the water like an eel. Feet kicking, he used the slimy, cold skin of the hull to guide him to the bow and over to the other side.

Through the water Remo should have been able to hear the sailors shouting at one another. But they weren't shouting. Even the howling sailor had gotten a grip on himself.

Surfacing on the other side of the sub, Remo reached up and found the ankles of the two still struggling to hold on to the deck. They came into the water screaming.

"Fun's over," said Remo, grabbing them by the scruffs of their necks. "Time to confess to Father Remo."

One threw a punch that Remo avoided with a quick bob of his head. The sailor tried twice more, with the same frustrating result.

"Give up?" Remo asked.

They said nothing. If clown faces could look sullen, these two managed a respectable impersonation.

"Last chance to talk freely," Remo warned.

They offered frowns, and their shoulders slumped dejectedly.

So Remo dunked their heads under the surface. Their hands groped and splashed wildly. When he lifted them, they gasped like frightened flounders.

"Okay, who are you guys?"

They gasped some more, so Remo dunked them again. Longer this time.

When he finally brought them up, they were jabbering some doggerel Remo didn't understand at all.

"You two just flunked Usefulness 101," he said, and brought their faces together so fast and hard they fused.

Like Siamese twins joined at the nose, they sank as one. They didn't even struggle. For them the light had gone out forever.

Remo stepped back onto the deck and found the ladder that led up the side of the great black sail. He started climbing.

The seaman on the sail was sweeping the seas with a small gimbal-mounted searchlight now. He missed Remo entirely every time. That was Remo's doing, not the seaman's fault.

Remo pointed out his error by slipping up to the top of the sail and tapping on his shoulder.

Startled, the seaman spun around.

The expression on his pale face was not so much surprise as it was a cartoon. The blue symbol spread outward like a flower coming to life. A black hole formed in the bottom of the gleaming white face. The black hole had blue lips and white teeth, with prominent incisors. Remo flicked the front teeth with a finger, and they flew back into the sailor's mouth.

The seaman grabbed his throat, eyes bugging out in shock.

"That's only a sample of what I can do if I don't get some answers from you," Remo warned.

The seaman doubled over, coughing.

"Uh-oh," said Remo, who then spun the man around and, jamming his fists into his stomach, Heimliched him.

With a grunt the seaman expelled the teeth lodged in his throat, then collapsed on the sail, gasping.

"Speak English?" asked Remo.

The sailor started to gurgle. Then he vomited up his last meal. It looked like potatoes, except they were bluish.

Reaching down, Remo picked him up by the collar and belt and deposited him down the sail's hatch.

He went down, limbs and other bodily projections banging off the spiral staircase. When he reached bottom, Remo started down after him.

It was a big sub. There had to be plenty more sailors to interrogate. And that one had unforgivably splashed vomit on Remo's shoes.

The stink of the interior of the sub was a mixture of oil, cooking odors and stale human sweat. Remo absorbed all these scents as he slipped down the spiral stairs. Fear-sweat was predominant. The air reeked of it.

That meant an ambush down below.

Remo processed the assorted scents. He got a whiff of inert, unburned gunpowder. Sailors with guns. He wasn't in a great position to dodge wild shooting. On the other hand, only idiots would shoot inside a sub on the high seas.

On the other other hand, Remo remembered, these guys were wearing clown faces. No telling what they would do.

He decided to smoke them out. He was coming down on silent feet, and deliberately he stumbled. The stairs rang like a tuning fork.

And up from the shadows they poured, silent except for their drumming boots. No shouting. No war cries.

"Are these guys all mute?" Remo wondered aloud.

The steps vibrated with their mad rushing as they circled up and around.

Remo reached out and took hold of the spiral rail corkscrewing around the stairs. Stepping out, he let his legs dangle and slid down on both hands.

The sailors saw him going past as they were going up. They collided, bunched up, and started to reverse course.

By the time they got themselves organized, Remo had reached bottom and ducked through a hatch. He dogged it shut. That let him in and kept them out.

Moving down the cramped corridor, Remo came upon a sailor with a white-and-blue face.

"Speak English?" he asked casually.

The sailor was unarmed. He ran. Remo grabbed him by the shoulder and began to squeeze his hard rotator cup.

"*¿Habla español?*" he asked.

The man screamed. No words. Just high, mindless screaming.

"*Parlez-vous Français?*"

More screaming.

"Sprechen Sie Deutsch?"

He apparently didn't speak German. So Remo tried Korean. *"Hanguk-mal hae?"*

The man's rolling eyes turned white. They matched his face. It created an interesting effect. While his mouth was open, Remo checked to see if he had a tongue. He did. A pink one.

Having exhausted his stock of languages, Remo put the screaming sailor out his misery with a hard tap to the temple. The man collapsed in the corridor, and Remo stepped over him.

Back the way Remo came, the trapped sailors began pounding on the dogged hatch. That was all they did. Pound. They said nothing. They might have been completely mute. Or what they seemed to be— mimes.

"What would mimes be doing with a sub?" Remo muttered to himself, wishing Chiun were here. The Master of Sinanju would have an answer. It was even money it would be wrong, but at least it would be something to argue about. This slipping around a submarine wasn't exactly Remo's idea of a productive evening.

Remo knocked on each closed hatch as he passed by, hoping to draw someone out. He got no takers. A white-faced sailor dogged a hatch after himself when he saw Remo coming.

That meant they were afraid of him—always a good way to start an interrogation. All Remo needed was someone to interrogate.

Behind him another hatch clanged shut. It was far behind. Then, not twenty yards down the passageway, a hatch opened and a hand tossed out a grenade.

Remo shot into reverse, knowing the blast radius would be small.

When the grenade let go, it did so with a pop, releasing a spurt of yellowish white gas cloud. The cloud had nowhere to go but Remo's way.

Remo smelled the first wisp of gas and understood he was not at risk. It was pepper gas. Nonlethal.

Pausing, Remo picked a hatch and tried to undog it. The wheel wouldn't turn. Someone had locked it on the other side. The same was true for the next hatch. He took hold of it with both hands and forced it to turn. It did give a bit, then it cracked and Remo found himself holding a broken section of useless wheel.

A hatch at the end of the corridor was locked, too.

And the white exhalation kept spreading Remo's way.

He pinched his eyelids shut, making them tear. That was to protect his eyes.

Closing his mouth, Remo sucked in a long breath of air. It stung a little, but was mostly good. Then he began to exhale in a long, slow release of carbon dioxide.

As long as he kept air flowing out through his nostrils, no gas could get in.

That left him practically blind and with limited oxygen. Remo just hoped the gas didn't work through the pores, too.

Turning to face the hatch, Remo found the exposed hinges. They were massive. Laying the side of his hand against the top one, he brought it back and chopped hard at the place his sensitive fingertips told him the metal was weakest. The hinge shattered. Remo chopped the other one. It broke, and a chunk of cold steel fell with a clang.

Grabbing the wheel, he exerted pull. The wheel remained locked, but without functioning hinges, it was useless. Remo wrestled the hatch off its shattered hinges, and the locking mechanism twisted out of its groove.

Dropping it on the floor, Remo moved on.

He found another hatch that was open. It led to a corridor. He moved down its length by feel, ears alert for the pounding of excited hearts. Every sense was alert.

After a while it felt safe to open his eyes. Remo squeezed out the last protecting tears as he tried to figure out his next line of attack.

Before, he had been headed toward the control compartment amidships. Now he was angling back toward the tail.

Remo could feel eyes on him. From time to time, he spotted ceiling video cameras. Remo waved at them where he could.

No one waved back. No one tried to stop him, either.

But a lot of hatches were hastily shut as he approached them. After he passed them, too.

Just to see what happened, Remo knocked on one hatch.

"All clear!" he shouted through the steel. He repeated the call, knocking loudly.

He heard a gunshot. A smooth spot on the hatch

abruptly bulged out, followed by two closely spaced ricochet sounds.

Remo decided to leave well enough alone. These guys were so nervous they were capable of sinking the sub with everyone aboard, including Remo.

He moved on. It was weird. The crew seemed pretty scared of him—which they should be. But this was a different scared. Usually Remo had to pile the bodies to the rafters to get this kind of reaction.

Finally he found himself under the deck hatch through which the two sailors first emerged to attack him.

Behind him a hatch clanged shut. The other hatches were also closed. Only the deck hatch remained open like a clear invitation.

Then, with a sudden gurgling of moving water, the sub began shifting and settling. They were blowing the ballast tanks.

Bitterly cold brine began slopping down from the open hatch. Remo saw he had two choices: close the hatch and sink with the sub or get topside and swim for it.

He decided to swim for it.

Remo went up the hatch like a moth on wing, gained the deck and sprinted through the sloshing water surging over the deck plates for his bobbing power boat.

He jumped into it, unhooked the line and pushed off.

The engine refused to start. Remo pressed the starter button again and again. Finally the props churned water.

"Great," he muttered darkly. "Maybe I should have stayed on the sub."

Remo succeeded just as the closing waters met along the dorsal spine of the submarine. The sail was slipping under the waves like a retreating deity of black steel.

Remo stayed with the power boat as long as he could. He felt the undertow drag and clutch at it. A vortex began to take shape.

In the end he was forced to face the same choice as seamen in distress face. Abandon ship—or go down with it.

The boat was sucked under the waves. Remo was, too. He allowed the cold waters of the Atlantic to close over him, then kicked with all his strength. Not up, which was impossible now, but sideways, out of the vortex.

Like an elastic band snapping, the downward tug relaxed, and Remo shot to the surface.

Reaching breathable air, he treaded water.

Then and only then did he realize he had made the mistake of his life.

"I should have stayed with the sub."

In the immensity of the black night, with the uncaring sea holding him in its frigid grasp, and the familiar New England stars looking down from their remote stations, Remo's own voice sounded surprisingly small in his ears.

7

The cold of the North Atlantic felt like bands of cold steel squeezing Remo Williams's chest. The air coming in through his nostrils, warmed by nasal passages and throat, was still too cold when it reached his lungs. They burned. It was a cold, life-draining burning.

He was losing body heat rapidly. His nerves were shutting down.

Yet somehow Remo was able to sense the upward ripple of the icy ocean water being pushed by the blunt snout of the shark.

Expelling the remaining air from his lungs, he slid under the waves. If a shark wanted to eat him, it was going to have to fight for its supper.

Under the water Remo's night vision came into play. He made out a blue-gray shape rising to meet him. Jackknifing, he went down to meet it.

Predatory eyes glinted toward him. A mouth like a grinning cave filled with needles showed dim and deadly. It yawned. Teeth revealed themselves, ragged and overlapping but wickedly sharp. Teeth that could snap off an arm or a leg cleanly, Remo knew.

The gap closed. Remo twisted his back to create torsion in his spinal column. He could no longer see the shark, but he could roll out of its path—if he timed it to the last second and the shark cooperated.

At the last second Remo felt the lack of oxygen and knew the maneuver was doomed. He was too weak. His nerves were like spidery icicles that would break under the simplest strain.

Sensing the weakness of its prey, the shark gave an eager, convulsive wiggle of its sleek body and lunged for Remo.

In that moment, with ugly teeth straining for his flesh, Remo noticed a loose shark tooth and remembered something.

Shark teeth are like baby teeth. They come loose easily and regenerate later.

Making a spear with one hand and a fist with the other, Remo kicked like a frog and made for those rows of ugly teeth.

A short-armed punch connected with the blunt snout. The shark recoiled under the unexpected blow. It rolled, twisted and Remo went for the gaping maw of teeth.

With a sweep of his hand, he cleared the upper gums of teeth. The maw snapped shut, squirting a mixture of blood, triangular teeth and angry bubbles. Too late. Remo's hand had already retreated.

On the return sweep he got most of the lower set. A few remained here and there. The lower corner was still heavily toothed.

Threshing about, the shark fought to regain its orientation.

Remo got under it, curled his body into a ball and, with the last atoms of oxygen still burning in his lungs, gave it an upward kick.

Shocked, the shark shot to the surface—as much from panic as from the unexpected blow.

Remo surfaced behind the shark, drew in air and got his mitochrondria—the part of his cells that functions like tiny energy furnaces—charged again.

The cold air felt like the cold water around him. He couldn't tell one from the other. His skin was cold and blue and unfeeling. In the moonlight he saw the skin under his fingernails turning a purplish black.

Kicking, Remo got to the shark's side, took hold of its sturdy dorsal fin and pulled himself on board.

The shark didn't resist. It was stunned.

Its tough bluish hide scraped skin from Remo's bare arms. But that hide could provide warmth by acting as a wet suit. Wrapping his legs around the shark's tail, Remo hugged it tightly, its fin nudging his crotch.

Gradually a bit of warmth was restored in his body. It wouldn't be in time. It would not save him. But as long as he breathed, Remo still had a chance.

Even if he couldn't exactly see that chance. Or where it would come from.

Time passed. The shark began to switch its muscular tail. Remo clamped down to inhibit its forward movement. Once the shark dived, it would be in its element. And it would be all over for Remo.

As they struggled, Remo focused on the will to live. A man fought for his life when his life had meaning. Remo's life had meaning to him. He wasn't always satisfied with it. Often not satisfied with it at all. But it was his life, and he intended to hold on to it.

He thought of Chiun, and how his life had been transformed and redirected through the training of the last Korean Master of Sinanju. He thought of the House of Sinanju, and the villagers who had survived for five thousand years because the Master of Sinanju had gone out into the known world to ply the trade of assassin, feeding the village that could not feed itself because the soil was too rocky to till and the waters too cold for fishing.

Remo saw the impassive faces of those villagers, unchanged down through the ages, with their suspicious eyes and alien faces.

On second thought, maybe staying alive for the sake of those people wasn't the way to go.

He thought of his own life. Of the women he had known and loved and mostly lost. He thought of Jilda of Lakluun, a Viking warrior woman with whom he had had a daughter, a laughing-eyed little girl named Freya. Over a year ago Remo had been visited by the spirit of his own deceased mother and was told by her that a shadow had fallen over Freya. The danger was not yet great, but it was growing.

Since then Remo had been on Harold Smith's back to find Freya, but even Smith's far-reaching computers couldn't locate a teenage girl whose last name was unknown and unguessable.

Shifting position to warm his left side, Remo recalled the image of little Freya. When he had last seen her, she was seven. Now she would be thirteen. A very young lady. Closing his eyes, he tried to imagine what her face would look like today. His imagination failed him. He couldn't envision the daughter he had seen only once in his life; he could only remember her as she was on their last meeting.

Over the lap and gurgle of water, he thought he heard her tinkling laugh. It came again. Clearer this time.

"Freya?"

"Daddy. Where are you?"

Remo's eyes snapped open.

"Freya!"

"Daddy, don't die. Live for me. Live for meeeeeee."

"Freya!"

But the voice was gone. Only the monotonous waters spoke.

Regathering his energies, Remo made a decision. He would live for Freya. If for no other reason, for Freya. Freya was somewhere in danger, and he would find her. Somehow.

The shark was threshing more now. Remo kneed it. It huffed, expelling water from its bleeding mouth.

Its triangular head twisted and bucked. Remo held on. He caught glimpses of the remaining teeth down in its lower jaw.

If the shark ever caught him in its mouth, those few ragged teeth would still saw through his flesh like razors.

"You wanna eat me?" Remo growled.

The shark threshed, one eye coming into view. It was flat, black and inhuman. But Remo sensed a cold, predatory intelligence that saw him as warm food.

"You want to eat me, you rat bastard?" Remo repeated, angrier this time.

The shark flexed its stiff cartilage tail.

"Well, maybe I'll eat *you* instead."

Reaching forward, Remo snapped off a shark tooth. It happened so fast the shark couldn't react in time.

Remo plunged the tooth into the tough hide. It went in. Sharks were not immune to shark bites. They frequently cannibalized one another.

Blood erupted, dark, almost black-red. Remo placed his lips to the wound and drank deep. It was salty and bitter but it was sustenance. It was fish blood, so he could drink it safely. Beef blood would probably poison his purified system.

After drinking all he could stand, Remo reinserted the tooth deep, then ripped it straight back.

The tough hide parted, exposing reddish pink meat.

With quick motions Remo sliced row after row of lines, filleting the shark alive.

It struggled. Remo quieted it by squeezing until its gills expelled water. And reaching in, Remo ripped out a slab of shark steak.

He began eating it raw. Taking big bites and gobbling the food down. There was no time for the niceties of chewing it correctly. He needed the energy from its meat, its life force, in his belly. Now.

The shark tried rolling. Remo steered its fin against the motion. The shark righted itself. It resumed threshing and twisting, but ultimately it was weak from loss of blood. Its blood oozed out, a reddish shimmer on the surrounding waters.

Remo ate on, ripping out fistfuls of tough meat. The taste was rank. Sharks ate the trash of the sea and they tasted like it. So even though Remo's diet was restricted by Sinanju training to certain varieties of rice, fish and duck, Remo rarely ate shark.

As Chiun had once explained to him, "He who eats shark eats what a shark has eaten."

"Sharks sometimes eat people," Remo had said, understanding.

"He who eats shark risks being a cannibal by proxy."

So Remo avoided shark. But this was life or death. His life and the shark's death. It was the law of the sea. The big fish ate the little ones.

Little by little the shark's struggles became noticeably more feeble. After a while it just floated, still alive but dying.

And inevitably the fins of other sharks, attracted by the smell of seeping blood, appeared in the water.

They came from the north, south and west. At first they cut the water in aimless, searching circles. Closing in, they would rip red chunks from the shark's inert carcass in a matter of minutes.

And from Remo, too, if he let it happen.

Remo Williams wasn't about to let it happen.

Fuel in his stomach, his body temperature stabilized, he got up on his hands and knees. Then, balancing carefully because the shark carcass was unstable, he found his feet.

The approaching fins slicing the heaving swells were only yards away now. They knifed the water with cold intent. Remo could almost hear the *Jaws* theme in his head.

Selecting one fin swimming away from the others, Remo faced it.

The first maws yawed upward and lunged. It was now or never.

Remo jumped from his perch.

Landing on the solitary shark's back, he dropped to one knee, grabbing the stabilizing fin in his hand.

Twisting, he steered it away from the carcass just as the feeding frenzy began.

"Get along, little doggie," Remo muttered as he fought the shark, steering it with its own fin.

In the beginning the shark wasn't exactly cooperative. But it was only a fish. Remo was a man. Remo stood on top of the food chain. No shark was going to disobey him.

He lined up the shark's fin with the western horizon and established a course.

The shark fought naturally. But to live it had to keep swimming forward. Sharks do not sleep. Sharks cannot rest. To keep breathing, they have to continue forward. Or they die.

And since the shark had to keep swimming, it was just a matter of controlling the direction.

Remo kept the shark on course. Sometimes with the fin, other times with a hard slap to its sensitive snout. When it tried to dive, Remo wrenched it back, and the shark would forget all about diving and try to bite the annoying thing on its back.

After a while the shark grew too tired to resist. But it wasn't too tired to swim. It had to keep swimming.

So it swam toward land, with its gills submerged just enough to scoop oxygen.

An hour passed, two, then three. During that time Remo digested the food in his stomach and started to hunger for more. His body was burning calories at a fierce rate. Sustaining his elevated body temperature in the cold North Atlantic was taxing his Sinanju powers.

When he felt strong enough, Remo broke the shark's spine with a single chopping bow. It coughed, an explosion of air. When it slowed to a glide, by using only his index fingernails Remo scored the dorsal hide, carving out a fresh shark steak. He ate two. Then he stood up.

Somewhere in the offshore breeze, Remo smelled land. He had no idea how near it was, but he was ready to make a run for it, especially because the heavy swells were calmer here.

Stepping back, he set himself, charged his lungs and, with tiny steps to create maximum forward momentum, Remo ran the length of the shark and stepped onto the water.

His toes touched, skipped, touched again and kept on skipping.

The art was in not letting his full weight break the surface tension of the water. Cold water was denser and better suited than warm. Otherwise water running might have been impossible in Remo's weakened condition.

But he wanted to live. And so he ran, step after step, sucking the cold, reviving air into his lungs, fighting the fatigue that threatened to engulf him.

He ran because, like a shark, if he stopped, he would die. He could not die, so he ran. And ran and ran and ran, his toes making tiny pattering slaps on the choppy gray-green surface of the Atlantic.

Remo smelled land before he saw it. Remo had no idea how much time had passed. But the smell of cooked food and burning fossil fuels and car exhaust pulled him on.

He saw rocks first. Cold, rockweed-covered New England granite half-eroded by relentless waves.

Remo ran for them. But somewhere in the last mile, his strength gave out. He misstepped, lost his footing and sank into the cold, unforgiving waters—within sight of land and life and safety....

8

She didn't know who she was.

Sometimes in the mirror, she thought she recognized her own eyes. Green eyes. Emerald green. Sometimes they were sapphires. Other times a dull gray. They looked familiar. Her hair did not, but she colored it so often she'd forgotten its true color.

She had been told she was Mistress Kali, but the name didn't fit. Somehow it didn't fit.

When she lay all alone in her great circular bed looking up at the mirrors on the ceiling, she knew she was not Mistress Kali. It was a persona she assumed when she donned the tight black leather that sheathed her supple form. She was Mistress Kali when the silver chains clinked and tinkled. She felt like Mistress Kali when she selected a suitable whip from her stock and donned the yellow silk domino mask.

When she stepped out of her private chambers with its implements of pain and discipline, she knew she was Mistress Kali. There was not doubt. Who else could she be?

But when the silken domino mask came off, the doubts returned. They crept into her mind unbidden.

"Who am I?" She wondered.

Once, she asked. "Who am I?"

"You are Mistress Kali," the sweet but distant voice replied.

"Before that?"

"Before that you were nothing."

"What am I when I am not Mistress Kali?" she pressed.

"Asleep," came the absent reply, dotted by the plasticky clicking of keys. The keys that were never still. The keys that were as much a constant in her life as the clink and rattle of chain. As familiar as the crack of the whip that brought a thrill of power control and sexual release whenever she laid it along a pale white spine and flicked an ass cheek into quivering spasm.

"What will I be when I am no longer Mistress Kali?" she wondered aloud.

"Of no use to me, Mother."

The slip had been strange. She put it out of her mind because the next words chilled her so.

"Do not forget this. Ever."

And the clicking of keys continued. Mistress Kali—she was Mistress Kali again—slid the watery blue-green glass panel back into place.

On the other side, the stunted figure at the computer terminal continued to type without rest. She never slept.

And so long as she never slept, the long, vague nightmare seemed to have no ending.

9

The cold water rose up to claim Remo Williams. His mind went blank. He had not the strength to process what was happening to him.

Water touched his lips, splashed into his nostrils, stung his eyeballs.

He held his breath—and his bare feet touched cold, silty sediment. And under it, hard, seaweed-slimy granite. Reflexively his legs straightened.

It took a few seconds for the truth to sink in.

The water didn't even cover his head.

Then Remo laughed. It was a laugh of sheer relief. Of pure joy. Within sight of land, he was standing in chin-deep water.

So he began walking, shivering once or twice when the natural protective defenses of the human body overcame his Sinanju training, which had taught that shivering wasted precious energy, even if the body's reflexes forced a person to shiver in order to stay warm.

The last few yards were rocky, and the rocks scummy under his feet. Remo didn't care. He had survived. Chiun would be proud. He had survived an ordeal that might have beaten some of the greater Masters of Sinanju.

But not Remo Williams. He was a survivor. He had survived.

Reaching shore, Remo clambered over the rocks and found a patch of dry, cold sand. His knees felt hollow.

There he lay down and slept until the rays of the morning sun touched his face and a voice asked, "Where the hell have you been?"

Remo blinked, lifted his head and saw a face that wasn't at first familiar, though the Red Sox ball cap was.

"Who are you?" he muttered weakly.

"Ethel. Don't you remember me? I gave you a lift. We had a deal."

"Oh, that. Sure."

Her lined face hovered over him, filling his field of vision.

"What kept you?" she asked.

"I was fighting off sharks."

"Where's the stuff?"

"Something went wrong."

"I kinda figured that." She stood up, eyed Remo critically and asked, "You know what?"

"What?" said Remo, not really caring at the moment.

"Last night I thought you were kinda cute."

"Thanks," Remo murmured tiredly.

"But now you look like something the cat dragged in, and I wouldn't have you on a stick."

"That's nice," said Remo, closing his tired eyes.

"So I guess I don't feel so bad about what I did."

"That's nice, too," said Remo, tuning her voice out.

Ethel stood up and called over her shoulder. "He's over here."

"Who is?" mumbled Remo.

"You are," Ethel replied.

The Maine State troopers surrounded Remo with their hands on their side arms. They looked unhappy, the way men look when they've spent a cold night on a long stakeout.

"Get up, sir," one said formally. "You are under arrest."

"For what?"

"Suspicion of smuggling."

"Smuggling what?"

"You tell us."

Remo got up, shivered one last time energetically and cracked a weak grin. "The only thing I'm smuggling is shark meat."

"Where is this contraband?" the second trooper demanded.

"In my stomach."

Nobody looked very amused.

Because it was the easiest way to go and it meant warmth and probably dry clothes, Remo allowed himself to be taken to the local state police barracks. He was issued a hot shower and blue prisoner denims. He took them in that order.

"We know you're a bad guy," a trooper told Remo in the interrogation room after Remo had gotten dry.

"Wrong. I'm a good guy."

"You're a smuggler. Ethel said so. She's well liked around here."

"You know, I thought she had an honest face."

"She does. Why do you think she turned you in?"

"Good point," said Remo. "I want my one phone call."

"We need your name and address first."

"Sure. Remo Mako." He gave a Trenton, New Jerscy, address.

"That a house or apartment?"

"House," said Remo. "Definitely a house."

"Any statement you care to make at this time will be counted in your favor."

"Thanks. My statement is I want to call my lawyer."

A clerical head poked into the interrogation room. "You don't have to. He's already on the horn, demanding to speak to you."

"His name Smith?" asked Remo, who was not about to fall for some trick and lose out on his lawful call.

"Ay-yah. And you must get into a lot of this kind of trouble if he knows where you are so quick."

REMO TOOK THE CALL in private.

"What took you so long, Smitty?"

"Your Remo Mako alias is not on my list of approved cover names. When it went out on law-enforcement wires, my system spit out the fact that the address you gave was that of the Trenton State Prison death house. That told me it was you being held in the Lubec barracks on suspicion of smuggling."

"Good catch."

"What happened, Remo?"

Dr. Harold W. Smith was grimly silent after Remo told him what had happened.

"You can spring me the polite way or I can spring myself," Remo told him.

"We need to do this quietly."

"Don't take long, or I'll take matters into my own hands," Remo warned.

Remo knew he was on his way home when he heard the helicopter rotors beating his way.

The chopper settled on the back lawn, where he could see it from his holding cell. It was a big orange-and-white Jayhawk rescue helicopter with the Coast Guard anchor-and-flotation-ring crest in red-and-white striping on the tail.

Coast Guardsmen in crisp whites came running out, holding their service caps against the rotor wash.

In less than ten minutes Remo was being processed out.

"You might have informed us you were with the Coast Guard," the arresting officer told Remo as he searched his pockets for the handcuff key.

Remo handed over the handcuffs, still locked tight, and said, "Lost my ID in the water. Would you have taken my word for it?"

"No," the trooper admitted.

"There you go," said Remo.

The Coast Guard chopper ferried Remo to the local guard station, where Remo was transferred to a Coast Guard Falcon jet. It took off screaming, and two hours later Remo was deposited at Logan International Airport in Boston.

He took a cab home, thinking that Chiun was either going to be very happy to see him or very angry. Possibly both. It was impossible to predict the Master of Sinanju's moods in advance.

But either way, Remo couldn't wait to see him again. It had been as close to death as he had gotten in a long time, and it felt good to be alive and kicking.

He hoped the Master of Sinanju would feel the same way about things. After all, a mission was just a mission, but Remo was next in line to head the House. How angry could Chiun be?

10

She wanted sex. Of course she did. He could tell it from the look on her long face when he walked in the door and from the filmy negligee that would drape a busty blonde wonderfully. But clinging to her scrawny, pale skin, it looked pathetic. Like spiderwebs on a corpse.

He avoided her kiss by striking first. A peck on the cheek, and sensing it would not be enough to avoid the tobacco breath, a second, more careful one on the brow.

She stepped back, spreading the gauzy wings of the negligee.

Lavender, for God's sake. Made her look like a harridan.

"I thought you'd never get home, dear," she cooed.

He wanted to slap her. Tell her to grow up. She was a mother, for Christ's sake. Why couldn't she settle for that? Not these pathetic attempts to rekindle the spark that was long past cooling.

"I had a difficult day," he said guardedly, his eyes going to the closed door of the den.

Her smiling face bobbed into view.

"Then you'll need a long, leisurely...what?"

"Soak," he said quickly.

"Soak. Yes, have a nice soak. I think I'll join you."

There was no way out. Divorce was out of the question. Without a wife he might as well pack it in. Throw away all hope, all ambition, all thoughts of the future.

"All right," he said, mustering up what passed for marital enthusiasm. "We'll share a soak."

The soak was as sexy as bathing with an Irish wolfhound. With her long face, thin arms and absolute absence of a bust or bottom, she more and more reminded him of an Irish wolfhound, an abysmally hideous canine.

When it was over, she toweled him down lovingly and led him by the hand to the bedroom, where scented candles flamed in glass jars. It was all very bewitching. All the tableau needed was a woman with some meat on her bones.

But he hadn't married her for her flesh, but for her mind, her good breeding, her impeccable character. A respectable wife was one of the inconvenient accoutrements for a man on the move.

He never stopped to think that even sex became boring if one did it often enough in the same two unimaginative positions with absolutely no props or enhancements.

So, once again he went through the motions. Foreplay consisted of a few chaste kisses, a perfunctory back rub and then he mounted her. He wanted to strangle her. Strangling her would have made it exciting for once, and it would have ensured that he'd never have to plumb these unpleasant depths again.

In the moment she gave before his first prodding thrust, he decided the hell with it and took her violently. It was madness, but he was desperate. It had been too long. And he was under such stress at the office, what with the latest Angus Reid polls and all.

To his astonishment, she loved it. She shrieked wildly, then began moaning as he pumped and pumped as if driving a stake through a vampire's heart. That was how it felt. Like driving a stake through the heart of the undead thing that his marriage had become.

Climaxing, she sank her teeth in his shoulder and shuddered uncontrollably.

It wasn't passionate, but as least he had climaxed. For once.

"You came!" she whispered, giving the word a slutty inflection.

"Miracles never cease," he said dryly.

Her smile was a dim porcelain glow in the wan light. "Admit it. It was wonderful."

"Shattering," he said, disengaging.

As he rolled over, she doused the bedroom light and blew the candles out. She was humming. It was some mindless Barry Manilow song he detested.

But at least it was over.

As he waited for sleep to come, he smelled a pungent odor. It was her. But it reminded him of something else. The sexiest smell in the entire world.

The smell of ripped and gutted fish.

It wouldn't let him sleep. He prayed for sleep, but the tuna smell in his nostrils was like scented cotton.

He waited until her snoring filled the room before throwing off the bed covers and digging his feet into his slippers.

He padded into the den and turned on the computer. The paneled walls were adorned with schooner prints. A varnished pine plaque over the monitor had a legend burned into it by a soldering iron: From Sea To Sea.

The system went through its interminable sign-on cycles, and finally he accessed his e-mail via the service.

There was no message from the one who haunted his thoughts. It had been nearly a month. Where was she?

The cellular telephone in his briefcase buzzed. Snapping it open, he lifted it to his face and spoke. "Yes?"

"Commodore."

"Go ahead."

"We had another inconvenient encounter."

"Details, please."

"A U.S. vessel in the Nose. We were conducting routine truffle operations, and the illegal spotted the Hound on his fish-finding sonar. We had to take action."

"Vessel status?"

"Scuttled."

"Crew?"

"Cat food."

"Witnesses?"

"None. As before."

"That will do."

"Aye-aye, Commodore."

"Continue herding operations. Report any anomalies."

"Aye, sir."

Closing the cell phone, he laid it beside the terminal. His eyes went to the screen.

And there, like a beacon, glowed a New Message prompt line.

To: Commodore@net.org
From: Kali@yug.net
Subject: Call me instantly

But the message area was only blank space.

"Bitch!" he muttered.

He had been warned never to call, never to visit, without being summoned first. No one gave a man of his stature orders, and that was part of the thrill, of course.

He punched out the number from memory and waited with pounding heart and an uncomfortable rising sensation in his crotch.

"If you dialed correctly, you know my name," her cool contralto voice said. "Speak."

"Mistress."

"Commodore."

"Er, I have your message."

"All is well, I trust," she said coolly.

"As well as it can be with the current situation."

"Still conducting tests?"

"Er, yes. We had an accident this evening."

"You must tell me all about it." It was not a polite invitation, but a firm command.

"Be glad to."

"In person."

"I would be delighted. Shall I bring something?"

Her voice dripped with contempt. "Bring your obedience, worm." And she hung up.

He changed from his stained pajama pants into fresh trousers and sped through the sleeping city to the place he knew as the Temple.

It was unlocked. He stepped into the anteroom and through double doors beside which danced barbaric carvings of bare-breasted females with ripe lips, lascivious hips and multiple arms poised to please. In the preparation room he removed his clothes down to the last stitch.

His manhood was already rising. He swallowed hard, presented himself to the mirrored door of one-way glass. He saw himself. Behind the obscuring glass, she was looking at him, he knew. He could feel her blazing blue eyes upon him.

Her cool question floated through the barrier. "Are you prepared to enter my presence?"

"I am, Mistress."

"Then assume the position of approach."

Falling on hands and knees, he crept toward the door, bumping it open with his head.

Like a scuttling crab, he entered the room.

He kept his eyes on the polished floor because the penalty for doing otherwise was severe, and it was too early in the encounter to expect the corporal delights to be visited upon him.

He stopped when his head bumped her stiletto boots and one lifted to press its steely pointedness into his bare back.

"Tell me," she said flatly.

"Anything."

"Tell me what happened tonight that disturbs you so."

"Another U.S. fishing vessel stumbled onto a test. It had to be disposed of for security reasons. Crew and vessel are no more."

"Very wise."

"No one will ever know."

Her tone turned sarcastic. "Except you and I and everyone involved. That is how many individual persons?"

"I imagine thirty, all told," he stuttered.

"Thirty people in on a secret that could ruin your career, if not your life. If only one percent of them tell one person, how big a leak is that?"

"Considerable," he admitted.

"How big?"

"Disastrous."

"That's better." Her voice shed its bitter sarcasm, though it could hardly be said to soften.

"It's a well-known axiom, Commodore, that if you tell one person a confidence, you must assume you told three. Because most people feel the urge to confide in their most trusted confidants, who in turn will confide in theirs, and so on several times over until the secret is fully out and no longer a secret but common gossip."

"Stories distort in the telling."

"It may be time to move to the next level."

"Escalation?"

"I have read your polls. They are sinking. *You* are sinking."

"I am receptive to your merciless counsel, as always, Mistress."

"Of course. How could it be otherwise?"

She dug her heel into his back, and the bull-whip—whose leather he smelled but did not see—unwound from her unseen hand to fall heavily over his head like a shiny, crinkled tentacle.

"I can see you are in need of convincing."

In fact, it was the contrary. But he had more-urgent needs. Already the bullwhip was being gathered up into a tense, tight coil of unreleased energy.

"Whatever you decree, Mistress."

"I decree pain!"

And the bullwhip cracked down on his back like a bitter, stinging kiss.

His face was pushed into the black floor. His hardness burned, sliding to one side under the pressure of his recoiling body. Later he would discover friction burns. He loved friction burns. They were like a badge of honor.

She was hectoring him mercilessly. "You will escalate. You will provoke and you will obey."

"I will obey."

"You will obey absolutely!"

"I will obey absolutely."

And kneeling before him, she lifted his head by the sweaty hair, thrusting her womanly face into his own. Her eyes burned like icy blue diamonds. Her golden hair was a wild cloud framing a perfect face made more perfect by the yellow silk domino mask. Her lips glistened with a bloody shine. They pulsed with her moist, confident exhalations, not an inch from his eager ear.

"I will tell you what you must do...."

11

Tomasso Testaverde was a survivor. From his earliest days of stealing fish off the slush-laden wheelbarrows and ice buckets on the busy Kingsport, Massachusetts, wharves of his youth to the day he crewed his first dragger, he was a survivor.

It was said of Tomasso Testaverde that he was a survivor to the day he died.

He died on a day just like any other. All of the days of Tomasso Testaverde's life were essentially the same. That was to say, larcenous.

Deep in his larcenous heart, though Tomasso didn't see himself that way, he was a low thief.

When he stole fish off the docks and cooked them over fires made in the crumbling, naked chimneys of Old Dogtown, where witches used to dwell in the long-ago days before his grandfather Sirio came from Sicily, Tomasso saw himself as simply an opportunist. One who took advantage of life's little opportunities. Nothing more. And besides, he was hungry. His father was away for weeks at a time fishing cod off the Grand Banks, or sometimes seining mackerel off the Virginia coast. Tomasso's mother was, as they liked to say, a woman whose heels grew rounder the longer her husband's shoes were not tucked under her bed.

Had he been born a fish, Tomasso Testaverde would have been a bottom feeder.

When he grew older, it was no longer possible to hide in small places or outrun the fishermen from whom he pilfered haddock and flounder. Tomasso discovered he had acquired an unfortunate reputation. And so crewing on the trawlers and draggers of his peers, as his ancestors had done, was not in his future.

But a resourceful boy invariably flowers into a resourceful adult. Denied the livelihood of a man, Tomasso shunned those who refused to let him crew on their boats and so found other, more creative ways to survive.

In those days they set lobster pots in the water just off the shore, lowering the pots in the morning and hauling them up again at night. The buoys were colored, so that no one hauled up a pot that was not his, but as far as Tomasso was concerned, any untended pot he happened upon in his rickety dory was his.

After all, he always replaced the pot just as he found it, keeping only the lobsters within. This was fair.

And so Tomasso acquired a new reputation, one more lasting than the old. For a wayward boy might be forgiven in time, but a man who stole the sustenance from the mouths of hardworking Italian fishermen was branded for life.

Having no overhead, and expending little labor,

Tomasso in time hauled up sufficient free lobsters that a more seaworthy vessel became his.

Here began his true career.

Fishing was hard work and hard work wasn't to Tomasso's liking. Not that he didn't try. He attempted dragging. He tried seine fishing and gill netting. He eked out a haphazard living, acquired a crew that often needed firing because it was cheaper to fire than pay a man regularly, and along the way Tomasso learned every draggerman's trick there was.

It was possible to survive by foraging off the coastal Massachusetts waters for many years.

Until the fish began to recede.

Tomasso refused to believe the stories that were circulating. He was unwelcome in the United Fishermen's Club, where these things were discussed. So he learned of them secondhand and imperfectly.

"Old ladies," he would sneer. "The oceans are vast and the fish free to swim. The fish are not stupid. They know they are sought. They swim farther out. That is all. We will go even farther out for them."

But the farther out the boats went, the harder it was to catch fish. Where in the days of not-so-long-ago, it was possible to lower a net and lift it bursting with pale-bellied cod, the nets straining because the innards of the cod were filling with raw air, by the early 1990s, a lowered net came up filled with wriggling, less desirable brownish whiting, some gray halibut and on a good day a mere bushel of silvery cod.

Tomasso, who had to sell his catch down in Point

Judith, Rhode Island, because his cargoes were unwelcome in Massachusetts fish ports, could not meet his expenses.

There were other inconveniences. The diamond-shaped mesh was outlawed. Only small square-mesh nets were legal now. But nets were expensive and Tomasso refused to throw his away. After he was caught for the third time hauling up endangered groundfish in forbidden biomass nets, he was told his license was forfeit.

"I don't care," he told them. "There is no more fish. The others have frightened them all away. I am going north, where the lobster is plentiful."

And it was true. Lobsters were plentiful up in the Gulf of Maine. Also, Tomasso Testaverde wasn't known up in Maine. Maine would be good for him. It would be a fresh start.

Up in Bar Harbor he was accepted. The lobsters were coming back after a short period of decline. Catches were exploding.

"The cod will come back, too. You wait and see," Tomasso often said.

They were harvesting other things in Maine. Rock crab. Eels. Spiny sea urchin was very lucrative, too. But it was intensive work, and urchin roe was not to Tomasso's taste. He refused to catch what he could not also eat.

"I will stick with lobsters. Lobsters I know," boasted Tomasso Testaverde. "I will be the King of Lobsters, you wait and see. I know them well, and they know me."

But Tomasso was surprised to discover that they had rules in the Gulf of Maine. The fisheries people down east, as they called Maine or Maine called itself, were concerned that the lobsters would go the way of the cod, although that was absurd on the face of it, Tomasso thought. Cod swam far. Lobsters were crawlers. They could only crawl so far.

In the early months he caught great red jumboes, some albinos and even a very rare fifty-pound blue lobster. It made the newspapers, this monster lobster of Tomasso Testaverde's. Marine biologists from the Woods Hole Oceanographic Institute said it was possibly one hundred years old and should not be sold to the restaurants for food.

A famous actress came to Bar Harbor to personally plead for the life of the blue lobster. Tomasso offered to spare if it the actress slept with him. She slapped him. Tomasso, cheek as red as a common lobster's, dropped the blue lobster into a boiling pot of water and ate it himself out of spite, dropping off the angry red discarded shell at the hotel where the actress slept in selfish isolation.

After that, people shunned Tomasso Testaverde. Other lobstermen especially. It did not matter to him, though. Tomasso cared only about taking lobsters from the Gulf of Maine. And the lobsters were there for the taking, to be sure.

He used all the tricks, such as soaking cloth in kerosene and baiting his lobster traps with the malodorous stuff although this was frowned upon for environmental reasons. For some reason no one knew, lobsters were attracted to the scent of kerosene in the water.

But it was the rules and regulations that bothered

Tomasso Testaverde the most. They were many and inconvenient.

Lobsters under a certain length could not be taken legally. These Tomasso dropped into a secret ice-filled chest in his boat. These he ate himself. Working with lobsters had not dulled his taste for the crustacean's sweet, firm meat. It pleased him to think he ate for free what rich men better than he paid good money to enjoy on special occasions.

Another rule said the egg-bearing female of any size must be returned to the sea to protect future generations of lobstermen by ensuring future generations of lobsters. Tomasso, who had no sons, thought the law should not apply to him. Only to men with futures. Tomasso cared only about today. Only about survival. Tomorrow would take care of itself.

"The law applies to everyone," a man in a bar once said to him over beer, Buffalo wings and complaints.

"Different rules for different men. That is my law," Tomasso boasted.

An unfortunate admission, because the man was from the Department of Fisheries and Wildlife in Portland and he followed Tomasso down to the docks and took down the name of his scunga-bunga jonesporter boat, the *Jeannie I*, named after a cousin Tomasso deflowered at a tender age.

The next time he went out, Tomasso was casually hosing off the jellylike black eggs from under the curled tail where female lobsters carry their tiny eggs. That made them legal. Technically.

A Coast Guard lifeboat came upon Tomasso as

he was about this activity, and he hastily finished what he was doing and tried to look innocent as he was hailed and boarded.

"What can I do for you fellows?" he asked.

A Coast Guard inspector stepped onto the *Jeannie I* and said in a very serious voice, "Inspection. Suspicion of scrubbing."

"I keep a clean boat," Tomasso said, trying to keep a straight face, too.

They took up the lobster he had just deposited into the holding bin. The hold was abrim with crawling red-brown crustaceans. There were a few pistols, too, as the one-claw culls were called.

"All my lobster are over the legal limit," Tomasso protested. "You may inspect them if you wish. I have nothing to hide."

Two inspectors dropped into the hold and did that, using caliperlike measuring tools designed for that purpose. They were very professional as they measured the carapace.

Tomasso watched unconcerned. He knew as long as they didn't find the secret hatch, he was all right.

But when they came up with one particular lobster and an inspector dabbed some indigo solution from an eyedropper onto the swimmerets under the tail, which the other held straight, Tomasso grew worried.

"This lobster has recently had eggs," he was told.

"I see no eggs," Tomasso said quickly.

"The eggs are gone. According to our tests, the cement that holds them on is recent."

"Cement? What would a lobster know of cement?'' And throwing his head back, Tomasso laughed uproariously.

The inspectors didn't laugh with him. They handcuffed him and towed his boat back to Bar Harbor, where he was warned and fined.

It was a bitter experience. Not only was it becoming impossible for a lobsterman to earn a good living in Maine, but it was no longer safe to have a convivial beer with a stranger. The bars were filled with spies.

For a while Tomasso avoided taking the eggbearers, but they were too great a temptation. He heard that chlorine bleach could erase all trace of the natural cement that lobsters secreted to hold their eggs in place. Tomasso found it worked. The next time he was caught, they had to let him go, though they weren't happy about it. The jugs of chlorine bleach lay in plain sight.

On the day Tomasso ran out of days, the *Jeannie I* puttered out of the harbor into the gulf with open cargo holds and many jugs of chlorine bleach.

In a zone where the Coast Guard seldom ventured, where the lobsters were not as plentiful and therefore it was possible to work without competition or interference, Tomasso set down his traps.

It was a cold, bitter, blustery day, and only because he drank his profits did Tomasso venture out. He often dreamed of wintering in Florida, where fishermen caught real fish like tarpon and swordfish. But he didn't have the savings to achieve this dream. Not yet.

Tomasso was lowering traps and pots and hauling them up again by stern-mounted block and tackle when a great gray ship came out of the low-lying fog. He took instant notice of it. One moment it was not there, and the next it was bearing down on him as big as a house, streamers of fog curling out of its way.

Tomasso had a dozen claw-pegged egg-bearers on the deck in wooden trays and was dousing them with bleach when the great gray ship showed itself like a silent apparition.

He had never seen one like it. Lobstermen didn't go out as far as deep-sea fishermen, so the sight of a behemoth factory ship was an unfamiliar one to Tomasso Testaverde.

The ship hadn't veered off course, and Tomasso gave his air horn a tap. It blared, echoing off the oncoming bow.

A foghorn blared back.

Tomasso nodded. "They see me. Good. Then let them go around me. I am a working man."

But the ship didn't change course. It came steaming directly at the *Jeannie I.* Its foghorn continued to blare.

Dropping his jug, Tomasso dived for the wheelhouse and got the engine muttering. He threw it into reverse because that seemed to be the quickest route out of harm's way.

Still the great gray ship plowed on.

Cursing, Tomasso shook a weatherbeaten fist as red as a lobster at them. *"Fungula!"* he swore.

Men lined the forward rails, men in blues and whites. Their faces looked strange from a distance.

Tomasso looked hard at these faces. They looked all alike. They weren't the faces of fishermen, which are raw and red. These were a stark white, and in the center of those faces splayed some blue blotch tattoo.

For a strange moment Tomasso's limited imagination made those blue blotches into rows of identical lobsters. And he thought of the blue lobster he had eaten, for which he was still reviled.

For a queasy moment he saw the identical impassive faces staring at him as men out to avenge the blue lobster that had been Tomasso's most famous meal.

But that couldn't be. The blue blotch must represent something else.

The great gray ship made a long turn, and its bow was soon lining up with the *Jeannie I.*

"Are these men mad?" Tomasso muttered, this time throwing his boat forward.

The *Jeannie I* avoided being struck by a good margin, but the other ship seemed determined to catch him.

There was no radio on the *Jeannie I.* A lobsterman didn't need one, believed Tomasso Testaverde. But now he wished he had a radio to call the Coast Guard. This mystery ship was playing with him the way a big fish plays with a little one.

It was possible to avoid the big ship whose name was some unpronounceable thing Tomasso didn't know.

But try as Tomasso might, it wasn't possible to outrun it.

Setting a heading for land, he ran the *Jeannie I* flat out. She dug in her stern, and the bow lifted as high as it could. But hard on her cold, foaming wake came the sinister gray ship with its ghost-faced crew.

It wasn't a long chase. Not even three nautical miles. The huge gray knife of a prow loomed closer and closer, and its shadow fell on the *Jeannie I*, drowning it like the Shadow of Death.

In his slicker, Tomasso Testaverde swore and cursed and sweated, hot and cold alternately. "What do you want? What do you bastards want?" he screamed over his shoulder.

The remorseless gray ship nudged the *Jeannie I* once. She spurted ahead, her fat stern fractured.

Tomasso let out a pungent wail. *"Mangia la cornata!"*

For the cold ocean was pouring into the *Jeannie I*, washing her decks. It happened very fast. Taking on water, the lobster boat slowed. The gray prow lunged anew, splintering the wounded boat.

Tomasso jumped clear. There was nothing else for him to do.

By some miracle he swam clear of the foamy upheaval that was the *Jeannie I* going down.

The cold made his muscles shrink and his bones turn to ice, it came upon him so swiftly. He was intensely cold. With sick eyes he watched the big ship glide on past, its sides bumping aside the fresh driftwood and kindling that used to be the *Jeannie I*.

The warmth of death came over Tomasso quickly. He knew how one would grow warm just before succumbing to the cold of exposure and hypothermia. It was as true for a child who falls asleep in the snowy woods as for a man adrift in the cold waters of the Gulf of Maine.

Tomasso was a survivor. But he knew he would not survive this.

His body like lead, he began to sink. He didn't feel the hands clutching his ice-rimed hair and flailing arms, nor did he know he was being hauled into a dory.

He only knew that some time later he lay in the fish hold of a ship. It was cold. He tried to move but couldn't. Lifting his head, he looked down and saw that his body was blue and naked. It trembled and shivered involuntarily. It was his body. Tomasso recognized it, but he couldn't really feel it.

I am shivering and I don't feel it, he thought in a vague, wondering frame of mind.

Men were hovering around him. He could see their faces. White. Gleaming white. The blue tattoo that went from forehead to chin and spread out over nose and mouth and cheeks wasn't shaped like a lobster. It was something else.

Tomasso did not know what the design was, only that it was familiar.

A man stepped up and began to apply something white and gleaming to Tomasso's unfeeling face.

They are trying to save me. They are applying some warming salve to my face. I have been saved. I will survive.

Then one of them stepped up with a living fish in one hand, a fish knife in the other. With a quick slash, he decapitated the fish and, without ceremony, while the other man was calmly applying creamy white unguent to Tomasso's features, he inserted the bleeding stump of the fish into Tomasso's open mouth.

Tomasso tasted blood and fish guts.

And he knew he was tasting death.

He did not feel them turn his inert body over and perform an obscene act upon his dying dignity with another fish.

He never dreamed, not even in death, that he was destined to be the spark in a confrontation that would shake the world from which he took much but gave back so very little.

12

Boston traffic was, for Boston traffic, almost normal. There were only two accidents, neither serious, although one looked as if someone decided to pull a U-turn onto the UMass off-ramp. The pickup truck in question had ended up on its back like an upset turtle, and the tires were nowhere to be seen.

When the cab he was riding swerved suddenly, Remo saw them rolling in different directions like big black doughnuts out for a stroll.

"Just another day on the Southeast Distressway," the cabbie muttered to himself.

Remo Williams never got used to turning the corner and seeing his house. It wasn't actually a house really. It was a condominium now, but the units were never marketed for several very good reasons, not the least of which was that before it had been converted, the building had been a stone church.

It wasn't a typical church. A typical church is typically topped by a witch's-hat steeple with a cross on top. Its lines were medieval, although it looked very modern with its fieldstone walls and double row of roof dormers.

Still, it had been built as a house of worship, not a dwelling. The Master of Sinanju had wrested it from Harold Smith during a contract negotiation several years earlier. Remo, of course, had had no say in the matter. Not that he really cared. After years of living out of suitcases, it was nice to have a permanent address. And he had one wing of the place all to himself.

What Remo hated most were the idle comments of the cabdrivers.

"You live here?" this one blurted when Remo told him to pull over. "In this rock pile?"

"It's been in my family for centuries," Remo assured him.

"A church?"

"It's actually a castle transported brick by brick from the ancestral estate in Upper Sinanju."

"Where's that?"

"New Jersey."

"They have castles in Jersey?"

"Not anymore. This was the last one to be carried off before state castle taxes went through the roof."

"Must be pre-Revolutionary."

"Pre-pre-Revolutionary," said Remo, slipping a twenty through the pay slot. He had replenished his cash supply at an airport ATM with a card he carried in his back pocket.

At the door Remo rang the bell. And rang it again.

To his surprise a plump dumpling of an Asian woman with iron gray hair padded up to the two glass ovals of the double doors. She wore a nondescript quilted costume that wasn't exactly purple and not precisely gray, but might have been lilac.

She looked at Remo, winking owlishly and opened the door.

"Who are you?" Remo demanded.

The old woman bowed. When her face came up, Remo studied it and decided she was South Korean, not North Korean. That was a relief. For a moment there, he was afraid she was some cousin of Chiun's come to visit for the next decade.

"Master awaits," she said in broken English.

"He in the bell tower?"

"No, the fish cellar."

"What fish cellar?" asked Remo.

"The one in basement," said the old woman.

"Oh, *that* fish cellar," said Remo, who had never heard of any fish cellar and was dead sure there hadn't been one in the basement before today. "What's your name, by the way?"

"I am housekeeper. Name not important." And she bowed again.

"But you do have one?"

"Yes," said the old woman, bowing again and shuffling up the stairs to the upper floor.

"Chiun better have a good explanation for this," muttered Remo, ducking through the door leading into the basement.

The basement was an L-shaped space, just like the building above. Patches of light streamed through casement windows. They fell on rows of storage freezers like the ones big families use to keep sides of beef and giant racks of ribs. They were new. They hummed insistently. There were also giant bubbling aquariums, also in rows. All were empty of fish.

"Chiun, where are you?" Remo called out.

"Here," a thin voice squeaked.

Remo knew that squeak. It was not a happy squeak. Chiun was upset.

He found the Master of Sinanju at the far end of the cellar, in what had once been the coal bin. It had been changed. The wooden sides had been torn out and the area bricked off. There was a door. It was open.

Remo looked in.

The Master of Sinanju stood in the dim, cool space wearing his face like a mummy's death mask. His bright hazel eyes were looking up at Remo. They glinted, then narrowed.

Chiun wore a simple gray kimono of raw silk. No decorations. Its skirts brushed the tops of his black Korean sandals. His hands were tucked into the sleeves, which met over his tight belly.

His button nose flared slightly and he said, "You stink of *sango*."

"*Sango?*"

"Shark."

"Oh, right. One tried to eat me."

Chiun cocked his head like an inquisitive bird, his expression unreadable in the gloom. "And...?"

"I ate him first." Remo grinned. Chiun did not. His head came back, throwing off the shadows that clung to the wizened parchment features. He was as bald as an Easter egg, with two white puffs of cloudy hair over each ear. A beard like the unkempt tail of a white mouse hung from his chin.

"Smitty tell you what happened to me?" Remo asked.

"He did not. No doubt shame stilled his noble tongue."

"I got to the rendezvous zone in time. But someone had sunk the ship."

"You allowed this?"

"I couldn't exactly help it. It was sunk before I got there."

"You should have been early."

"But I wasn't."

"But you avenged this insult?"

"I tried to. A submarine torpedoed it. I went looking for it, but it found me first."

"You destroyed this pirate vessel in the name of the House?"

"Actually it kinda got away," Remo admitted.

"You allowed a mere submarine to elude you!" Chiun flared.

"I know what a sub is. I got aboard, but they chased me off. I did my best, Chiun. Then I found myself floating in the ocean without a pot or paddle. I almost drowned."

Chiun's face remained severe. "You are trained not to drown."

"I came that close. Sharks circled me."

"You are stronger than a shark. You are mightier than a shark. No shark could best you whom I have trained in the sun source that is Sinanju."

"Thanks for taking all the credit, but it was a close call."

"The training squandered upon you brought you home alive," said Chiun, stepping out and closing the door behind him with abrupt finality.

"Actually I don't think I would have made it, but I remembered Freya," Remo admitted.

Chiun lifted his chin in unconcealed interest.

"I remembered that I had a daughter and I wanted to see her again. So I found the will to survive."

Chiun said nothing.

"I'm sorry I blew the mission," Remo said quietly. He rotated his freakishly thick wrists absentmindedly.

Chiun remained quiet, his face stiff, his hazel eyes opaque.

"So, what did we lose?" asked Remo.

"Our honor. But it will be regained. You will see to that."

And Chiun breezed past Remo like a gray wraith.

Opening the door, Remo stuck his head into the bricked-off end of the cellar. It was bare, except for row upon row of cedar shelving.

Shrugging, Remo reclosed the door and started after the Master of Sinanju, and they mounted the stairs together.

"The old lady said you were in the fish cellar. But I don't see any fish."

"That is because there is no fish."

"Happy to hear it. Because I'm in a duck mood tonight."

"This is good because duck will be served tonight and every night for the foreseeable future."

"That's more duck than I was looking forward to."

They reached the top of the stairs.

"That is because there is no fish," said Chiun, without elaborating further.

They ate in the kitchen at a low taboret. The rice was white and sticky, steamed exactly the way Remo liked it, and served in bamboo bowls.

The duck lay supine in a light orange sauce.

Remo was surprised when the old woman who padded about the kitchen like a mute served Chiun a bowl of fish-head soup.

"I thought you said there was no fish," said Remo.

"There is no fish. For you."

"But there's fish for you."

"I did not fail in my mission," Chiun said aridly.

"Usually we eat the same thing."

"From this day until the honor of the House is avenged, you are reduced to duck rations. You will eat roast duck, pressed duck, steamed duck and cold, leftover duck. Mostly you will eat cold duck. And you will like it."

"I'll put up with it, but I won't like it," said Remo, poking at the duck's brown skin with a silver chopstick. "So, what's with the housekeeper?"

"I decided this today."

"She's South Korean, not North."

Chiun looked interested. "Very good, Remo. How can you tell this? By the eyes? The shape of the head?"

"By the fact that she hasn't eaten her way through the cupboard."

Chiun frowned. "Southerners make proper servants, but are of low character. I would not make a servant of a Northerner. Since she is Korean, but not of our blood, she is tolerable."

"You know, this might be a security problem."

"Her English is imperfect."

"I noticed," Remo said dryly.

"And I am weary of cooking for you and cleaning up after you."

"I pull my load."

"Not today. Today you lost an entire ship and its valuable cargo."

"That reminds me," said Remo, "what's *Ingo Pungo* mean?"

"You understand Korean."

"I don't know every word."

"You know *ingo.*"

"Sounds familiar."

"You know *kum.*"

"Sure. *Kum* is 'gold.'"

Chiun lifted one chopstick. "This is *ingo.*"

"I remember now. It means 'silver.'"

With his silver chopstick, Chiun speared a fish head from his soup broth. "And this is *pungo.*"

"A fish?"

"Not a fish. Fish is not fish. Fish have names. They have tastes and textures and even ancestries. River fish are different from ocean fish. Pacific fish are superior to Atlantic fish."

"Since when?"

"This soup is made from the heads of Pacific fishes."

Remo leaned over the taboret and scrutinized the fish head. It stared back.

"Don't recognize it," he admitted.

"It is carp."

"*Ingo Pungo* means *Silver Carp?*"

"Yes. It is a very worthy name for a vessel."

"Maybe. I never much liked carp."

"No, you are an eater of shark."

"It was a necessity," grumbled Remo.

"Not as much a necessity as bathing."

Remo looked at the Master of Sinanju.

"You smell of shark," Chiun reminded him.

"Better than the shark smelling of me," said Remo, who grinned even after the Master of Sinanju refused to return the grin.

It felt so good to be alive he even enjoyed the duck, greasy as it was.

13

Although outwardly Dr. Harold W. Smith looked like a cross between an aging banker and an undertaker, there were days when he resembled an embalmed banker. This was one of those days.

Midwinter did nothing for Harold Smith's complexion. He was well past retirement age, and his hair had turned gray. Not white. A crisp white head of hair would have looked good on Harold Smith. It would have offset the unrelieved gray of his person.

Harold Smith was gray of hair, gray of eye, gray of demeanor and even gray of skin. The gray tinge to his skin was the result of a heart defect. Smith had been a blue baby. He was actually born blue. Like all newborn humans and kittens, Harold Smith had blue eyes at birth.

This soon changed. His eyes turned gray naturally. Silver iodine treatments for his condition had left his skin looking gray. It was as if, his mother had thought at the time, some dour cloud had come along to steal all the blueness from her dear little Harold.

No one knows exactly what forces dictate a man's destiny. Perhaps a man with a colorless name like

Harold Smith was destined to enter some colorless field. His preference for Brooks Brothers gray and his chameleonlike ability to blend unobtrusively into social settings probably made the course of his life inevitable. No one named Harold Smith ever ran off with a busty starlet or broke the sound barrier or played music anyone wanted to hear.

It would have been the undeniable fate of Harold Smith of the Vermont Smiths to enter the family publishing business and toil steadily and doggedly and competently yet never brilliantly, but for Pearl Harbor. Harold Smith had enlisted. Smiths did not wait to be drafted. Smiths served their country in time of war.

Harold Smith's serious qualities were recognized early, and he spent the war in Europe with the OSS. This led to a postwar role with the new Central Intelligence Agency. Smith fit into the CIA perfectly. During the Cold War era, it was really a giant bureaucracy. There Smith learned computer science and gained a reputation and an inconvenient nickname, the Gray Ghost.

Smith would have retired from the CIA in the fullness of time were it not for a young President of his generation who saw the nation he loved spiraling into uncontrollable chaos. That President created a simple concept. CURE. An organization with no staff, no congressional mandate or sanction, but the ultimate power to right the keeling ship of state before the American experiment foundered on the shoals of dictatorship.

The President reached out to the supercompetent Harold Smith and offered him the responsibility for saving his nation from ruin. Smith responded to the challenge as he had responded to Pearl Harbor twenty years before. He undertook his civic duty. That was how he saw it, as a duty. He did not desire the post.

That was long ago. Many Presidents, many missions and many winters ago. Smith had grown grayer behind his desk at Folcroft Sanitarium, the cover for CURE. He would never see retirement now. He would die at his desk. There was no retiring from CURE. And there was no end to the missions or the crises.

Now in the winter of his life, with the leaden skies making his gray personality seem beyond gray, he toiled at his desk and the computer terminal through which Harold Smith monitored the nation he was sworn to safeguard.

Smith had called up a simple data base, Flags of the World. Sometimes the deepest mysteries could be solved by simple resources.

Remo Williams had described to him a submarine with a white flag painted on its sail, framing a blue fleur-de-lis.

Smith had already looked up fleur-de-lis on his data base. It was French for "flower of the lily." There was some historical confusion, he found. Because the flower represented by the fleur-de-lis was actually the iris, it was thought that the iris was originally called a lily. Thus the confusion.

It had been a symbol of French royalty since the reign of the Frankish King Cloris. The trouble was that the French royal flag was a gold fleur-de-lis against a blue background. A quick computer search of the flag data base showed no national flag depicting a fleur-de-lis of any color. The modern French flag was the simple tricolor. No fleur-de-lis.

Smith wasn't surprised. He possessed a photographic memory and recalled no such flag among modern nations.

Absently Smith plucked the rimless spectacles off his patrician nose and polished them with a disposable tissue. Decades of close computer work had made his eyes extremely sensitive to even the smallest dust particles on the lenses. He was forever polishing them.

Replacing them, Smith attempted a wider search. He called for any flag of any color depicting the fleur-de-lis.

The computer, its screen hidden under the black glass of his desktop, showed the colorless outline of a simple flag with a basic fleur-de-lis in the center.

Instantly it began absorbing color. Smith leaned closer.

He got the Boy Scout emblem. Remo had mentioned that. But the Boy Scout emblem was gold against dark blue. That was not the flag Remo had described. But of course it wouldn't be. The Boy Scouts don't operate submarines, much less attack shipping without cause.

Tapping an illuminated key, Smith instructed the system to continue its search.

After five minutes he came up with assorted heraldic flags, none of which matched the one described by Remo.

Frowning with all of his face, Smith leaned back

in his cracked leather executive chair. Dead end. What could it mean?

Snapping forward, he ordered the system to call up any flag depicting any number of fleurs-de-lis. It was a long shot. But he had to know who was behind the sinking of the *Ingo Pungo* and if there was any reason to suspect a threat to CURE.

Almost at once, a blue flag divided into quarters by a white cross appeared. Each quarter framed a white fleur-de-lis exactly as described by Remo.

His mouth thinning, Smith studied it.

Of course, he thought. He had lived in Vermont, not very far from the Canadian border, and he should have recalled this particular flag. It was the provincial flag of Quebec, Canada.

Each quadrant matched the flag Remo had described, except the colors had been reversed.

Reaching for the blue contact phone on his desk, Smith dialed Remo's number.

A strange voice answered. "Who calls?"

Smith froze. "Who am I speaking to?"

"I ask first, sour mouth."

"I, er, am trying to reach Remo."

"Remo eating. Call back later. In meantime, go to hell."

And the phone went dead.

"What on earth?" Smith muttered.

Smith called back instantly, saying, "Please inform Remo that Dr. Smith is calling."

"I will. After dinner."

"It is important that I speak with him now."

"It is important that he eat. Go back to hell." And the line went dead again.

A rare flash of anger welled up in Harold Smith's gray, colorless soul. He quelled it. There was nothing to do but wait for the call back.

It came twenty minutes later.

"Smith. Remo. You called?"

"Who answered the telephone earlier?" Smith demanded in his lemoniest voice.

"Chiun's housekeeper."

"Chiun hired a housekeeper!" Smith said in surprise.

"Don't ask me why. She was guarding the door when I got back. And what happened to telling Chiun about what happened?"

"He did not answer the telephone."

"Okay, you're off the hook this time. But he's pretty steamed."

"Remo, the flag you described. Did it have a white cross in the center?"

"Nope. Just that flower symbol. Got anything?"

"My search failed to bring up an exact match, but the provincial flag of Quebec consists of a white cross framing four designs similar to what you described."

"Sounds right, though. They just got the color scheme reversed. But if they can't handle English, why should we expect them to know their colors? Hey, Smitty. Does Quebec have submarines?"

"No. But the Canadian navy has. They are old World War II-vintage diesel-electric submarines."

"This was an old pigboat," Remo said. "And why would Canada sink the *Ingo Pungo?*"

"Of course they would not. Canada is our ally,

and the ship was in U.S. waters, well within the two-hundred-mile limit.''

''That's good because now that I've eaten, Chiun wants me to go chasing subs.''

''Locating that submarine is your next mission,'' said Smith.

''I was afraid that was what you were going to say. Look, can it wait? I just spent a night in the water playing with the sharks and I'd just as soon not see open water for a while.''

''A hostile submarine operating in U.S. waters is a security problem. Remo, those sailors you encountered. Did they speak at all?''

''No. The sub might as well have been crewed by Marcel Marceau and his Merry Mimes. Hey, he's French, isn't he?''

''I can think of no reason for a French submarine to be attacking U.S. shipping,'' Smith said dismissively.

''Maybe it's Quebec after all. They mad at us for any reason?''

''No. Quebec is currently at odds with English Canada over the secession question. But that issue has nothing to with the U.S.''

''Then they had to be after the *Silver Carp*.''

''The what?''

''That's the English name. I'm sick of saying '*Ingo Pungo*.' It sounds like I go pogo.''

''No one other than her crew knew of the *Ingo Pungo*'s mission and cargo,'' said Smith.

''What exactly was it, by the way?'' asked Remo.

''Fish.''

''Fish!'' Remo exploded.

Harold Smith cleared his throat. "Yes, during the last contract negotiation, the Master of Sinanju requested and I agreed to supply regular shipments of fresh Pacific fish."

"Fish?"

"As you may have read, there is a global fishing crisis. Coastal fisheries have been exhausted worldwide, forcing fleets to go fishing in deeper and deeper waters. The quality of catches is in sharp decline. Prices are skyrocketing. Master Chiun has been unhappy with the varieties available to him and requested that I remedy it."

"Let me get this straight—instead of more gold, he held you up for *fish* this time?"

"Actually the fish will end up being more expensive than gold on a per-pound basis, once all costs are factored in," Smith admitted.

"How's that?" asked Remo.

"The *Ingo Pungo* was a factory ship. It plied the high seas catching and processing fish. It made a Pacific crossing from Pusan, harvesting varieties of fish on the way. Many varieties."

"That's a lot of fish."

"Yes, of course it is," said Smith. "Master Chiun insisted these fish be delivered alive so as to be as fresh as possible."

"And it might explain the fish cellar."

Smith made a curious sound in the back of his throat.

Remo explained, "Chiun's got the basement set up for what he calls a fish cellar. I never heard of one, have you?"

"No. But Koreans do salt and pickle fish for winter storage."

"It also explains why I had to eat duck while Chiun gorged himself on fish-head soup. Not that I'm complaining, but he threatened to deny me fish forever. I can't live on duck. I gotta have fish."

"Inform Master Chiun I have contacted another fishing concern. The fish clause of the contract will be honored, of course."

"Don't you feel silly saying 'fish clause'?"

"I stopped being self-conscious about my dealings with the House of Sinanju back in 1980," said Harold Smith with no trace of humor detectable in his colorless voice. "Go to the Coast Guard station at Cape Cod, Remo. I want that submarine found."

"If you say so, Smitty. What do I do with this sub if I catch it?"

"Interrogate the captain and report back to me."

"After I kill him."

"Report to me. I will instruct you of his disposition."

"Forget his disposition," said Remo. "He tried to kill me. I'm the one with the disposition. If I find this guy, I'm going to feed him to the fishes."

With that, Remo hung up.

Replacing the blue receiver in his Folcroft office, Harold Smith addressed his keyboard. He had to make the arrangements with the Coast Guard if Remo was to expect any cooperation.

As he worked, Harold Smith wondered if this incident could have anything to do with the recent rash of missing fishing boats. There had been a surge in lost commercial-fishing vessels of late. He was aware of it because his ever-trolling system constantly offered up clusters of coincidences or related events for his analysis.

Smith had dismissed the cluster of lost vessels as occupational hazards of deep-water fishing during these lean times.

Now he wasn't so certain.

14

Coast Guard Lieutenant Sandy Heckman didn't want to hear it.

A swab of a cadet came running up as she made sure the cutter *Cayuga* was ready to go out. The *Cayuga* had just returned to the Coast Guard air station at Cape Cod from search-and-rescue duty, and they were knocking the ice off her spidery electronics mast and superstructure while the hundred-and-ten-foot vessel was being refueled.

"The commander wants to see you in his office."

"Tell him the sea waits for no man or woman," Sandy retorted.

"It's important."

"So is search and rescue."

And Lieutenant Heckman went back to overseeing preparations to depart. She was in her glory. Unfortunately her glory meant that out there in the cruel ocean, there was a boat in distress.

This time her name was *Santo Fado,* an otter trawler out of Innsmouth and missing for thirty-six hours now.

There had been no distress call. That was a bad sign. The boat hadn't returned to port, nor had it been sighted or spotted adrift.

A Coast Guard Falcon surveillance jet was crisscrossing the North Atlantic looking for it. But jets can't land on water, so the entire complement of the Coast Guard stations at Cape Cod and Scituate were out there, too. White-hulled cutters and black-hulled buoy tenders and lifeboats and bright orange Jayhawk and Pelican helicopters.

After a day of around-the-clock searching, nothing had come to light. It didn't look good for the *Santo Fado* or her crew.

The cadet came huffing and puffing back, and this time the word was, "Commander is ordering you to the operations building."

"I'm about to go back out," Sandy protested.

"Someone else will take your watch. You're needed."

"God damn his hairy ass."

"Don't let him hear you say that. Sir."

"I don't care who hears me say it," Sandy snapped.

At the operations building, there was a white Falcon jet warming up, the diagonal red stripe of the U.S. Coast Guard on her forward fuselage and stabilizer.

An orderly said over the climbing engine whine, "You're on drop-master duty. Orders."

"What the hell is going on?"

"We have two VIPs. The commander wants to present the guard's prettiest face, I guess."

"Is that so? Well, I can fix that!"

Marching to the waiting Falcon, she mounted the air-stairs two at a time and thrust herself into the cabin. "Since when am I an airman!" she bellowed in her best fog-piercing voice.

A hand reached out and slammed her into a seat. Not hard, but very firmly. Sandy sat, very surprised.

The hatch was hauled up and the cabin closed. Whining, the Falcon moved out onto the main runway and, without any preliminaries, went screaming down its length and into the air.

Sandy was getting a good look at the VIPs as her bottom got over the shock of the sudden sit-down.

One was a skinny guy dressed for shooting summertime pool. The other was as old as the hills and dressed for a rousing game of mah-jongg. He looked Chinese, but he wore a turquoise Japanese-style kimono with facing sea horses on his thin chest. Out from his sleeve hems peeked the longest, wickedest fingernails Sandy had seen this side of Fu Manchu.

"I'm Remo Pike," said the tall white one. "This is Chiun." He showed her a card. It said National Marine Fisheries Service.

"So?"

"We're looking for a submarine lurking out there."

"Whose sub?"

"That's the question of the hour."

"Isn't this more of a Navy mission?" Sandy demanded.

"We want this kept quiet."

"Look, all available CG vessels are on search-and-rescue duty right now. You're diverting important resources from their mission."

"No problem. While you search for a rescue, we'll look for our sub."

Sandy eyed the pair with what she hoped was her

most skeptical look. "What's NMFS's interest in a submarine?"

"That's classified," said the one named Remo.

"All right," she declared, taking a jump seat next to a window. "You do your job and I'll do mine."

"No problem. The pilot has his orders."

"I swear, my commander must suffer from myxololus cerebralsis."

"Isn't that the stuff that regrows hair?"

"You're thinking of Monoxidil. Myxololus cerebralsis is Whirling Disease. Fish get it sometimes. They lose their orientation and just spin and flop out of control. I'm surprised you don't know that."

"We are new to the National Marines," said the Asian blandly.

Sandy said, "Uh-huh," and asked, "Ichthyologists?"

"That's classified, too," Remo answered quickly.

Sandy said, "An ichthyologist is a fish expert."

"We just know subs," explained Remo.

"I am the fish expert," said Chiun.

"What's your specialty?"

"Eating them."

Sandy looked twice to see if he were joking. His face was a wrinkled map without any humor in it. She decided he was some kind of inscrutable humorist and turned her attention back to the waters below.

Under her breath she cursed softly and feelingly. "God damn these fucking fishermen."

"You have the mouth of a fishwife," said the elderly Asian.

"Keep your opinions to yourself. I have a job to

do, and so have you. Like we say, 'You have to go out, but you don't have to come back.'"

"That the Coast Guard motto?" asked Remo.

"No. Our motto is *Semper Paratus*. Always Ready."

"Be ready to call out if you spot that sub."

"Like I said, keep out a weather eye for your stinking sub and I'll do the same for my pain-in-the-ass fishing boat."

"You have a salty tongue," said Chiun. "Perhaps you should spare our gracious ears and still it."

"Stow it," said Sandy. "I spend half my time policing fishermen who are either breaking maritime law or getting their screws caught in foul weather. They've dragged their nets along the ocean floor until it's as barren of life as the moon and won't be satisfied until they've eaten every last fish in the sea."

"The greedy swine," said Chiun.

"Damn right," said Sandy, stationing herself beside a port and taking up a clipboard and binoculars.

Remo took the opposite porthole and hoped the jet didn't have to ditch. The last thing he wanted to do was go for another enforced swim.

15

Sea gulls swooped and wheeled in the sunless sky. From time to time they dipped and splashed their wingtips against the gray Atlantic, then lifted up again with flapping sardines in their sharp bills.

And far above them, the Master of Sinanju was counting his grievances.

"I was promised char," he lamented.

"Char?"

"Arctic char," said Chiun, consulting a rice-paper scroll on his lap. "Twenty weights suitable for salt curing. Char is best eaten dry." His right index finger, capped by a filigreed horn of jade, tapped the slashing Korean characters on the scroll. "Cod and croaker were promised. Pollock and pogy, shad and salmon from both great oceans. Sea bass. Sea bream. Mullet and menhaden. Trout and tilapia. Lemon sole and ling. Swordfish exceeding the length of a tall man."

"No shark?" asked Remo.

"Of course not."

"Good. I hate shark. I never want to eat it again."

"You smell of shark."

"That's one reason why I hate it."

They were over the Atlantic now. The Coast

Guard Falcon jet flew low. The pilot paid them no heed, and neither did Coast Guard Lieutenant Sandy Heckman, much to Remo's surprise.

"You know," he confided to Chiun, "she doesn't seem to be attracted to me."

"Why should she be? You stink of carrion *sango.*"

"I showered."

"*Sango* exudes from your pores. It is inescapable."

Remo glanced toward Lieutenant Heckman curiously. So far she hadn't expressed a single ounce of interest in him. That was pretty unusual, especially these days. For almost as long as Remo had been under Chiun's tutelage, he had exerted a powerful effect on women. It had gotten worse in the past year or so—to the point where Remo was fighting them off. Sometimes literally. He'd gotten so tired of it he decided to go with the flow and ask them out first.

So far it hadn't been very successful. The one woman who hadn't tried to jump his bones from a cold start turned out to be gay.

Remo was starting to wonder about Lieutenant Heckman.

Remo wandered over to her at her jump-seat station.

Sandy Heckman was looking down through a port with her eyes clamped to a pair of binoculars. She was scanning the crinkled, greenish gray surface of the Atlantic for fishing boats.

A rust-colored trawler churned a path through the

water below. The jet tilted one wing toward the laboring vessel.

Abruptly Sandy snapped a switch and yanked a cabin microphone to her mouth.

"Fishing vessel *Sicilian Gold*, this is the U.S. Coast Guard. Your vessel is over a closed area in violation of the Magnunson Act. Charges may be filed and your catch seized later. Proceed out of the area immediately."

Grabbing a clipboard, she took down the trawler's name and went back to searching the sea.

"What's the Magnunson Act?" asked Remo.

"A congressional law regulating commercial-fishing takings. When it was first enacted back in '76, it stopped foreign fishing vessels—mostly Canadian—from plundering U.S. waters. But Congress got around to making it law too late. The Canadians had made a big dent in the stocks. Now it regulates where our fishermen can go, how long they can go out and how much fish they can take. But most coastal areas are pretty much fished out now."

"It's a big ocean. Can't be that bad."

"It's a crisis. And some of these damn fishermen don't seem to be getting it. This is supposed to be a rescue mission. If I don't get some more rescues under my belt, it's back to buoy tenders for me. Or worse, Alaska and the halibut patrol."

"Halibut patrol?"

"They're scarce, too."

"Mind if I ask you a personal question?" asked Remo.

"I don't date civilians. Sorry."

"That wasn't my question."

"Then what was your question?"

"Are you gay?"

"No!"

"Great!"

"Forget it. I don't date."

"I wasn't asking for a date."

"Good, because you weren't going to get one. Now, will you take a seat? Like I said, this is a search-and-rescue mission. If we happen upon your mystery sub en route, fine. If not, you're just so much supercargo. So kindly shoo."

Suppressing a smile, Remo turned to the Master of Sinanju. "She doesn't want to date me. Isn't that great?"

Chiun nodded sagely. "It is the shark smell."

A flicker of interest crossed Remo's high-cheekboned face. "Little Father, are you telling me that eating shark acts like a female repellent?"

"It is obvious that it does, slow one."

Remo brightened. "No kidding?"

"Truly."

"All I gotta do is keep eating shark, and women will leave me alone?"

"If that is your wish..."

"It's my wish to pick my dates and not vice versa."

"Your desires are your own vice, Remo."

Chiun sat by a port and was examining the open water now. It was cold and choppy and about as inviting as open sewage.

"If you spot that sub, I got dibs on the captain," Remo remarked.

"I will allow you to dispatch him once I have

flayed the meat from his bones and fed it to him,"
Chiun said coldly.

"You sure take your fish seriously these days."

"Have you been to the fishmonger of late?"

"You mean the supermarket. No, you've been doing food buying lately."

"They have been foisting inferior fish upon me.
Mealy, unpalatable fishes the like of which I have
never before heard, with names like monkfish, cusk
and hagfish."

"I hear they're getting popular."

"In the newspaper they are called junk fish. I do
not eat junk. I am Reigning Master of Sinanju. You
may eat junk, but I will not."

"Good fish are getting scarce."

"Which is why I have prevailed upon Emperor
Smith to comb the deepest seas for the sweetest fish
so that I may eat as my ancestors have. Sumptu-
ously."

"You eat better than your ancestors, and you
know it, Little Father."

"I will not place junk fish into my belly. Did you
know that one fishmonger attempted to convince me
to eat spiny dogfish? I have never heard of dogfish.
It looked suspiciously like shark."

"Dogfish *is* shark," Sandy called over.

"Eavesdropper," Chiun hissed. "Have you no
shame?"

"You're shouting. I can't help but hear you. But
what you say is true. The quality of food fish has
gotten terrible since they closed Georges Bank."

"What's Georges Bank?" asked Remo.

"We just passed over it. It was the best fishery

of the East Coast. Maybe they'll reopen it in a few years, but right now it's a disaster for our fishermen. A lot were forced out of business. The government has been buying their boats and licenses. But as bad as it is here, it's worse for the Canadian fleets. They've been banned from taking cod from the Grand Banks.''

"Where's that?''

"Where we're headed. It's only the richest cod fishery on the planet. It's where they had that turbot war two years ago.''

"What turbot war?'' asked Chiun.

"Before you answer, what's a turbot?'' added Remo.

Lieutenant Sandy Heckman turned in her seat. "Turbot is another name for Greenlandic halibut. The Turbot War was between Canada and Spain.''

"Never heard of it,'' said Remo.

"It wasn't so much a war as an international incident. Spanish fishing trawlers were taking juvenile turbot from the end of the Grand Banks called the Nose. That's where the fishery stuck out past Canada's two-hundred-mile limit into international waters. The Spanish were technically legal, but they were taking fish that swam in and out of the Canadian side of the fishery. Ottawa got pretty hot about it and sent cutters and subs to tear up the Spanish fishing nets. A serious high-seas brouhaha was brewing until the Spanish caved in and hauled up their nets. Since then it's been pretty quiet, although Canada makes a lot of noise about U.S. fishermen taking cod from the U.S. side of the Grand Banks while their own fleets are forbidden to touch them.

They seized a couple of scallopers a while back, but lost their nerve for a showdown. They're making noises about doing something about U.S. fleets taking salmon in the Pacific, but so far it's only cold Canadian air.''

"No one owns the sea or the fish in them," sniffed Chiun.

"If the groundfish crisis continues, pretty soon there'll be no more fish to argue over.''

Remo looked to the Master of Sinanju. "Do you know about any of this?''

"Of course. Why do you think I am hoarding fish?''

"I'm glad *you* said 'hoard' and not me.''

"Hold it!'' said Sandy. "There's something in the water.''

She called up to the pilot, "Kilkenny, take us around. I want to check something out.''

The Falcon leaned into a slow turn, dropped and was soon skimming the cold, gray, inhospitable waters.

They saw the thing in the water clearly in the fleeting second they passed over it.

"Looks like a body!'' Sandy shouted.

"It's a body, all right,'' said Remo. "Floating facedown.''

Sandy got busy on her radio. "Coast Guard cutter *Cayuga,* this is *Coast Guard One* requesting assistance at this time. We have a floater at position Delta Five.''

They circled the spot for some twenty minutes until a Coast Guard cutter showed up and took on the body.

They watched the procedure, Sandy through her binoculars and Remo and Chiun with their naked eyes.

Divers entered the water and brought it up like a sack of wet, dripping clay.

"Man alive, I never saw a floater with a face so deathly pale," Sandy muttered.

"I have," said Remo.

They looked at him.

"And if that isn't a fleur-de-lis on his face, I'll eat the next shark I see."

"Glutton," sniffed Chiun.

THERE WERE three strange things about the body when it was taken off the cutter at the Coast Guard station at Scituate.

First it was completely nude, and as blue as a human body could get. The blue was from exposure.

The corpse's face was the white of chalk, and spread over the dead man's features was a livid blue fleur-de-lis put on with what looked like clown greasepaint. The nose was completely blue, as were the lips. The upper and lower spears of the design touched hairline and chin, respectively. The wings curved over the cheekbones in perfect symmetry.

Clenched between the man's teeth was something thin and black. With a pair of pliers, Lieutenant Heckman extracted the thing. It turned out to be the tail of a small gray fish without a head.

"This is damn weird," she was saying.

"Nothing weird about a guy trying to stay alive as long as he can," Remo remarked.

Sandy looked at him dubiously.

"He was adrift in the water. Naturally he'd eat whatever he could catch to keep himself alive," said Remo.

"Nice theory. But unless he had stainless-steel teeth, it won't float. A knife cut off this fish's head."

"Open up his stomach, and I'll bet you find the fish head," Remo said.

"At least he did not stoop to shark," Chiun said aridly.

When they turned the body over to look for wounds, they discovered the third weird thing. It was definitely the weirdest of the three weird things.

There was a gray fish tail projecting from the bluish crack of the dead man's rear end.

"I have seen some pretty odd things, but I have never seen *that*," Sandy muttered.

"Maybe the fish tried to eat him and got stuck," said Remo in a voice that suggested he wasn't exactly embracing the theory.

"That's a turbot, if I know my fish. They aren't flesh eaters, and I don't see how, left to his own devices, one could cram his head into a human rectum."

"What other way could it have happened?"

"Two. The guy was queer for fish or someone jammed it up in there."

"Why would anyone do that?" asked Remo.

"Your guess," said Sandy, "is as good as mine."

"My guess is the fish tried to eat him and got stuck."

The Master of Sinanju reached out with delicate fingers and took the fish by the tail. He pulled. With an ugly sucking sound, the fish came loose. So did a cloud of gases that mixed the stink of blocked bowels and decomposition.

Everyone retreated several yards, Chiun still holding the fish. He lifted it so everyone could see. It was a small, putrid, gray fish with bulging eyes and nothing appetizing about it.

"Whatever it is," Remo said, "it's no prize."

"Halibut," said Chiun.

"Turbot," amended Sandy.

"If you say so," said Remo, holding his nose.

Everyone saw the fish's throat had been cut, making a pinkish smile under its gaping mouth. Chiun then tossed it so it landed on the body with a light smack.

"Someone cut this fish's throat and stuck it in," Sandy said slowly. "Probably the same someone who cut off the other turbot's head and stuck it in his mouth. This is not good."

"Not for the fish anyway," said Remo.

"Not good for anyone. This is a message. The question is from who and to whom?"

Remo looked at her skeptically.

"Look, the turbot is the symbol of Canada's victory over Spain and other high-seas poachers. This dead guy has callused claws for hands. That tells me he's a fisherman."

"So what's the design on his face mean?" asked Remo.

"Beats the living pooh out of me."

"It is the symbol of Frankish kings," said Chiun. He gestured across the room to the bluish corpse.

"Come again?" asked Sandy.

"The French. This man is French."

"The French don't fish these waters. They're mostly in the Gulf of St. Lawrence."

"Nevertheless, this man wears the mark of the French."

"Maybe it's the other way around. Maybe the French have marked him," suggested Remo.

Sandy Heckman shook her sun-bleached head. "Wouldn't be the French. French-Canadian more than likely. Though Quebec hasn't much of a deep-water fleet."

"Maybe we should kick this upstairs to our boss."

"Do it quick. I've still got to locate the *Santo Fado*."

AT FOLCROFT SANITARIUM, Harold Smith listened patiently and digested every morsel of information. At the end of Remo's recitation, he frowned so deeply Remo thought he heard his dry skin crackle. It was probably only line noise.

"Something is very wrong here," he said in his astringent, lemony voice.

"So what do you want us to do about it?"

"I will have identification of the body expedited on this end. I want the search for that submarine to go forward. There is something very wrong in the North Atlantic. And we must get to the bottom of it."

"In a manner of speaking," Remo said dryly.

"I am attempting to locate it by satellite. Remain in close touch at all times."

Hanging up, Remo turned to Sandy Heckman and

said, "We gotta sweep for that submarine. Orders from on high."

"Okay, let's go," she said, grabbing her helmet. "Maybe we'll find that missing trawler while we're at it."

When they left the operations building, they found the white Falcon jet had taken off without them.

"There goes my damn rescue," Sandy fumed.

Remo looked at her. "What rescue? The guy's dead."

"We don't know that's him. And if it is, there's still his boat to be found." Her eyes fell on an idle Coast Guard Jayhawk helicopter. She started for it at a dead run.

"Pilot, we need a lift to the *Cayuga*."

"She's at sea."

"That'll save us some travel time," Sandy said, climbing aboard. "Hope you can handle a deck landing."

"It'll be my first."

"Mine, too," she said grimly as Remo and Chiun climbed aboard and the Jayhawk's main rotor started to scream.

16

The Jayhawk pilot did an excellent job of dropping the bright orange rescue helicopter onto the pitching helipad. The Coast Guard cutter *Cayuga* came to a dead stop to accommodate it but immediately got underway again, so the chopper pilot had to take off from a moving deck. After a couple of false stabs, he got out and hung his head over the cutter's rail until his stomach was completely empty.

When he finally took off, it was without a hitch.

On deck the Master of Sinanju continued to enumerate his grievances. "*Yono,*" he lamented, his hazel eyes bleak as the surrounding seas.

"What's *yono?*" asked Remo out of boredom rather than real interest.

"Salmon."

"Never cared for it much."

"It is better than skate."

"Anything tastes better than skate...."

"I was promised salmon of all kinds. The sockeye. Coho. Chinook. And pink and golden."

"All salmon tastes pretty much the same to me."

Chiun squeezed his eyes with a mixture of pain and yearning. "Orange roughy. I was promised orange roughy."

"Never heard of orange roughy. Is it anything like red herring?"

"I have never heard of red herring. I will see that red herring goes into the next contract."

Remo smiled. "You do that, Little Father."

"Orange roughy. Red snapper. Yellowtail flounder. Bluefin tuna. Gray sole. Black crappie."

"Don't forget purple smoothie."

"Yes, purple smoothie. And redfish and sablefish and bluegill and amberjack and striped bass and rainbow trout. And exotic mahimahi," continued Chiun in a plaintive voice.

"Isn't that porpoise?" asked Remo.

"Dolphin-fish," corrected Lieutenant Sandy Heckman. She had just emerged from belowdecks. A vivid orange Mustang survival suit encased her blue flight suit, its multiple pockets full of flares and other mariner's emergency equipment. A side arm slapped her thigh. "We're approaching the longitude and latitude of your phantom submarine."

"Can you find the sub if it's submerged?"

"Maybe. But if it comes to a fight, we're not exactly equipped for antisubmarine warfare."

"You leave the fighting to us," said Remo.

Sandy eyed them skeptically. "What are you two going to do—blow bubbles at them?"

"We'll think of something. Won't we, Little Father?"

"*I* will think of something," Chiun said sternly. "You will do the thing I think of."

"Just remember what's important—me, or getting that sub."

Chiun steepled his long-nailed fingers before his

chest and made his eyes menacing. "Drowning the submersible vessel is very important. If you follow my instructions to the letter, possibly you will not drown, too."

Twenty minutes later the helmsman called from the pilothouse, "Contact!"

Rushing to the pilothouse, they found the helmsman monitoring the sonar scope.

"What do you make of this?" he asked Sandy.

She stared at the greenish scope. It showed a green grid with a bird's-eye view of the cutter's outline in its center. Ahead off the port bow was a tiny but very distinct green blip.

"It's not a sub. Too small," Sandy decided.

"It's metallic. Maybe it's a one-man sub."

They watched it for several minutes. The object was tracking an undeviating course.

"If it's a one-man sub, it's off a mother ship," Sandy said firmly. "We'll follow it and see where it goes."

The cutter stayed in its easterly heading, cleaving through the waves with only a slight bumping when they struck larger swells.

Abruptly the object changed course, and Sandy snapped out orders.

"Starboard. One degree!"

The helmsman spun the wheel expertly, and the cutter dug in as it moved to stay with the mystery contact.

"It's either a small sub or a torpedo," Remo suggested.

Sandy shook her head. "Torpedoes don't change course, not that I know of."

''This thing just did,'' Remo muttered.

Chiun drifted away, evidently bored. Remo found his thoughts wandering. The smell of the open sea was causing him to flash back to the previous night. He was trained to feel fear when fear was a useful survival tool. After a crisis was over, he discarded fear like a used Kleenex. But the memories of the previous night kept coming back.

He joined the Master of Sinanju at the rail. ''I almost bought it out here,'' he told Chiun.

Chiun eyed a solitary petrel that was eyeing him back. ''You did not.''

''Been a long time since I came that close.''

''Purge your mind of all such considerations. The past is the past.''

''I gotta find Freya.''

''And you will. If she does not find you.''

Not long after that, the sonar scope began pinging excitedly, and Remo and Chiun returned to the pilothouse.

''What's happening now?'' asked Remo.

''Our contact just ran into a schooled-up pod of fish,'' Sandy told them.

''What kind?''

''Hard to say. Maybe whiting.''

''Whiting is not quality fish,'' Chiun said disdainfully. ''Its bones do not digest well.''

''You're not supposed to eat the bones,'' Sandy said absently.

''If you cook fish right,'' Remo told her, ''you can eat the bones, too.''

''And the heads,'' added Chiun.

''Must be whiting,'' Sandy remarked, her eyes

intent on the scope. "It's about the most plentiful kind you could catch out here these days."

"Maybe it's turbot," said Remo.

"That's weird," Sandy suddenly stated. "The contact is changing course, and the fish are moving with it."

"Looks like they're running from it," the helmsman said.

"No, it's following them. They're not scattering before it."

"Then it's gotta be a fish," said Remo.

Sandy frowned deeply. "No, that's a metallic blip. We can tell these things."

"So why is it following those fish?"

"That," muttered Sandy, "is the question of the hour."

They watched the cluster of sonar blips as the cutter *Cayuga* thundered along.

"We're approaching the Nose," the helmsman warned.

"The part of the Grand Banks that Canada doesn't lay claim to," Sandy explained. "We're not exactly welcome in these parts, but it's still international waters, so we're out of our jurisdiction."

"The Canadians are our allies. What could they do?"

"Complain to our superior officers and get us cashiered out of the guard." Sandy frowned. "What do you think, helmsman?"

"Can't hurt to follow this thing a few knots more."

"Why do you not seek to catch it?" asked Chiun.

"Be interesting to try, but there's no way. If we

could drop a net in front of it, at this speed it would pop right through.''

"Remo can catch it," Chiun offered.

Sandy Heckman laughed, and up in the dead gray sky the petrel joined in raucously. Their voices had about the same tone.

"With what—an undersea butterfly net?" she scoffed.

"We have our ways," Remo said defensively.

"Remo, I command you to catch this mysterious fish that is not a fish," Chiun said sternly, pointing at the water.

"Aw, c'mon, Chiun. Don't bust my chops."

"Remo, you are commanded. Obey."

Remo sighed and said to Sandy, "Get ahead of it. I'll see what I can do."

"We have diving gear aboard," she offered.

Remo shook his head. "I don't need it."

"You can't go down without scuba gear."

"I do it all the time." Then, remembering the previous night, he added, "But I'll take a wet suit."

Sandy looked to the helmsman, who said, "Orders are to assist in any way possible."

"It's your lungs," Sandy said.

The *Cayuga* spurted ahead, got ahead of the underwater contact, then came to a slow, easy stop.

Stepping out of his Italian loafers, Remo donned a night black neoprene wet suit, drawing in a deep charge of oxygen as he stood on the afterdeck. He disdained the gloves and flippers.

He waited until everyone was looking the other way. Only Chiun was watching him. Then, from a standing start he back-flipped into the water. He made no discernible splash.

The water closed in on him, and the first cold clutch of fear took hold of his mind. Remo pushed the thought back.

His face tingled from the shock of the cold, then it went numb. He diverted warmth to his hands and feet, where he really needed it.

Remo let himself sink, eyes adjusting to the lessening light. Seawater filtered out the red-orange end of the spectrum. The blues and indigos soon shaded to a uniform gray.

The first thing Remo looked for was a submarine. The water was completely free of subs. Remo was not surprised.

But the school of small fish showed with increasing clearness. They formed an ellipse of well-spaced ranks over the ocean floor. In the filtered daylight, Remo was surprised by one thing. Other than the school, there were no fish in sight. This far out, that was unusual.

The school, its multitudinous cyes gleaming like perfectly matched silvery coins, swam toward him. Remo was impressed by the whiting's orderly lines. They might have belonged to some fishy army, they were so disciplined.

He spotted the thing following them at an even speed and distance.

Seen head-on, it looked as dull as a big blunt bullet. It was not a fish. What it was wasn't exactly clear.

Setting himself, Remo achieved neutral buoyancy

by releasing air from his lungs while he waited for the blunt nose to come to him.

The whiting—if that's what they were—grew agitated when they came upon Remo. Still, they held their course, their tiny fins waving rhythmically.

Remo let the leading fish pass over and around him. They seemed to take his presence in stride.

It was a torpedo, Remo saw as the pressure of its approach touched his benumbed face. Remo scooted out of the way slightly and, as it passed, trailing a bubbly wake, he snap-kicked at its tail.

The torpedo shuddered and veered, churning water. Abruptly its steady mechanical whir sputtered out. It slowed. Tail first, it began to sink.

Reaching out, Remo wrapped his arms around it and, as the pod of whiting broke in every direction, clearly startled, Remo pushed to the surface.

The torpedo was heavy, but it responded to his upward thrusts. Feet kicking furiously, Remo followed it, pushing at intervals to keep it moving along. Finally he got it to the surface.

Treading water, one arm wrapped around the middle, Remo called up to the cutter deck. "Hey! Lower a net!"

Sandy Heckman's startled face showed at the rail.

"Where did you come from?"

"I dived."

"I didn't hear you. We thought you'd ducked belowdecks."

"How about that net? My toes are turning blue."

A net was lowered. It was studded with orange flotation balls, and after Remo got it wrapped around the torpedo, he climbed a stainless-steel hull ladder while the crew hauled up the long object.

On deck Remo said, "It's a torpedo. I disabled it."

"With what?" Sandy wondered aloud, looking the thing over.

"A side kick."

"You *kicked* it out of commission?"

Remo grinned stiffly. His face was still numb. "You should see me stun a shark with a flick of my finger."

Sandy Heckman seemed unimpressed.

They uncovered the torpedo on the afterdeck and looked it over with cautious respect.

"I don't see a detonator," the helmsman was saying.

"It's a torpedo. No question about that," said Sandy.

"The fish were swimming ahead of it like it was their mother," Remo advised.

"I don't see any manufacturer's mark or serial numbers."

"Maybe they were burned off," said Remo.

Sandy looked up. "Burned off?"

"Yeah. You know, when thieves steal a gun or a car, they burn off the serial numbers with acid so it can't be traced."

"Nice theory. But this doesn't look like an explosive torpedo. The nose is as smooth as an egg."

"Could be a proximity fuse. They don't need to strike a target to blow it up," the helmsman offered.

Sandy stood up and adjusted her gun belt grimly.

"Well, it's ours now. We'll let the experts figure it out."

"Anybody got a cellular phone?" asked Remo.

"Sure. What for?"

"I want to contact my boss. Maybe he has a satellite fix on that sub. If the torpedo was launched from a sub, it can't be too far from here."

A cell phone was produced, and Remo dialed Harold Smith's contact number from the privacy of the bow.

In the middle of the third ring, the phone picked up. And an unfamiliar voice said, "We have lost contact, Commodore."

"Smitty?" asked Remo.

Chiun, hovering close, hissed, "That is not Emperor Smith."

"Shh," said Remo.

A second voice, smooth and almost without accent, said, "Repeat, please."

"There is no telemetry coming from the Hound."

"Take the usual precautions."

"Understood, Commodore," the first voice said, fading slightly. Then it called out, "Transmit self-destruct signal."

Remo said, "Self—?"

His eyes went to the iron thing on the afterdeck. Sandy Heckman was looking it over with her bone white fists on her orange hips.

Dropping the handset, Remo covered the distance from midships to the afterdeck in two seconds. He took Sandy by her big floppy collar and sent her spinning backward. Her yelp of surprise was lost in the clang of the torpedo after Remo punted it with his naked big toe.

The torpedo shot off the deck, dragging netting along with it, and slipped over the side.

It made a healthy splash, and the salt spray was no sooner pattering on deck than the stern gave a convulsive leap.

A geyser of salt water roared a solid dozen feet over the rail and came down on deck to immerse the spot where Remo had stood. Remo was no longer there. He had faded back, grabbing Sandy Heckman by the waist while on the move.

They were in the shelter of the pilothouse when the cutter's stern finished bucking and wallowing.

"What the hell happened?" the helmsman shouted over the after roar.

"Later, I gotta check the stern," called Remo.

Remo flashed back to the stern and leaned over.

He was looking for diesel fuel and oil. There was neither, just sea foam boiling. A few dead whiting popped to the surface, their eyes looking stunned and incredulous.

Dropping over the side, Remo grabbed on to a coil of nylon line. With this he lowered himself under the waterline, away from the screws.

From below, the cutter looked a little ragged. One screw was turning with a slight wobble. But there were no ruptures, no serious damage.

Going back up the ladder, Remo reached the deck.

Sandy Heckman confronted him. "How did you know it was going to explode?"

"The cellular picked up some kind of transmission about a self-destruct signal. I figured it meant the torpedo.''

Sandy frowned. "A cellular shouldn't pick up ship-to-ship radio traffic. It's on the UHF band."

"I know what I heard, but if you want I'll go get the torpedo back and we can try again."

"No, thanks."

The Master of Sinanju came bustling up with the cellular, saying, "Smith desires to speak with you."

Remo took the handset. "Smitty. Is that you?"

"Of course," Smith snapped. "You called me."

"I tried to. I got some kind of intercept."

"I heard it, too. One party calling another 'Commodore.'"

"We almost went down out here, Smitty. We hauled up some kind of dingbat torpedo and it blew up right after the commodore gave the self-destruct signal. I got the torpedo into the water just in time. Not that there's a lot of gratitude floating around," Remo added dryly.

Lieutenant Sandy Heckman pretended not to hear him.

"Listen, Smitty. Can you get a new fix on that sub?"

"I have its position as of four minutes ago."

Remo relayed the coordinates to Sandy.

"We can be there in ten minutes," she said crisply.

"Get us there."

Smith broke in. "Remo, if you intercepted a cellular phone call on the high seas, it had to have come from a boat or submarine."

"My money's on the sub."

"A submarine cannot broadcast while submerged. Therefore, it should be visible on the surface. If you move quickly, you will catch it while it is most vulnerable."

"Great. I'm itching for another crack at that pigboat."

"I want answers first, bodies second."

"You'll get both," Remo promised, snapping the phone off.

Facing the Master of Sinanju, Remo said, "We're about to have our showdown."

"Bodies first, answers second."

"Smitty wants it the other way around," Remo said.

"I am certain you will be able to explain your errors to Emperor Smith without bringing dishonor on the House you have shamed by your abysmal failure," Chiun said thinly.

"You're pretty pissed for a guy who only lost a boatload of fish."

"My soul yearns for good fish."

"Hope tin fish will satisfy you."

The Master of Sinanju looked puzzled. "I have never tasted tin fish. Is it like steelhead trout?"

17

Finding the submarine proved the easy part.

The USCG cutter *Cayuga* hammered along on a dead heading for the coordinates Harold Smith had provided, and abruptly there it was, wallowing in the trough of a wave like a wet black cigar.

"Thar she blows!" said Remo.

They stood in the bow beside the sixteen-inch gun, which was coated with a rime of frozen salt spray.

Lieutenant Sandy Heckman, the floppy collar of her orange Mustang survival suit pulled up to her ears, trained her binoculars on the sub and said, "I never saw a flag like that before."

Chiun's eyes thinned, and he said, "It is a French vessel."

"That's not the French flag."

"It is the flag of Clovis and the Frankish kings, although the hues are wrong," Chiun insisted. "It should be gold against blue."

Calling back over her shoulder, Sandy said, "Sparks, see if we can raise these submariners."

In the radio shack the radioman got busy.

"Why are radiomen always called 'Sparks'?" Remo asked.

"Beats remembering names," Sandy said distantly.

Sparks raised the sub—but not in the way intended.

A hatch popped and up from the sub's innards came seamen wearing insignialess white uniforms. Their faces were white, too. Remo saw clearly the fleur-de-lis squatting on greasepainted faces like flat blue crabs.

They applied pry bars to a deck hatch, and up came a big steel deck gun on a revolving mount.

"I don't like the looks of this," Sandy muttered.

They got the gun turned in the *Cayuga*'s direction, and Sandy shouted, "Helmsman! Evasive action! Looks they mean business with that deck gun."

Slapping her binoculars to her eyes again, she muttered, "What the hell is their problem? We're in international waters." Then she grabbed the bow rail to keep from being flung into the water.

The cutter heeled and all but reversed course. It began charting a slashing S course on the surface of the Atlantic. Wild spray spattered the superstructure, freezing almost instantly.

A dull shot boomed. They heard the whistle of the shell as it jumped from the smoking muzzle. It whistled over the radar mast and smacked into a cresting swell about thirty yards aft of the quarterdeck, vanishing completely with a gulping sound.

"Sloppy shot," said Remo.

"It was a warning shot," Sandy called back over the climbing roar of the engine. "Sparks, did you raise them?"

"No answers to our hails."

Under the busy guidance of the three ghost-faced seamen, the deck gun continued to track them.

The gun coughed again. A smoking shell dropped out of the breech to roll off the deck into the sea with a sizzling sound like a hot poker being doused.

This time the shot struck ahead of their bow. The cutter ran into the cold uprush of seawater. It washed over the bow, dousing Sandy in bitterly cold brine.

Remo and Chiun had retreated to a safe remove ahead of the sloshing downpour.

Sopping wet and turning blue, Sandy Heckman sputtered, "That's it! We're returning fire."

"I got a better idea," said Remo, stepping out of his shoes again. "Let me handle this."

"How?"

"By knocking out that gun."

"With what?"

"Surprise tactics."

And Remo back-flipped into the water.

SANDY HECKMAN WAS watching this time. She saw Remo standing there, still in the black neoprene wet suit, then suddenly he'd vanished. She heard the splash this time. It wasn't much of a splash. Porpoises sliding back into the water make a smooth entrance almost as devoid of sound.

She leaned over the bow rail. The water was already regathering at the point where Remo cut the surface. There was no sign of him.

Sandy turned to the Master of Sinanju. "He'll be killed."

"He will succeed. For he has been trained by the best."

"The best what?"

"There is no *what* when one speaks of the best. The best is the best."

"And who or what is the best?"

"I am," said Chiun.

Sandy trained her binoculars on the submarine. They were jockeying the deck gun around again, looking very determined. Or as determined as a trio of clown-faced sailors could look.

"We can't wait for them to get lucky." She raised her foghorn voice again. "I need a gun crew here."

Coast Guardsmen came running up to man the sixteen-inch gun.

JUST UNDER THE OCEAN surface, Remo arrowed toward the sub dolphin style, feet flippering like a frog long enough to create momentum. The rest of the way he simply glided. That way there was no wake or surface disturbance to betray his line of attack.

The sub was a big target. He reached it, slipped under the hull using his hands to guide him. This got him to the other side of the rolling U-boat, unseen and unsuspected.

The gun crew had just lobbed its third shell at the zigzagging cutter when Remo's wet head came out of the water. He lifted his hands and took hold of the hull. It felt slimy to the touch, but he got up onto deck with a smooth pulling motion.

Pausing to let water drain from his suit, Remo raised his body temperature to take care of residual wetness and crept toward the preoccupied gun crew.

He took them out the easy way.

Two were hunkered over the swiveling mount mechanism, and Remo just grabbed them by the backs of their heads, bringing them together before they registered they were in trouble.

Their heads split open with a dull, pulpy crack, and the two seaman dropped from Remo's grasp, their exposed brains mingling like two flavors of pudding.

That left the gunner. He had his hand on some kind of pull-cord trigger and was getting ready to yank it again.

Slipping up, Remo tapped him on the shoulder.

Startled, he turned.

"It's not nice to shoot at the good guys," Remo said.

The man's blue-rimmed mouth dropped open in his white face. It looked like a toothy red cavern, and he started making inarticulate fish sounds of surprise.

"Can you say myxobolus cerebralsis?" Remo asked.

"Buh-buh-buh."

"I didn't think so," said Remo, who shook the man by the head so fast his brain discombobulated into cold gray scrambled eggs. The seaman stepped back, eyes rolling in opposite directions, while staggering and stumbling about the deck as his nonfunctioning brain gave his body unrecognizable neural signals.

When he walked off the deck and into the brine, Remo figured he got what he deserved.

Stepping away from the gun so he could be seen,

Remo lifted both arms, crossed them and waved broadly.

The cutter was bearing in on them, and Remo started to wave it in.

A second later he was ducking. The bow deck gun shed a shower of icicles, and out of a sudden cloud of gunpowder came a smoking shell.

On either side M-16s began spraying bullets in stereo.

Remo hit the water ahead of the storm.

The din of striking rounds penetrated the cold ocean water. There was a dull boom. The sub shuddered and rolled, and when Remo lifted his head out of the water, he saw the cutter had scored a direct hit. The amidships hull was perforated at the waterline. The sail had taken a direct hit and was a smoking tangle of ruptured steel. Waterline bullet holes were drinking seawater and giving back air, making the sea bubble and bloop drunkenly.

A seaman poked his head up from the deck hatch. Remo put two fingers in his mouth and whistled to get his attention.

The seaman blinked, looking around in confusion. Remo whistled again and he crept as close to the water as he dared.

With a kick Remo came up out of the water like a dolphin standing on its tail. He grabbed the sailor's blouse with one hand. When gravity pulled Remo back down, the seaman came with him.

Underwater, he fought Remo with a flurry of kicking arms and legs. Remo ignored him. The cold quickly made his struggles feeble.

Resurfacing, Remo started back toward the cutter

with the captured seaman in tow, his head held above the water.

The man sputtered something Remo didn't catch.

"*Parlez-vous* French?" asked Remo.

If the man's response was in French, it was impossible to say. It sounded like sputtering to Remo.

A dull boom sounded behind them.

Looking back, Remo saw the sub start to list and said, "Great. I had them where I wanted them and now they're going down."

The sub's decks were awash with frantic seamen. Someone got a collapsible aluminum lifeboat out of a hatch and was putting it into the water when another sailor came out and shot him in the back without a word of warning.

The sailor and his boat slipped into the water to sink from sight. Only a thin blot of blood showed he had ever existed.

The rifleman lined up on Remo, and Remo pulled his prisoner under water with him.

Rifle bullets started striking the surface immediately above them.

They hit true, but veered crazily once they slipped underwater. One angled toward Remo. He released his prisoner and, sweeping out with his bare palm, created a wall of deflecting water. The bullet met the wall. The wall won. The bullet lost the last of its punch. Spent, it sank like a lead sinker, which for all practical purposes, was what it was.

Kicking, Remo reached down for his prisoner, who was sinking, too.

A lucky bullet got the man in one leg. He curled up, grabbing for the wound. Dark blood threaded out as he convulsed. Air vomited from his open mouth through pain-tight teeth.

A second bullet hit him in the chest.

Grabbing him by the hair, Remo pulled him to the surface and got his face in both hands, holding it close to Remo's own.

"Look, your own guys just shot you. Give it up. Who's operating that sub?"

"Ga ta hell, bloody Yank!" the man spit in a thick, heavily accented English.

The effort seemed to sap the last of his life force. He jerked, turned blue and his eyes rolled up in his head. His final breath was cold and foul. It smelled of some of hard liquor Remo didn't recognize.

Remo let him sink.

Striking back for the cutter, Remo caught a thrown line and pulled himself aboard.

Dripping wet, he stormed up to the bow. "What's the idea?" he demanded of Sandy Heckman.

"We were defending ourselves," she said tartly.

"I knocked out the gun crew before you got off your first shot."

"I didn't see you."

Remo turned on the Master of Sinanju, "Chiun, why the hell didn't you stop her?"

"Because."

"That's it? Because!"

"Yes. Because." And Chiun showed Remo his disdainful back.

They watched the sub sink. The stern went down, throwing the bow high above the water. It was as if the sub were straining to keep its head out of the water like a living thing.

Then, with agonizing slowness, the forepart of the submarine slipped beneath the waves.

But not before they could read a name on the bow:

Fier D'Être des Grenouilles

"What's it say?" asked Remo.

"You are not blind," sniffed Chiun. "Merely myopic."

"I can see the words, but I don't recognize the language."

"It is French."

"No wonder I can't read it. French isn't a language. It's mumbling with grammar. What's it say?"

"Fier D'Être des Grenouilles."

"That much I can make out. What's it mean in English?"

"'Proud to be frogs.'"

"That's the name of the submarine? *Proud to be Frogs?*"

"That is what the vessel is called."

Remo looked at Sandy Heckman. "What kind of submarine is named *Proud to be Frogs?*"

Sandy Heckman shrugged and said, "A French one?"

They watched the ocean settle down. Air bubbles, some as big as truck tires, popped the troubled surface. Nothing else. There were no survivors.

"Why didn't anyone get out?" Sandy asked of no one in particular.

"They didn't want to. They wanted to go down with the ship," said Remo.

"That's crazy. We're the U.S. Coast Guard. We

would have taken them alive. Everybody knows that."

"Obviously they did not wish to be taken alive," intoned the Master of Sinanju.

That cold thought hung over the water as they watched the last blooping bubbles break the surface. Finally a rainbow slick of oil began to appear, marking the spot where the *Fier D'Être des Grenouilles* had gone down.

18

Remo got Harold Smith on the first ring.

"Sighted sub. Sank same," he said.

"What information did you extract?" asked Smith.

"We're pretty sure it was French. Either that or someone has a weird sense of humor."

"What do you mean, Remo?"

"When the sub went down, we caught a glimpse of the name. *Fier D'Être des Grenouilles.*"

Chiun cut in. "That is not how it is pronounced."

"You say it, then."

"Fier D'Être des Grenouilles."

Smith's voice was full of doubt. "That cannot be correct."

"What's it mean to you?" asked Remo.

"'Proud to be Frogs.'"

"That's what Chiun says, too."

"No French vessel would possess such a name."

"This one did."

"You have prisoners?"

"Had. He got away. His own people wasted him."

"What did you get out of him?" asked Smith in a sharp voice.

"'Ga ta hell, bloody Yank.' Unquote."

"No Frenchman would say 'Yank.' He would say 'anglo.'"

"You know better than me," said Remo. "His accent wasn't particularly French, either. It was more Irish or Scottish."

"Which? Irish or Scottish?" asked Smith eagerly.

"Search me."

"Was it a brogue or a burr?"

Remo's forehead wrinkled up. "I know what a brogue is, but what's a burr?"

"Scotsmen speak in a burr. Irishmen affect a brogue. Was what you heard a brogue?"

"Kinda."

"You must be certain, Remo. This is important. If it was not a brogue, it must have been a burr."

"You'd have to hum a few bars."

Smith made a noise in his throat.

"No, it wasn't like that."

"I was not attempting a burr," Smith test testily. "I was clearing my throat."

"Whatever you were doing, it was kinda in the ballpark, but not exactly right."

"Never mind," said Smith, his voice tart.

"Listen, Smitty," Remo continued, "the sub went down with all hands. They could have saved themselves but they didn't want to."

"Only a very determined crew chooses death over capture."

"We're looking at professionals, all right."

Smith was silent for the better part of a minute. "Return to land," he finally snapped.

"Can't. We're still on search-and-rescue duty."

"I will fix that."

"That's up to you. Want me to hand the phone over to Lieutenant Queeg here?"

"No," Smith said sharply. "I will do this through channels."

Less than fifteen minutes later the radio call came from the Coast Guard air station at Cape Cod.

"We've been ordered to return to port," Sparks reported.

"The way this wind is picking up, I'm surprised you could hear them through all that static," Sandy remarked, casting a weather eye toward the cumulus clouds that scudded across the sky like a flock of dirty scared sheep.

"What static?" asked Sparks.

"I'll show you."

In the radio shack Sandy tried to raise Cape Cod. She was having trouble being heard over the ball of crumpled paper she was holding up to the mike.

"Say again?" she shouted. "I'm getting interference."

"If that's static, I'm a penguin," a voice called back.

"I can't hear you."

"Then stop squeezing whatever it is you're squeezing."

"Coast Guard Station Cape Cod. Come in, Cape Cod. You're breaking up. This is CGC *Cayuga.* Come in, Cape Cod."

"Your passengers are urgently required on land, Heckman, and if my ass is in a sling over this, your ass is in an even bigger sling," a radio voice barked.

At the radio shack door, Remo said, "We're in no big rush."

Sandy snapped off the radio set. "Make sure that's your story when we make landfall."

"You're a real grateful sailor."

"I'm a professional on a search-and-rescue mission who's wondering what the hell is going on out here."

"You know as much as we do," said Remo.

Back on deck the wind was biting. As they raced through the turbulent green-gray waters, Sandy took up a bow position and was scanning the threatening horizon with her binoculars.

"There's big trouble on the horizon," Sandy muttered half under her breath.

Remo looked in the direction she had her binoculars trained. Chiun did, too. Neither of them saw anything unusual.

"What are you looking at?" asked Remo.

"Nothing in particular. I'm thinking out loud. We're smack in the middle of what may be the battleground for the twenty-first century the way these waters have been overfished."

"Maybe."

"Look around you. Show me the difference between sovereign Canadian waters and U.S."

"Can't. It all looks the same to me."

"How about international waters? Can you tell it apart from the others?"

"No," Remo admitted.

"No. Not by color of sea or sky. Not by the crinkling of the waves. Nor by the peaks of the waves or the depths of the troughs or the taste of the salt spray. You can't fence it off or build on it or grow food on it, but you're looking at something that other nations have fought over before. The right to take fish. NAFO's got this area treatied up pretty well now, but it can't hold. The center cannot hold.''

"What center?" asked Chiun.

"Figure of speech. NAFO treaties stipulate the takings. But the way the groundfish stocks are dwindling, it's only a matter of time before those treaties are discarded. People have to eat. And fishermen are going to fish. It's in their blood.''

"Don't you mean NATO?" asked Remo.

"No. NATO's the North American Treaty Organization. NAFO stands for Northwest Atlantic Fisheries Organization.''

"Never heard of it," grunted Remo.

"You will. Everyone will. When I joined the Coast Guard out of Ketchikan, I thought I'd be rescuing boaters and breathing clean salt air. Instead I ended up chasing drug runners and gunrunners and trading shots with low-life scum who figured it was better to burn their own boats to the waterline than be boarded. Finally I got so sick of it I requested to transfer to Atlantic duty. I have a feeling deep in my nautical bones that I'm on the front line in the next great global war, and before long all this foggy salt air is going to be full of hot, burned gunpowder''

"Not a chance," said Remo. "People don't kill over fish.''

Sandy looked at him steadily. "You were down there. See much life?''

"No.''

"Seafloor looked like it had been dredged clean, correct?"

"Yeah. But it's winter."

"Where do you think the fish are? Wintering off Florida? Hah! The big factory ships just come along with nets the size of football fields, weighted down with chain and tires, and scoop everything up. The fish they don't want, they throw back dead. They call that the by-catch. Only now people have to eat by-catch trawler trash because the prime fish are gone."

"It's a big ocean and it's not the only one," Remo said defensively.

"Today was Fort Sumter. Tomorrow we'll have Pearl Harbor," Sandy replied, turning her gaze back on the seemingly limitless sea. "And it's happening the world over. The Pacific salmon catch is verging on collapse. In the Gulf of Mexico red snapper is down. Russian trawlers are trading shots with Japanese and Korean poachers in the Sea of Okhotsk. The Scots are shooting at Russians in their waters. French and English destroyers have faced off over Channel Islands fishing rights. So have Norway and Iceland up in the Arctic. The Palestinians and Israelis are at each other's throats in the Mediterranean over grouper. The marine food web is coming part, and we're all responsible."

"Fishmongers!" Chiun hissed venomously. "I will not be denied my rightful share of the ocean's bounty."

"Another port heard from," Sandy said quietly.

Remo said nothing. He was thinking of how close he had come to being fish food.

As DUSK DESCENDED, they came upon a great gray ship.

"Take a look," Sandy said. "You are looking at the prime reason fisheries are falling to ruin. That's a factory ship. A floating butcher shop for unlucky fish."

Remo sniffed the air. "I can smell it."

Sandy trained her glasses on the gray vessel's fat stern. "Let's see if she belongs in these waters or not."

Remo read the stern. *"Hareng Saur?"*

"French," said Sandy.

"What's it mean?"

"Don't know. My French is stuck in the fourth grade."

Remo looked down at the Master of Sinanju. "Little Father?"

Chiun's hazel eyes were on the name on the boat's stern. "Pah! It is only a red herring."

"What's that supposed to mean?" said Remo.

"That is the name of the vessel. *Red Herring.*"

Sandy made a face. "Strange. I never heard of red herring."

"Nor have I. I do not care for herring. Too many bones."

"A red herring is a fake clue in a mystery story," said Remo. "What kind of ship would have a name like that?"

"A ship of death," grunted Sandy, turning her field glasses elsewhere.

They left the *Hareng Saur* behind them, where it was swallowed by the gray of the sea and the lowering leaden sky.

An hour later the sonar scope started to ping strangely.

"What's wrong with this thing?" the helmsman wondered aloud.

Sandy Heckman took one look and said, "The scope's blank. It's pinging."

She grabbed up a set of hydrophones. "It's even worse on this." She listened intently.

Chiun leaned in, interest on his parchment mask of a face.

"Pingers," Sandy said, snapping her fingers suddenly.

"Is that like static for sonar?" asked Remo.

"You'll see." She lifted her voice. "All engines stop. Bring out the grapples."

Floating over the spot minutes later, they lowered grappling hooks, swirling them around until they encountered drag, and winched them up.

Up came a clump of netting festooned with seaweed and orange flotation balls and two wooden panels the size of doors.

"Otter net," Sandy said, examining it. "Looks like it was cut or released in an awful hurry. Only a few cod in the cod end."

"So what made the pinging?" Remo inquired.

Sandy fingered a small electrical stud sewn into the net.

"See these? They're radio transmitters called pingers. They're attached to the nets to scare off porpoises. Environmental regulations mandate them to keep porpoises from getting caught with the cod."

"Very wise," said Chiun.

"Think this is off the missing boat?" asked Remo.

"I'd bet my sea legs on it," Sandy said. "The *Santo Fado* was in this area." She stood up. "Maybe it still is."

They trolled the area until the sonar scope came up with a big undersea contact.

They lowered an underwater camera by a cable and found the wreck.

"That's it. The *Santo Fado*. No sign of storm damage. Maybe a big wave capsized her."

"So where are the crew?" asked Remo.

"Maybe drowned. Hypothermia got them otherwise. Bad way to go. All alone in the drink with no hope of rescue." She frowned. "Still and all, they should have gotten off a distress signal."

Ordering the underwater camera recalled, Sandy Heckman gave the order to return to the Cape Cod Coast Guard station.

"So," Remo said after the cutter was charging back toward land, "you interested in dinner when we get back?"

"No."

"How about a movie?"

"Not a chance."

"Then I suppose sex is out, too?"

Sandy Heckman looked at Remo as if he were a bug. "I wouldn't have sex with you if you came with a winning lottery ticket."

Remo grinned. "Great."

She looked at him, then stomped off.

After she disappeared below, the Master of Sinanju joined Remo at the rail.

"I cannot believe your crudity. That was inexcusable," Chiun scolded.

"Had to make sure it was the shark scent and not her sweet disposition," said Remo happily.

"If you desire a woman who does not desire you, take her. Do not ask. Asking is the same as apologizing. It shows weakness. Women are not attracted to weakness, not that it matters what they want or do not want. Unless, of course, you intend to marry the female you desire. Wives matter. Other women do not."

"I'll keep that in mind. Meanwhile I'm enjoying a break from being chased around the quarterdeck."

"It will wear off," Chiun warned.

"There's plenty more shark in the sea...."

"You will eat duck until I say otherwise," Chiun said darkly.

19

Harold Smith sat on the horns of a dilemma.

In actual fact he sat in the cracked leather executive's chair with his back to Long Island Sound and his pinched, patrician face washed by the amber glow of his computer terminal.

Smith was waiting for the medical examiner's report on the body pulled out of the Atlantic by the Cutter *Cayuga.* While he waited, he created a simple table of organization.

What had begun with the inexplicable sinking of the Korean fishing vessel *Ingo Pungo* had apparently been going on for some time. Smith saw that clearly now. Commercial-fishing-vessel losses were at a twelve-year high. Statistically that was significant. The winter had been cold, but not particularly stormy.

The list of lost vessels filled the screen:

Maria D.
Eliese A.
Rimwracked II
Doreen G.
Miss Fortune
Mary Rita

Jeannie I
Santo Fado

All had been lost without a trace. All had vanished in a period of less than six weeks. No survivors found. The white-faced corpse now being autopsied by the Barnstable County medical examiner in Cape Cod was the first. And the turbot inserted into his rectum was at least as significant as the blue fleur-de-lis smeared on his dead face.

Up in Canada, Parti Quebecois separatists were inching toward another referendum on separation. It was impossible to say this many months before the event whether it would result in the secession of Quebec from the rest of Canada. It wasn't impossible.

In Ottawa the Canadian federal government was busy appeasing the separatists. This was only causing English Canada to grow more resentful of French-speaking Canada.

The political situation was approaching flash point once more. Even if Quebec did not secede this time, there would be another referendum in another year or two at most. Not even the efforts of the current French-speaking prime minister could stave off that storm forever.

For U.S. concerns, this had serious ramifications. Quebec was a major trading partner with New England. A significant amount of its electrical power was purchased from Quebec Hydro. Beyond that, the most stable nation on the U.S. border—the longest undefended border in world history—threatened to come apart. In the most civilized country of the modern world, civil war wasn't out of the question.

The prospects were difficult at best. Unforeseeable. And it was the unforeseeable that was most troubling. Secessionist rumblings were starting to be felt in British Columbia, the westernmost Canadian province. Created by the enormous distance from Ottawa, resentment had been fueled by the federal decision to closely curtail the Pacific salmon fisheries, throwing many out of work, just as the Maritime crisis had devastated the economies of Nova Scotia and Newfoundland in the east.

Smith's thoughts veered back to the matter of the submarine christened *Fier D'Être des Grenouilles*. It seemed incredible that a naval vessel manned by French or French-speaking crew would adopt such an undignified name. But Smith had punched up the phrase on his computer. And up had popped the fact—*intelligence* was too serious a term for the datum—that it was the name of a saloon song popular in France. It was possible the song had migrated to Quebec. Probable, in fact.

Smith accessed the *Jane's Fighting Ships* data base for the names of Canadian navy submarines.

The list was short. Canada did not have much of a military in geopolitical terms. There were only three subs:

The Whitehorse/Le Chevalblanc
The Yellowknife/Le Couteaujaune
Le Jacques Cartier/The John Carter

Smith blinked at the list. It indicated twice as many ships as *Jane's* reported. Then he noticed that the slash mark separating both columns, and recalled the federal law designed to appease French-speaking Canadians that required all Canadian signs and labels to carry bilingual names. The submarines, already commissioned when the law had been passed by the Canadian parliament, had been renamed with the most appropriate English and French equivalent names permissible.

"Absurd," Smith muttered. But there was no other explanation.

But none of the vessels had been designated *Fier D'Être des Grenouilles/Proud to be Frogs.*

The French submarine fleet had no such vessel, Smith quickly determined.

Smith decided to look elsewhere. The more links the better. There were too many threads that went nowhere.

Using a paint-box program, Smith created a white fleur-de-lis against the blue background and executed a global search of the World Wide Web, using multiple-search engines. It was a very long shot. He wasn't accustomed to searching for iconography, only language strings. He didn't anticipate useful results.

Smith was astounded three minutes into the execution when the Altavista search engine displayed a wire-service photo of the previous Quebec secessionist referendum. An AP color photo showed two supporters wearing white greasepaint on their faces. The blue fleur-de-lis spread over mouth, lips and both cheeks just as Remo had described.

"Could it be this simple?" Smith muttered.

He decided it was time to bring this matter to the attention of the Oval Office.

THE PRESIDENT OF THE U.S. was feeling relaxed. It was the first time he felt really, truly relaxed in a very long time. The election was behind him. The campaign over. The long swim out of perilous political white waters to clear, untroubled seas was at last over.

Now all he had to do was survive the next four years.

From the standpoint of midwinter, it looked pretty good. Better than he expected, in fact.

Then his beeper beeped. The beeper was tied into a baby monitor up in the Lincoln Bedroom. But it wasn't monitoring a baby but a fire-engine red telephone nestled in an end table next to the bed Abraham Lincoln had slept in so many Chief Executives ago.

Snapping off the beeper, the President took the cramped White House elevator to the top floor and locked the Lincoln Bedroom door behind him.

"Yes?" he said into the red receiver.

The President recognized the tight, lemony voice. He did not know where Dr. Smith held forth, only that in times of crisis he could be counted on.

Smith calling him was another matter.

"Do we have a crisis?" the President asked in a hoarse, hushed tone.

"I do not know," Harold Smith said frankly.

The President relaxed. "Then everything is all right?"

"No."

"Explain."

Harold Smith cleared his throat. His voice was respectful but not awed. It was the voice of a man whose government position was all but unassailable. Rather like the White House valet staff. Presidents came and went. True continuity lay in those who knew where the keys were and how to change the White House fuses. Harold Smith, appointed in secret by a previous President, could not be fired or replaced. CURE could be disbanded by presidential decree, but to date no President had had the courage to issue that order.

The current President didn't plan to be the first.

Still, it wasn't pleasant to hear from Harold Smith, who never had good news unless it was a curt "Mission accomplished."

"Mr. President," Smith began, "we appear to have a foreign submarine operating off New England. It may be interfering with commercial fishing."

"Did you say fishing?"

"Yes. You are aware of the fishing crisis."

"It's global now, isn't it?"

"For our purposes it is also a domestic problem," Smith said. He went on. "An event in the North Atlantic caused me to send my people into the area. They encountered this submarine, and after a brief engagement in which a Coast Guard cutter was fired on by the aggressor, they sank it."

"They who? Your people or the Coast Guard?"

"It was a joint sinking," Smith answered truthfully.

"Sank a foreign submarine? My God," said the President, thinking the worst. "Was it Russian? Was it nuclear?"

"At this time, unknown. The name was French. *Fier D'Être des Grenouilles.*"

"I left my French behind in college," the President said dryly.

"It means *Proud to be Frogs.*"

"Why would the French be mucking about out there?"

"It may not have been a French naval vessel. The vessel flew a flag that suggests the provincial flag of Quebec, and their sailors wear greasepaint disguises portraying the fleur-de-lis.

"Suggests? What do you mean by 'suggest'?"

"It was not the Quebec flag, but a quadrant of it with the colors reversed."

"Why would Quebec be cruising for an international incident?"

"That is precisely my point. It is unreasonable to think that they would. If Quebec's current push for nationhood succeeds, they will need friendly relations with the United States. Their highest priority beyond official recognition by France itself would be remaining on good terms with America."

"Yet they're sabotaging it."

"That is not a conclusion I am willing to jump to," Smith cautioned, letting the line hang empty for a long breath, "unless there exist factors I do not know. I am forced to conclude that this is an operation designed to embarrass Montreal.''

"I can think of only one place that could be coming from,'' said the President.

"Ottawa,'' said Smith.

"I think I might give the prime minister up there a courtesy call.''

"I would be discreet,'' Smith warned.

"I don't have time for discreet. I'm going to ask him flat out what's going on.''

"That would not be diplomatic.''

"Maybe not,'' the President said tightly, "but if I can head off a fishing war by scaring the starch out of Ottawa, I think that would be a good thing. What could go wrong?''

"Anything,'' Smith said quickly, but since his role was advice not consent on these matters, that was all he would say.

The President thanked Smith and hung up.

When he got back down to the Oval Office, the President of the United States asked his personal secretary to place a call to Ottawa. Politically this was a matter that required a certain guarded tact, a calculated finesse. But this was neighborly, diffident, good-natured Canada. He'd just go boo, and they'd scurry for cover like a possum under a porch.

THE PRIME MINISTER of Canada was happy to take the call from the President of the United States. He exchanged convivial greetings and pleasantries of the day. Then the President's voice turned vaguely steely.

"I have a report on my desk of a Canadian submarine that fired upon a Coast Guard vessel. We had to sink it. No choice. We realized it was yours only after it had gone down.''

"Our submarine. What vessel?''

"I'd only mangle the French, but the English translation is *Proud to be Frogs.*''

The fiber-optic line was deathly silent. "Mr. President, have you been—how shall I put this—imbibing?''

"You have subs in your navy bearing French names?'' the President questioned.

"We do. But—''

"Your sub is on the Atlantic floor,'' the President went on in a cool tone. "This office will convey formal regrets, of course. But I want it perfectly understood that such aggressive Canadian naval maneuvers will not be tolerated.''

"We have *not* been aggressive!'' the prime minister exploded.

"Then if that wasn't your sub, you have nothing to worry about,'' the President said.

"It was not, and we are not concerned. Except for the regrettable loss of life, of course.''

"Down here we call that deniability.''

"And up here we call it poppycock,'' the prime minister said, his voice tense.

"Well, whatever the truth is, you and I understand each other clearly. Isn't that right?''

"We,'' the prime minister said tightly, "understand ourselves only too well. Thank you for the courtesy call. Good day to you, Mr. President.''

"Have a good one,'' the President returned in an unconcerned voice.

The call terminated with simultaneous clicks, and in the Oval Office, the President of the United States leaned back in his chair and breathed out a cool release of air. It felt good to do that. No point in letting anyone push him around now. Not even friendly, forgiving, top trading partner to the end, Canada.

20

In Ottawa the prime minister of the Dominion of Canada replaced the office telephone with an expression on his face like that of a man who had his lips seared unexpectedly by a friendly kiss.

Tapping his desk intercom, he snapped, "Get the minister of fisheries on the line."

"Yes, sir."

The phone lit up a moment later, and the intercom said, "Fisheries Minister Houghton on line 3, Mr. Prime Minister."

"Thank you," he said, punching the lighted button and snapping the handset to his displeased face.

There was snow on the ground, and the Rideau Canal was frozen solid, much to the delight of ice skaters. The Winterlude Festival, with its influx of tourists, was now a pleasant memory. This made what he was about to do more practicable. No loss in upsetting the free-spending Yanks after their dollars had been dispersed into the Canadian economy.

"I have just had a peculiar call from the United States President," the prime minister said in his distinctive French-Canadian accent.

"Yes?"

"He called to warn me that a submarine of ours

fired on a U.S. Coast Guard vessel. He was forced to sink it, he said.''

"A submarine of *ours?*"

"So he claims. I know nothing of any lost submarine. Do you?"

"No."

"He claimed the name translates as *Proud to be Frogs.* Ring a bell?"

"Of course not. There is no such vessel in our fleet."

"He was very curt with me."

"It sounds as if he were," the fisheries minister agreed.

"I did not care for his tone of voice. It reminded me of the Spanish."

"Those philistines."

"I think there should be a response. Measured but pointed. Will you see to it?"

"U.S.-flag vessels continue to slip in and out of the Grand Banks illegally."

"I think we might wish to see a simultaneous Pacific response. It will be easier to handle, in the sense of disengagement."

"We are having problems with U.S. vessels in our Pacific salmon fisheries."

"We are having problems with every flag and vessel, including our own," the prime minister said tightly.

"I have matters under control."

"I know you do, Houghton." The prime minister was very quiet as his curled lips gradually resumed their normal contours. "Do you suppose Quebec could have acquired a submarine?"

"You would know more about that than I, Mr. Prime Minister."

"I would. But I do not. I imagine that I shall have to make inquiries. I would not excuse the French from poaching again. Your predecessor had difficulties with their fishing fleets, as I recall."

"Actually that was my predecessor's predecessor."

"Of course." The prime minister's voice grew reflective. "Strange, is it not, that we live in times where the minister of fisheries and oceans should control such a potent portfolio?"

"I am equal to the task," said Fisheries Minister Houghton.

"Get right on it, Gil. I look forward to the coming news reports."

"Thank you, Mr. Prime Minister..."

IN HIS OFFICE overlooking Parliament Hill, Canadian Fisheries Minister Gilbert Houghton dropped the receiver into its hard plastic cradle and dry-washed his haggard face with both hands....

The word from the PM was like a blow to the pit of his stomach. The *Fier D'Être des Grenouilles* lay at the bottom of the North Atlantic. If true, it was a grave setback. That left only the *Hareng Saur* to conduct Maritime operations.

He went to the bank of windows that looked out over the Ottawa River and Quebec, soon to be an enemy province, if the infernal secessionists got their damn way.

Well, they would not get their damn way if Gil Houghton had anything to say about it. While the appeasers gave and gave and conceded all but sovereignty to a bunch of mumble-mouthed cultural rebels, true Canadians like himself would do what they could to hold the dominion together.

When the previous fisheries minister had resigned to become premier of Newfoundland, some said his successor Gilbert Houghton would—if he so chose—follow in his footsteps and ascend to the premiership of his native Nova Scotia. But that wasn't the plan. Gilbert Houghton had accepted the portfolio with a more important agenda in mind.

The immediate problem had been that of the Pacific salmon fisheries. In a bold stroke that garnered him international headlines, Gil Houghton did what his predecessor hadn't dared. He cut back severely on the British Columbia fishing industry. There were howls of protest, of course. But with so many cod men in the Atlantic provinces out of work, what could the salmon fishermen say? It was simply their time.

The reaction had been more strident than calculated, however. The bloody fools in Vancouver—Hongcouver, they were calling it now that all the Asians had swarmed in—were flinging secession talk about as if it were a casual thing. And the talk kept growing.

Gilbert Houghton realized he had a problem.

He found the solution on the Net, of all places. One day he received an invitation for a thirty-day free trial of a cyber-talk forum with the tantalizing name of Mistress Kali's School for Corrective Action.

How someone had learned of his peculiar but

well-concealed tastes, he didn't know. But the service was anonymous. No one would know, especially his wife. It was a godsend. Since attaining ministerial office, he had had to dispense with Mistress Fury's services.

Mistress Kali had accepted him into her cyberschool without hesitation. Soon he was growing hard at his desk and keeping a spare set of trousers in case of accidental emissions. Which happened often.

Before long he was begging for private sessions. These were granted...eventually. She seemed to delight in denying him, and he delighted in the denial. It made the eventual fulfilment all that more exquisite.

He poured out his heart and secret soul to her.

"I want to be prime minister. That is my goal," he said one day while licking her yellow-painted toenails as she toyed with his testicles with the other foot.

"First you must take full control of the crisis on both coasts," she said.

"Those out-of-work fishermen will be my ruin."

"Give them work."

"I dare not reopen the fisheries," he said, switching feet. "I will be pilloried."

"They are sailors. Put them to work on your behalf. Are you not minister of oceans, as well as fisheries?"

"Yes..."

"A minister of oceans should control his dominion. If there was a way to replenish the Grand Banks, would that not advance your career?''

''It would,'' he agreed.

Tucking the handle of her black whip under his chin, she said, ''There is...''

And he listened. The technology existed. A phantom fleet could be assembled cheaply and secretly. And best of all, a scapegoat was ready-made, so the glare of blame would not fall upon Gilbert Houghton, minister of fisheries and oceans and secret supplicant of Mistress Kali, the most brilliant and ruthless tactician he had ever known.

But now, only months into the operation, the fleet had been cut exactly in half, with the loss of all hands.

Houghton knew that communicating this dire setback to his mistress must be the first order of business. And she was not going to be pleased.

Perversely he looked forward to her displeasure....

THE OFFICE DESKTOP SYSTEM was always running. He would not want to miss her summons, should it come.

Bringing up his e-mail folder, Gil Houghton executed a quick communication.

To: Mistress Kali@yug.net
From: Commodore@net.org
Subject: Grave development
The PM has just called me. The Americans are claiming to have sunk a Canadian submarine, the *Frog*. The PM has asked me to initiate a

stiff response in the Pacific. The loss of the *Frog* aside, this throws my plan into a cocked hat. How can we lay proper blame on Montreal through a Pacific action? No one would believe that. Not even the Yanks in Washington.

Adoringly yours, Gil.

After checking the spelling, he sent it. Mistress Kali detested poor spelling and denied her supplicants corrective punishment for such minor infractions.

An answer came very soon. Somehow Fisheries Minister Houghton was not surprised. It was as if the woman possessed multiple eyes that saw unerringly in all directions at once.

To: Commodore@net.org
From: Kali@yug.net
Subject: Do as you are bid

The message was empty when he brought it up.

"Damn that woman!" he swore. Did she have to deny him even the most paltry of acknowledgments? Furiously he typed out a reply.

To: Kali@yug.net
From: Commodore@net.org
Subject: Can we discuss this in person?

Then, in the body of the letter, he added a lower-case, perfectly centered "Please?"

A lonely hour passed before he gave up waiting for a response. Then he picked up the telephone and set in motion events that had not been factored into the master plan...

At least, not in *his* master plan...

21

UN Secretary-General Anwar Anwar-Sadat returned from a dismal day of resolutions and Security Council foot-dragging and temporizing to an e-mail message that made his heart leap with undisguised joy. If the members of the international community could have seen Anwar-Sadat in his Sphinx-decorated Beekman Place high-rise apartment dropping into the chair before the blue terminal, they wouldn't have recognized the profile of the diplomat who was called Old Stone Face behind his back.

His dusky features were wreathed in joy. His fingers leaped for the keyboard he had for years disdained. Functionaries formerly input his commands for him. He was above such tasks. As the son of an upper-class Cairo politician, he had been born with a silver spoon in his mouth. Until he was packed off to military school at the age of twelve, his hand never touched that spoon or any other with his mouth. Servants fed him by hand.

But not here. Not in the privacy of his private world of romance and desire. Here he moved his own mouse and input his own commands.

The message was from Mistress Kali.

The subject line read, "Opportunity."

Anwar-Sadat brought up the message. Its crisp blue lines made his heart sing, but it was no message of longing and love. Rather, it was a very serious communication:

> I have it on the highest authority, my Anwar, that U.S. Coast Guard forces last night sank a Canadian submarine in disputed waters.

"All waters are disputed," Anwar-Sadat muttered, his features resuming their stiff, stony lines. Such a face the Great Sphinx of pharaonic Egypt wore when it was whole and uneroded and complete of countenance.

He absorbed the remainder of the message.

> This incident is being suppressed by both sides to spare diplomatic feelings, but it may be but the opening skirmish in a wider conflict. It might behoove you to bring this to the attention of the international community, so that your views are given the proper credit and respect they so richly deserve.

Anwar-Sadat nodded in agreement. "I will do it," he announced. Then, remembering the medium of communication, he guided the cursor to the reply icon and tapped out his very words, adding a "My Sweet Sphinx."

The message sped through fiber-optic lines to its unknown destination. As he watched the system perform its sacred duties, Anwar Anwar-Sadat only wished he were a beam of light that could follow it to the waiting arms of his love-to-be.

He yearned for those arms and the gentle caresses of Mistress Kali's fingers. He could almost feel them on his brow, his lips and in other places it was not good to think about when he was alone.

Still, the thoughts had come unbidden.

Going to a bookcase, he took from its place a book of old erotica, the *Kama Sutra.*

It was going to be a long night. There was no telling when Mistress Kali would reply again, if at all. But for his mind to concoct the speech he planned to give on the morrow, it must be agile.

Certain hormones facilitated his thinking processes. He only wished that their release did not require a naughty book and his own manipulations....

It was very undignified. If only he had a snake-hipped, kohl-eyed personal slave to apply the necessary unguents to the needy portions of his anatomy, which more and more felt the distress of a fish caught on a hook.

A very stimulating hook, he had to admit.

22

The death of Tomasso Testaverde would have amounted to as much as his ill-spent life were it not for the fact that Tomasso Testaverde was of Sicilian blood.

After the autopsy his bluish corpse was released to his next of kin.

The trouble was no one wanted the remains.

Not his mother, from whom he was estranged.

Not any of his hardworking uncles.

Finally his father's father, Sirio Testaverde, agreed to take possession of the late Tomasso Testaverde. Sirio showed up at the Barnstable County morgue and said simply, "I have come for my grandson, Tomasso."

"This way," the bored morgue attendant said.

They walked the antiseptic corridors of death in silence. The still, cool air smelled of pungent chemicals. These things did not bother Sirio, who had skippered Grand Banks schooners in the golden era of the cod schooners. Although he hadn't gone to sea in two decades, there were still fish scales under his fingernails and salt grime caking his hairy nostrils. He was a greaser, as Sicilian-born fishermen were known.

The body was slid out of the morgue drawer and a sheet thrown back.

Sirio saw the blue design on the unrecognizable face of the only son of his only son and said, "*Minga!* This is not Tomasso."

"Dental records say it is."

"What is that on his face?"

"That's how he was found. The funeral home will clean him up for interment."

"He was found this way?" Sirio muttered, his old eyes squinting.

"Yes."

"That means someone did this thing to him," he growled.

"You'll have to take that up with the Coast Guard. They have the full report on file."

Sirio Testaverde did. He learned the unpleasant details of his grandson's passing, the fish inserted where fish should not go, the face painting, all of it. And although he had disowned his grandson many years ago for dishonoring the proud Testaverde name, the thin blood in his thready veins leaped hot and fast.

"I will avenge this outrage," he said, voice low with feeling.

"We have no suspects at this time," the Coast Guard information officer stiffly informed him. "Anyone could have done this."

"The sign on his face, it has meaning?" Sirio pressed.

"He may have painted his face this way."

"For what reason?"

"Maybe he was a hockey fan. They like to paint their faces to show support for their favorite team."

"Hockey! Tomasso is Sicilian. We do not follow hockey. That is for others."

"I think that blue symbol is a French-Canadian team's emblem or something. I don't follow hockey, either."

Sirio Testaverde took possession of Tomasso's abused body and, after turning him over to the Kingsport Funeral Home, went to the United Fishermen's Club and began speaking to any who would listen in a low, urgent voice.

"It is the damn Canadians that did this to my son's only son. The Testaverde name stops in this century because of what these scum have done," raged Sirio Testaverde.

"Canadians?" someone asked incredulously.

"Have they not seized our boats?" Sirio countered.

This was allowed.

"Do they not compete for the same fish as we?" Sirio added.

This, too, was admitted.

"They have come into our waters for as long as I am alive and on the seas, and after they exhaust our waters, they close off their own. We are excluded from the Grand Banks. Did we exclude Canadians from our waters? No. We did not. This is inherently unfair. Something must be done."

"It is their waters to close," a reasonable voice said.

"The waters belong to no one but the strong. To those strong enough to take fish from them. We are

Sicilians. And Americans. We are strong. Canadians are weak. We will take their fish if we so wish.''

"What if they try to stop us?"

Sirio Testaverde shook his sun-shiny fist in the smoky club. "Then we will take their boats and their lives.''

On any other night Sirio Testaverde's exhortations would have been dismissed as the bitter grievings of an old man who has come to the end of his bloodline.

But in one corner of the club, set high on a rude shelf, a television set poured down its flickering kinetic light. The network news was on. No one was paying much attention to it. Neither was it being ignored entirely.

"We will take what is ours because we are men,'' Sirio was saying. "For too long we get a poor price for our landings because we compete with Canadian fish that is trucked in to the Boston Fish Pier, already dressed and cooled. First they overfish our waters, then they overfish their own. Now they send their damn fish to our markets. They are swine.''

A fragment of a report caught the attention of a man seated closest to the TV. He turned up the volume.

"...In New York, UN Secretary-General Anwar Anwar-Sadat has made a claim that is creating quite a stir in diplomatic circles,'' the mellow-voiced anchor was saying. "It seems, according to the Secretary-General, that a U.S. Coast Guard cutter and a submarine suspected to be of Canadian origin— French-Canadian origin, to be precise—clashed in disputed waters on the Grand Banks with the result that the sub was sunk with all hands aboard. In Ottawa, Canadian officials vigorously deny this story. From Montreal, additional denials. Yet the Secretary-General is insisting the report is true and furthermore that, like the current fishing crisis, it is a sign that individual nations cannot be trusted to oversee their own territorial waters, and that a UN high commission be established to patrol and safeguard the high seas, incidentally protecting the much-overfished stocks that are the cause of so much international friction these days.''

"See!" Sirio said, pointing to footage of the UN Secretary-General addressing a group. "See. The damn wog is correct. No one owns the sea. Let us take what is ours!"

In other times Sirio Testaverde's demands would have fallen on deaf ears. For these were hardworking men who rose with the sun and, when they at last returned to port, slept for days afterward.

But times were tough. Massachusetts had surrendered to Maine the distinction of being the most successful fishing state in the nation. These were men who owned their own boats, their own businesses, but had no control over their product. They were farmers of the sea, and their crops were in perpetual failure.

"We must take!" Sirio ranted.

Others began to vent their own grievances.

Soon Sirio's gravelly calls were taken up by younger, more vigorous seamen.

The hour grew late and the voices grew angry and, as word spread, the smoky hall filled with many out-of-work fishermen.

"I say," Sirio Testaverde shouted, pounding the table at which he sat, "that we assemble an armada and take what belongs to us by virtue of our superior might."

The scarred and cigarette-burned table shook with the vehemence of Sirio Testaverde's slamming fist. All around the room, other fists struck old wood, and voices, low and sullen, grew high and agitated.

That night an armada was assembled. It slipped out of the Kingsport waterfront and made its way north to the richest fishery in the entire world.

They were sailing into history.

In St. John's, Newfoundland, Canadian Coast Guard Petty Officer Caden Orlowski received his orders by wireless and asked that they be repeated.

"You are to arrest and detain any United States vessels operating near our waterways."

"*In* our waterways? Or did I hear incorrectly and you said 'near.'"

"Upon any pretext board and detain any and all U.S. vessels you encounter near our waterways."

"Fishing vessels, you mean?"

"Any and all U.S. vessels," his commander repeated somewhat testily.

"Aye, sir," said Petty Officer Orlowski, who then turned to his helmsman and said, "Steer a straight course south. We are hunting American vessels."

The helmsman turned from the wheel and made dubious eye contact.

"You have your orders, as I have mine," Orlowski repeated.

The helmsman fell to his duties.

Aboard the Canadian Coast Guard cutter *Robert W. Service*, the word spread. They were hunting American maritime vessels. No one knew why, for certain. But all understood where the order had come from.

It could only originate from the office of the minister of fisheries, who had only a year before closed off the Pacific salmon fisheries to Canadian fishermen. Obviously that had been only phase one. This, then, was phase two.

Orlowski had another word for it.

Damage control.

He hoped that no U.S. commercial-fishing vessels were operating over the line. Otherwise he was about to become the pointman in an international incident.

As he saw it, it wasn't a likely prospect for career advancement.

For politicians did what politicians did. Often without weighing the consequences.

Men like Orlowski were convenient scapegoats for such men as Gilbert Houghton.

"Damn bluenose," he muttered. "Damn him and his Ottawa thinking."

23

The Master of Sinanju was adamant. He presented his silken back to his pupil in his spacious kitchen where a wall clock in the shape of a black cat switched its eyes and tail like a lazy metronome.

"No."

"Aw, c'mon, Chiun. One night," pleaded Remo.

"I have hired at great expense a woman who cooks passably. I will not eat in a restaurant just because you crave fish. You will eat duck."

"What are *you* having?"

"I do not yet know. The fish cellar is bare. I must hie to the fishmonger's and discover what is fresh today."

"You can order anything you want at a restaurant," Remo suggested.

"I do not trust restaurant fare. They serve fish whose names cannot be found in cookbooks on fish."

"Name one."

"Scrod. I have never heard of scrod before I came to this cold province."

Remo frowned. "I think scrod is some kind of little cod."

"Others have claimed it is something else entirely."

"Well, you can order anything you want besides scrod. And it'll be on me."

"You will remain home and eat duck," Chiun insisted.

"Not if I go to the fishmonger's and buy my own food."

"You will have to cook it. I will forbid my personal cook to prepare it for you."

"I can cook."

"And you *will* cook. Now I must be off."

"I'm coming with you. No way I'm hanging around here with that old battle-ax you call a housekeeper. She won't even tell me her name."

"I cannot stop you," said the Master of Sinanju, who floated out the door and began walking at such a fast clip that his kimono skirts shook and swayed with every step of his churning pipe-stem legs.

Remo followed along with brisk but casual steps. He wore his habitual T-shirt and chinos because it saved making decisions in the morning and, when they got dirty, he just threw them away and donned new ones. The cold air caught the warm carbon dioxide escaping from between his thin lips and made white plumes with it.

As they walked, Remo tried to strike up a conversation. "I wonder where Freya is?"

"I wonder where my fish are. I was promised veritable riches in fishes."

"There's plenty of fish in the seas. To coin a phrase."

"That is exactly what Bamboo-hatted Kim said," spit Chiun.

"Who's Bamboo-hatted Kim?"

"The seventh Master of Sinanju."

"The bigamist?"

"No, that was the eighth."

Remo looked thoughtful. "Was Kim the one with the bamboo leg?"

"There were no wooden-legged Masters of Sinanju, although Gi limped during his end days."

"Keeping track of past Masters is as tough as counting phantoms," Remo muttered.

Chiun looked up. "Phantoms?"

"You know, the Ghost Who Walks Phantom. The comic-strip character who passes his name and costume down from father to son, just like we pass our skills down. They made a movie about him a year or so back."

Chiun made a distasteful face. "I am considering suing those people for theft of intellectual property."

"So tell me about Bamboo-hatted Kim. I take it his name comes from the kind of hat he wore."

Chiun shook his head. "No, from what he did with it. For many Masters wore hats of bamboo."

"Okay..."

"I have told you that the first Masters took to plying the assassin's trade because the land was rocky and the seas too cold for fishing."

"Seventy billion times," Remo said wearily.

"You were but a child in Sinanju when I first told you this. The truth is more complicated."

"Truth usually is," Remo said ruefully.

"You have swam in the waters of the West Korea Bay many times."

"Yeah," said Remo, in whose mind's eye flashed a chilling image. It was one of the last times Remo had seen his daughter. Remo still remembered running across the bay chasing a flying purple pterodactyl that was carrying off little Freya in its talons. It was an illusion created by an old enemy. Freya had been in no danger. Now it was a different story.

"The waters are very shallow," Chiun noted.

"Yeah."

"Very shallow for many *ri* out."

"If you say so."

"In such waters it is possible to walk for several *ri* without one's head being submerged in water."

"That's why the sub has to wait pretty far out while rafts bring in the gold."

"Do not speak to me of gold when a more precious commodity is under discussion," Chiun said, his voice tinged with bitterness.

"What's more precious than gold?"

"Fish. For without fish we cannot live."

"With gold you can buy all the fish you want," Remo countered.

"Not from a hungry man. A hungry man will spurn gold if he possesses but one fish. For one cannot eat gold, only hoard it. Or if necessary, spend it."

"Man cannot live by rice and duck alone," Remo said.

"In the beginning, Masters subsisted on rice and fish exclusively," Chiun went on.

"No duck?"

"Duck was unknown in those early days. Common Koreans do not eat duck."

Remo raised an astonished eyebrow. "I didn't know that."

"You know this now." Chiun walked on in a tight silence.

Up ahead a stooped Vietnamese man came hobbling along. Spotting Chiun, he hastily crossed the street. By that, Remo assumed the Master of Sinanju had been out terrorizing the city's Asian population again.

"In those days the soil had not been exhausted. Certain foods could be grown. And fish were plentiful in the shallow waters by the village. In the winter not as much fish as during the warm season, but for our tiny village there was a sufficiency of fish."

A cold wind brought to Remo's nostrils the heavy smell of nearby Wollaston Beach at low tide in winter. It smelled of dead clams and beached seaweed. The beach at Sinanju smelled like that on good days.

Chiun went on. "Now in those days, as now, the villagers were afflicted with the lassitude of indolence. They fished when their stomachs required them to fish. In the winter they did not fish at all because the waters were inhospitable and the fish, being intelligent, seldom ventured close to the rocks from which my ancestors threw their nets and hooked lines."

"Smart fish," grunted Remo, noticing a Chinese woman duck back into her house at their approach.

"All fish are smart."

"That's why they call it brain food," said Remo.

"That was what Wang the Greater said. Eating

fish improves the brain. It is one reason why Masters of Sinanju use their brains fully.''

"It's rich in omega-3 fatty acids, too."

"I do not know what white voodoo it is you speak," Chiun said darkly.

"That means it's lower in cholesterol."

"Cholesterol is good for some people."

"Not for us."

Chiun lifted a finger skyward. The light caught his nail protector of imperial jade. "It is good for us if our opponents wallow in it. For then the advantage is ours."

"Good point," said Remo, who was starting to relax.

They passed an apartment building where the words Go Home Gook were scrawled on the asphalt driveway. Remo recognized Chiun's slashing strokes—not that there was any doubt. The words were gouged in the asphalt as if by a very sharp knife.

"You been trying to stampede the local Asians?" Remo asked.

"If they are easily frightened, they should not try to dwell among their betters."

"Tell that to the mayor's Task Force on Racial Harmony."

"As I was saying," Chiun continued, "the fish who dwelled off Sinanju, the carp and the tuna and the corbina, understood that they were food. So they avoided the shore waters, forcing the fishermen to go into the far waters to seek them. In the warm months this was only a bother. But in the winter months it could kill. For it was not possible to stand in bitter ice water waiting for a cunning fish to succumb to a lapse in judgment.''

"Fish are smart because they eat other fish, right?"

"Correct. Now Bamboo-hatted Kim was in his dotage when the hunger of the villagers began to vex him. For he had ventured out many times to Japan and Cathay to serve the emperors who held sway over those realms. Kim grew weary of the long journeys that brought the gold that paid for the rice the villages could not grow and the fish they could not catch.

"It occurred to Kim, not yet known as Bamboo-hatted Kim, that there might be a better way. In those days he wore a hat like a great rice bowl of bamboo that was tied to his head by a catgut string so it would not fall off. One day, seeking his own supper, he waded out into the frigid waters of the bay with his line and hook of fish bone—for the best way to catch a fish is with one of its own sharp bones, Remo.''

"I'll try to remember that."

Chiun resumed. "Kim was forced to wade out three entire *ri* because many fish had sought warmer waters. But at last he came to a place where the carp and the corbina swam in promising numbers. There he dropped his hook and waited.

"When a fish larger than the usual snapped at his hook, Kim thought the Dragon King had smiled on him. You know of the Dragon King, who lives under the waters, Remo?"

"Yeah. He was the Korean Neptune."

"The Romans mangled the truth as usual," Chiun

sniffed. "No sooner had the carp taken Kim's line than Kim jerked his wrists to snap the fish living out of the water, where he would break its spine and claim it for his dinner."

"But the line snapped, right?"

"How did you know this, Remo?"

"Wild guess."

Chiun touched his tendril of a beard. "The line snapped. And the carp splashed back into the water to escape, leaving Kim with a three-*ri* walk back to his home and another three-*ri* wade back to his favorite fishing spot with a new line and still another three-*ri* trudge back to cook his dinner."

"That's a lot of *ri*."

"It was too many *ri* for Kim, who stood in knee-deep water and puzzled out a solution that would fill his belly with carp without tiring his legs. He wore the simple garments of those days, for the kimono had not been discovered. He was without sandals. Nor had he a belt. Kim had only his hat, which he removed from his head and contemplated at length.

"At that moment a silvery carp swam by, not suspecting that Kim's immobile legs belonged to one that sought its cold meat. With a flourish Kim dipped his bamboo hat into the cold water and lifted it high. As the water drained through the hat's coarse weave, the fish gasped and flopped and so trapped, it surrendered its life without Kim resorting to the cruelty of a hook.

"Carrying his meal in his hat, Bamboo-hatted Kim returned to his home and ate well that day."

"Good for him."

"The next day, Remo, he repeated this feat and was successful. Each day the villagers noticed that Bamboo-hatted Kim walked out in the cold water without hook or line and returned bearing a fish in his hat. And being the lazybones that they were in those days, they fell upon Bamboo-hatted Kim to return to the frigid water and bring them fish, too."

"Sounds like the Sinanju gene pool hasn't improved much in the last five thousand years."

Chiun let the comment pass.

"At first Kim was naturally reluctant. But the villagers plied him with honeyed words and promises of adoration. To these Kim was at first deaf. But one cunning wench with apple cheeks prevailed upon him in the end."

"It wouldn't be the first time someone traded a little nookie for food," said Remo.

"I have never heard of nookie. Is it an ocean fish or a river fish?"

"It's kinda like tuna," said Remo with a straight face.

"I will add it to the list under purple smoothie, another fish unknown in those days," Chiun said somberly.

"You do that," said Remo. "So that was the story of Bamboo-hatted Kim."

"No, that was the story of how Bamboo-hatted Kim earned his nickname. The lesson of Bamboo-hatted Kim is as follows—all that winter Kim went out into the frigid water to gather up the unsuspecting fish because the apple-cheeked wench had whispered a notion that appealed to Kim's lazy instincts. If he walked the three *ri* every day and brought back fish, he no longer needed to walk the hundreds of *ri* to Cathay or Egypt or Japan to ply his true trade. For in the those early days, it was the first duty of the Master of Sinanju to feed the village, who depended upon his fish-earning skills.''

"Kim took a shortcut, huh?"

Chiun nodded. "An unfortunate one, for as time went on, he softened and grew indolent. Kim allowed himself to be reduced to a fisherman.''

"Sounds like a reasonable approach to me.''

Chiun eyed Remo critically. "No doubt some of Kim's indolent blood flows through your susceptible veins. We will work on this.''

"So what happened?'' asked Remo.

"Time passed. Weeks and months followed one another, and Kim found he had to wade farther and farther out because the intelligent fish soon learned to swim farther away, for they noticed that their numbers were dwindling. In time Kim was walking twelve *ri*. Then twenty. Then thirty. Eventually he reached the point where the water was over his head and his bamboo hat found no fish.

"When after three consecutive days Bamboo-hatted Kim returned to the village forlorn of countenance, wearing his empty hat instead of carrying it before him laden with carp and corbina, he was jeered by the lazy ones, including the apple-cheeked wench. And his heart was heavy. For there were no more carp or corbina to be scooped up. What had not been eaten, had fled, Remo. The villagers had waxed fat through the bounty Kim had brought back. But instead of living off their fat, as they did some winters, they hooted and jeered and spit upon Empty-headed Kim.''

''You mean Bamboo-hatted Kim.''

''He was both. For he was soon forced to walk the hundreds of *ri* to foreign thrones to ply his proper trade. By that time he had grown thick of waist and flabby of muscle.''

''He die?''

''Not all at once. He fulfilled a contract with a minor Siamese prince and brought back sufficient gold to purchase sufficient dried yellow corbina from another village to carry Sinanju through the winter. That winter Kim began training his successor in earnest. When the next Master of Sinanju was well on his way to Masterhood, Bamboo-hatted Kim burned his unlucky hat—although nothing could consume his poor reputation.''

They walked past several markets and shops, disdaining them all. Quincy had a growing Asian population, but Chiun ignored Chinese- and Vietnamese-owned establishments, too.

''You are very quiet,'' Chiun prompted.

''Okay, catching too many fish is an old problem. But that was just the West Korea Bay. It's a big planet, and most of it's water. That's a lot of fish.''

''How many hungry billions are there now?''

''Seven.''

''That is a lot of billions.''

''There's still more fish.''

''Not if the fish live short lives and the billions enjoy long ones.''

''I see your point,'' said Remo.

They turned a corner of Hancock Street onto a

side street. Two blocks down they came to the Squantum Fish Market and they went in.

Ignoring the lobsters in aereated tanks, they went to the glass cases where assorted iced fish lay in halves and fillets.

"What is good today?" asked Chiun of the proprietor.

"We have fresh mudfish."

Chiun's hazel eyes went to the trio of dull black fish that might have been made out of old rubber. "I do not like their eyes."

"The cusk is fresh, too."

"I have had cusk. It is a very tough fish."

"You have shark?" asked Remo.

"Sure. One shark steak?"

"Make it two."

While the shark was being weighed, Chiun eyed Remo and asked, "You eat gross fish. Always with you it is heavy slabs of shark and swordfish and tuna. You eat fish like it is beef steak."

"I'm a big eater."

"Carp is a nice fish."

"You can't get it around here. You know that."

"Soon we will have carp in profusion."

"Could be a long wait," Remo reminded him.

Chiun turned his attention back to the fish case. His wrinkled face gathered up in deepening lines of unhappiness. "I was promised carp and I am reduced to deciding between mudfish and lumpfish."

Remo grinned. "Like it or lump it."

Chiun shot him a withering look, then his face brightened. "Do you have turbot?" he asked the proprietor.

"Sure."

"I will take a pound of your best turbot. For I have heard that fierce wars have been waged over its singular taste, yet I have never tasted it before now."

"It's like halibut."

"Halibut is an acceptable fish. It is better than oily mackerel or bony alewife."

Remo was looking down the rows of fish fillets. His eye fell on a bulge-eyed, blubber-lipped blue fish speared by a white plastic sign on which was written a name in green Magic Marker.

"Wolf fish. What's that?"

"It's good."

"Not with that face," growled Remo. His eye fell on a short-bodied reddish fish with very scared eyes.

"Scup?"

"It's real popular down south," said the proprietor, setting Remo's wrapped shark on the counter, then carefully wrapping up Chiun's turbot.

When his shark was rung up, Remo said, "Since when is shark almost ten dollars a pound?"

"Since fish became scarce."

Reluctantly Remo paid the bill. Together he and the Master of Sinanju walked out of the shop.

"This shark ought to last me a few days," Remo said.

"You will cook it yourself," Chiun warned.

"Anything to keep the wenches out of my waters."

BACK AT CASTLE SINANJU, the phone was ringing.

"Hey! Somebody answer that!" Remo shouted as he stepped in.

"It is same man who called before," shouted down Chiun's nameless housekeeper from the top floor.

Dropping his fish on the counter, Remo grabbed up the telephone.

Harold Smith's voice was hoarse and haggard. "We have an urgent situation developing in the North Atlantic."

"What's that?" asked Remo.

"The Coast Guard cutter *Cayuga* has been detained by Canadian Coast Guard gunboats."

"What did they do wrong?"

"I do not know, but if what I fear is true, the United States is now at war."

"War? War with whom?"

"That is what you must find out. Fly to St. John's, Newfoundland, immediately. The *Cayuga* is under Canadian tow, and that appears to be their ultimate destination."

"Sure. Once I wolf down a slab of shark."

"Now," said Smith.

"I'll eat it raw on the way. Without shark I doubt if I can make it through the flight."

24

Lieutenant Sandy Heckman would never have fallen for it, but the Canadian Coast Guard captain was so damn polite.

She should have known better. She cursed herself a blue streak when she realized how badly she had screwed up, but by then she was in over her head and the bubbles were breaking the surface.

She had dropped off the two crazies from the National Bureau of Fisheries, or whatever it was. And promptly turned around before her commander could stop her.

This was going to be her last patrol. There was no getting around it. She had in the heat of action sunk a foreign sub in open waters. It was self-defense, but as soon as the gurry hit the screws she knew it was back to halibut patrol off Alaska or worse, stripped of her commission and set adrift among the landsmen.

Either way she wanted one last rescue.

Off New Brunswick she was searching for the missing *Jeannie I* out of Bar Harbor, Maine, when a Canadian fisheries-patrol boat showed up, its decks thick with green-uniformed inspectors from the Ministry of Fisheries and Oceans.

They hailed her in very polite terms. "Can we speak to you a moment, Lieutenant?"

"Is this about the submarine?"

"Again, please?"

Maybe it was the brisk tone of his voice or the natty uniform. But Sandy Heckman fell for it hook, line and sinker. Especially line.

"Never mind. Helmsman, throttle down and prepare to make her fast to the cutter."

"Aye, sir."

She had her misgivings, but their politeness had disarmed her completely. Back in her Pacific days, she used to lull drug runners into letting themselves be boarded by just such casual words, crisply spoken. She had taken a course in being crisp and disarming at the same time. Truthfully she'd rather threaten and, if necessary, fire across their damn bows. But drug smugglers tended to be better armed that the average CG cutter, so she'd learned to do it by the book.

Besides, these guys were Canadians. The last oceangoing power they wanted to screw with was the U.S. of A.

The Canadian patrol boat bumped against the *Cayuga* and a boarding gangplank was laid between the two vessels. Three fisheries inspectors stepped aboard, flashing diffident smiles and announcing that the *Cayuga* has being seized in the name of the crown.

"This *is* about the submarine, isn't it?" Sandy asked in a tight voice.

"I know nothing of that," returned the captain, "but this vessel is coming to St. John's." He pronounced it "St. Jahn's," and Sandy Heckman had to suppress the urge to knock the officer on his polite rear.

"These are international waters," she argued stiffly.

The captain made a show of looking about the gray, heaving ocean. "Oh, I believe you are mistaken. My charts show these to be Canadian waters. You are in our Maritimes, and your boat must be brought in for a safety inspection."

"You have no legal authority to inspect a U.S. vessel," Sandy flared.

"Why don't we leave that to the lawful agencies that govern such things?" the captain said smoothly.

Sandy Heckman dropped one hand to her side arm, and the moment it touched the flap, a bullet whined past her left rear.

She saw a smoking M-16 on the other deck. Behind it was a stiff face looking at her down the dark-eyed barrel.

She let her hand drop loosely to her side. It hung there shaking. "It's your party. But you know there will be hell to pay," she said in a grating voice like seashells being chewed slowly.

"Be so good as to order your crew into my boat. I will see that your vessel arrives in St. John's safely."

"Well," Sandy muttered as she turned to address her expectant-faced crew, "they can't boot me out of the guard any harder for losing my ship than for sinking a Canadian sub."

Her crew seemed not to share her nonchalance. They looked worried.

The transfer of crew was executed with expert smartness. The gangplank was recovered.

Soon the Canadian fisheries-patrol boat was thundering north to Newfoundland, the *Cayuga* bringing up the rear.

There was one bright spot. The Canadians served the shivering *Cayuga* crew paper cups filled with very strong and bone-warming tea.

But then, they were a pretty polite lot. For pirates.

25

On the Air Canada flight north, Remo kept asking for water.

"One moment, sir."

"Please wait your turn, sir."

"We're coming to your aisle."

One stewardess actually ignored him outright.

"Isn't this great?" Remo asked Chiun.

"You will never get your water this way."

"Who cares? I can fly in peace now."

"Your breath smells of carrion."

"I only took one bite."

When the meal-service tray finally reached them somewhere over Maine, Remo lifted his rewrapped shark and asked a stewardess if she would zap it in the microwave oven for him.

"Not enough to toast it. Just warm it. I like my shark on the raw side," he said.

"I'm sorry, sir. It is against airline policy to cook a nonregulation meal."

"Please," asked Remo.

The stewardess's voice turned as frosty as her hair. "Sorry. But no. Do you want the chicken or the fish?"

"What kind of fish?" asked Chiun.

"Scrod."

"What is that, exactly?" Remo wondered aloud.

The stewardess looked at Remo as if he was a imbecile. "Scrod is scrod."

"I will have the turbot," said Chin.

The stewardess looked blank. "Turbot?"

And from the sleeve of his kimono, the Master of Sinanju produced a neatly wrapped packet of turbot fillet.

The stewardess took it with a smile and said, "Be happy to, sir."

"How come he gets special service and I don't?" Remo wanted to know.

"Scrod or chicken?" the stewardess asked, ignoring the question.

"Scrod," said Remo, folding his lean arms unhappily.

"I will have scrod, as well, since it is free. But see that my turbot is not too dry," Chiun admonished.

"Of course, sir," the stewardess said smilingly.

The scrod was served with baked potatoes and kernel corn. The potatoes were little bigger than Concord grapes, and the corn was pale and scant. They ignored both and tasted the scrod gingerly, not certain how it was prepared.

"Tastes like cod," said Remo.

"Mine brings to mind haddock," said Chiun.

"Can't be both."

They exchanged bites, which only confirmed each other's contrary opinion.

When the stewardess came back their way, Remo

asked her, "How come my scrod is cod and his is haddock?"

"Ask the fish," the stewardess said tartly, without breaking stride.

Chiun fumed. Remo grinned.

"Stewardesses couldn't care less about me," Remo said happily.

"They are in good company. For how will you sire a proper heir to the house if women do not open their willing wombs to your pollen?"

"I'm saving my pollen for the right woman," Remo muttered.

An hour into the flight, the seat phone rang.

"It's not supposed to do that," a stewardess said, her shocked face jerking around.

Remo inserted his credit card into the slot and freed the phone from its receptacle in the seat-back before him.

"What's up, Smitty?"

"Remo, here is the latest. The *Cayuga* has been taken to the Canadian Coast Guard station at St. John's, Newfoundland. It will be your task to liberate the vessel and its crew."

"Gotcha," said Remo.

When he replaced the phone, the stewardesses were grouped around the seat, and Remo began experiencing an acute attack of déjà vu.

"It's not supposed to do that," the first one reiterated.

"It just did," Remo contested.

"But they're not designed for incoming calls."

"Yeah. Only outgoing," another stewardess chimed in.

"There's a reasonable explanation for all this," said Remo.

They looked at him with expectancy on their lip-glossed faces.

"Be happy to explain it over dinner after we land," said Remo.

Expressions ranging from disdain to disgust overtook the stewardesses' faces and, without answering, they broke in three directions, returning to their duties.

"Isn't this great?" said Remo.

"Not if one is forced to sit next to you, shark breath."

"At least we know one thing for sure."

"And what is that?"

"Scrod is cod."

"No, it is haddock."

"Cod. It rhymes with scrod. That's why it's called that."

"You were given inferior fish by mistake. I was given true scrod, which is a kind of haddock."

"Remind me to ask Smitty about scrod next time. He's a New Englander. He'll know."

AT THE AIRPORT in St. John's, Remo noticed that the customs officials were members of the Royal Canadian Mounted Police. They wore brown serge coats instead of the traditional red. Since he was waiting in line, Remo decided to pass the time by asking why.

"You have been watching too much television, Yank," the Mountie said stiffly.

"I hardly watch any," Remo protested.

"Our red uniform is ceremonial."

"I liked the red better," said Remo, trying to be friendly.

"The red is strictly ceremonial."

"I heard you the first time."

"Please spread the word among your fellow Yanks. We are tired of answering this particular question. Here is your passport."

"Thanks," said Remo. "And try Ex-Lax for your problem."

The Mountie shot Remo a withering look from under his big yellow Stetson hat, and together Remo and Chiun went off to rent a car.

The rental clerk was more polite—by about three degrees centigrade.

"You must return the vehicle to this office and to no other office. If you cannot return the vehicle to this office, your deposit is forfeit. And in addition you may incur criminal penalties."

"Hey, I'm only renting a car," Remo protested.

"I am familiar with American television. You people are childish, irresponsible and frighteningly violent."

"Where do I check my Uzi?" Remo asked conversationally.

The clerk blanched, and Remo said, "Only kidding."

"Violence is never funny," the clerk admonished.

"You haven't seen me inflict Whirling Disease on a mammal," Remo said.

The St. John's waterfront smelled of fish, age and boredom. Waterfront shacks were bright red mixed with dull gray. Fishermen puttered around their docked boats. Nets were slowly drying in the cold sunlight. And no one looked happy.

Remo pulled up beside a friendly-looking seaman and asked, "Where's the Coast Guard station?"

"Eh?"

"I said where's the Coast Guard station?"

"Talk slawly," the man said in a strident accent. "Cannat understand you."

"Huh?" asked Remo.

"I cannat understand you, Yank."

"Same here," said Remo. "Coast Guard station. Where?"

The man pointed vaguely. "Yander."

"Where?"

The man leaned in, and Remo received the full force of his fermented breath. It smelled familiar, but Remo put that out of his mind. He had places to go.

"Yander. As the craw flies."

"Are you trying to say 'Yonder. As the crow flies'?"

"I did say it," the fisherman returned.

"Thanks. By the way, is that a burr or a brogue you're speaking?"

"What?"

"It is a brogue," said Chiun.

"If you say so," said Remo.

"If it were a burr, this would be Nova Scotia. It is not."

"What's the difference?"

"It is the difference between New Ireland and New Scotland."

"Oh."

"Did that one's accent fall upon your ears like the one you consigned to his watery death?"

"Hard to say when everyone all sounds like they have a knot in their tongue," said Remo.

AT THE ST. JOHN'S Coast Guard station, they were denied entrance.

"No admittance," the guard said, jabbing his finger at a sign.

"It says, *Entrée Interdite,*" Remo argued.

The guard then pointed to the opposite sign, which did say No Admittance.

"We're here about the Coast Guard Cutter you people are detaining."

"There is no Coast Guard cutter here. Other than Canadian cutters, of course."

"Of course," said Remo politely.

"Of course," agreed Chiun equally politely.

"Sorry. Our mistake," added Remo with a disarming smile. And they turned to walk away.

Abruptly they spun, taking out the guards with open-handed chops that brought both men to their knees. Remo chopped again, and their faces smacked the cold, hard ground.

They entered otherwise unchallenged.

"Now all we gotta do is find Sandy Heckman," undertoned Remo.

"Listen for cursing," suggested Chiun.

"Good idea," said Remo.

They walked through the grounds until they came upon a Coast Guardsman walking along all by his lonesome. Security seemed lax at best.

"Excuse us," said Remo.

"You are excused," the man said, walking on by.

Remo reached back and arrested him by the neck. He squeezed. The man froze in place. Then Remo turned him around with a casual spin.

"I asked a polite question. What's wrong with a polite answer?"

"Nothing."

"Where's your brig?"

The man pointed with the only appendage that seemed to function. His left ear. "The white building. But it is off-limits at the moment."

"Not to us."

"To everyone."

"If I point you in the general direction, will you take us there?" asked Remo.

"No."

"Good," said Remo, who pointed the man in the general direction of the brig anyway.

To the Coast Guardsman's surprise, he began walking. Remo urged him along with ungentle squeezes and pinches of his spinal column.

"Why am I walking toward the brig when I don't want to?" the man asked nervously.

"Because I am playing hell with your motor nerves," Remo responded.

"I confess this is a strange, rather puppety sensation."

"It can get stranger if you don't cooperate," Remo warned.

"I am trying not to cooperate. Why won't my body cooperate with me?"

"Because I own your neck and your spine and your snotty attitude."

As they approached the brig, Remo could hear loud and colorful cursing.

"If you miserable sons of sea cooks don't grow working brains and cut us loose, I'll personally convert you all to assorted chum and fish bait!"

"Sounds like Sandy is giving the Canadians salty heck."

"She is well named, then."

As they approached the door, the guardsman pointed out the obvious. "We will all be shot."

"You're taking point, so you'll be shot first. I'd think fast if I were you."

There were two guards framing the entrance with M-16s at the ready. They snapped their weapons down, and the familiar "Who goes there?" rang out. Only to Remo's ears it sounded more like "Wha gaz hair?"

Remo gave his captive a squeeze.

"Petty Officer Duncan," he yelped.

"State your business," a guard demanded at gunpoint.

"I am a prisoner of a cruel Yank bent upon unspecified mischief."

"Thanks," said Remo, who lifted the guardsman off his booted feet and ran him forward like a shield.

The guardsman somehow got turned sideways en route, and both ends of his flying body caught the two guards in their exposed midriffs. All three made a midair mess, falling to the ground in a tangle of arm and leg and rifle.

Remo stepped over them and into the brig after flinging their M-16s onto the roof.

"Sandy! Sing out!" he yelled.

"What the hell are you?" Sandy Heckman called back from somewhere inside.

Remo veered for the unmistakable roar.

Various guardsmen attempted to intercept him. They were intercepted first. Remo intercepted them with fists and smacking palms and kicking feet, and after he had intercepted them, they stayed intercepted. A few lapsed into snoring.

Sandy Heckman was clutching the iron bars of a holding cell, looking very, very angry when Remo located her.

"What are you two landlubbers doing here?"

"Rescuing you," Remo said.

"Shouldn't the diplomats be doing this?"

"They're too busy being diplomatic." Remo made his index finger stiff and inserted it into the lock.

"Now what are you doing?" Sandy wanted to know.

"Picking the lock."

"With your naked finger?"

Remo shrugged. "Why not? It fits."

A second later the lock made a grating sound, and the cell door swung open.

Shaking off her disbelief, Sandy stepped out. "Still no soap on that date, if that's what's motivating you," she warned.

"Deal," said Remo pleasantly.

"Do you even *want* a date with me?" Sandy demanded.

"Not really."

"Then why do you keep asking?"

"I don't. You're the one who brought it up."

Sandy eyed Remo skeptically. Finally she threw up her hands and exclaimed, "The Canadians have gone crazy. They commandeered my boat on the high seas."

"We're commandeering it back," said Remo. He got the rest of the crew out of their cells, and they formed a tight, whispering knot behind Remo and Chiun.

Outside there was no sound of alarm or commotion.

"This is too easy," Remo muttered.

"This is Canada, where a street-corner mugging is national news and for a winter thrill they tune in to hear the temperature in Florida."

"If you say so," said Remo, leading them toward the water.

There were guards stationed around the *Cayuga.* They looked relaxed, or as relaxed as armed guards can look on post.

"So what do we do about them?" Sandy hissed.

"We will give them something to transcend," said Chiun.

"Like what?"

But Chiun had gone. So had Remo. Sandy and her crew exchanged worried glances and waited in the shelter of a marine storage shed. The air smelled of wet nylon lines and copper hull paint.

On either side of the *Cayuga* sat the Canadian cutters *Robert W. Service* and the *Gordon Lightfoot.* They rode the mooring lines quietly in the gently tossing tide, their red hulls and white superstructures the exact mirror image of the *Cayuga*'s hull panoply.

Without warning, they began to sink. First there was a low bubbling from each boat. Then abruptly they hit bottom as if they had become tired and given up all thought of buoyancy.

This dual phenomena brought the guards running, looking both ways. An alarm was raised. The crews of the two scuttled cutters began howling in dismay.

While the *Cayuga* was momentarily unguarded, Remo and Chiun returned and led the crew back to the ship. Lines were cast off. No one noticed. They were too busy with their histrionics.

At the bow Remo and Chiun each set one foot against a concrete retainer wall and pushed off. The *Cayuga* surged away from its dock in complete silence. This wasn't noticed, either.

In the pilothouse Lieutenant Sandy Heckman ordered the engines started. They rumbled to life, and kicking up dirty white sea foam, the *Cayuga* came about smartly and made for open water.

There was no immediate pursuit.

"I still say this is too easy," said Remo, looking back from the stern.

"Try to think of Canadians as Brits without the balls, and it'll go down easier," advised Sandy. "They just aren't used to violence."

"So how come they seized your boat?"

"Screw with their fish and they'll cut your throat with the edge of a Canadian dollar bill."

After a while a Royal Canadian Mounted Police de Havilland Otter flew overhead. From a loudspeaker, a cold voice shouted down a warning.

"Can you make out what he's saying?" Sandy asked Remo.

"Sounds like 'Deaf boast fins fun.'"

"I don't think he's saying that."

"Maybe," Remo said with a grin. "But it sounds like it to me."

"Me, too," she said. "And if they can't communicate their intentions, we don't have to obey them."

The RCMP Otter circled and buzzed them angrily but attempted no interception.

Under cover of darkness they headed out and steered a course south.

"If we can reach U.S. waters, we should be okay," Sandy said.

But somewhere off Nova Scotia, they saw lights on the water. Many lights.

"Oh-oh. Looks like the fleet is moving to intercept us," Sandy said tensely.

"Whose fleet?" asked Remo.

"Whose else would it be?" returned Sandy.

But Remo's supersharp eyes were picking out details. "I see a flag, and it isn't theirs or ours."

"Whose would it be?" asked Sandy.

"I'm not good with flags," Remo said to Chiun. "Help me out, Little Father."

Chiun shaded his eyes with a palm. "I see the flag of Rome."

Sandy Heckman frowned. "Rome?"

"He means Italy. You do mean Italy?"

"And the flag of Portugal," added Chiun.

"What kind of fleet is that?" Remo asked.

"A fishing fleet. And I think it's ours," said Sandy.

"If they've come to rescue you, they're a day late and a line short."

"We'd better head them off before this thing gets any bigger and badder than it is."

"Canada is threatening us all over the place. How could it get any bigger?" Remo asked.

Lieutenant Sandy Heckman made no answer to that.

The *Cayuga* fell in on a straight intercept heading.

As it approached the oncoming fleet, the enormity of the vessels beating their way became apparent.

Sandy Heckman knew sailcraft. She saw Maine draggers, Chesapeake Bay skipjacks, assorted trawlers, shrimpers and scallop boats. It was a veritable armada of fishing craft, and all were pointed northward, maintaining an equal distance from one another like a pod of surface-feeding baleen whales.

"Helmsman, steer a careful course," Sandy warned tightly.

"Aye, sir."

The radioman was signaling their identity and intentions. He quickly received an answer.

"This is Captain Sirio Testaverde of the *Sicilian Vengeance*," a gravelly voice growled. "Get the hell out of our fucking way."

"*Sicilian Vengeance*, you are in Canadian waters. U.S. vessels are definitely not welcome at this time."

"We do not care. We come to avenge my Tomasso and take what is rightfully ours."

"What is rightfully yours?"

"The fish. The cod. Even the turbot, nasty as it is."

Sandy and Remo swapped glances, then Remo picked up her microphone to ask another question when suddenly they were riding into the teeth of the fleet.

Boats broke left and right to let the *Cayuga* pass.

Sandy rushed to the starboard rail and called out, "Are you people crazy? Don't you know tensions are running high? Canadian Coast Guard cutters are in hot pursuit of this vessel with the intention of recapturing it."

"Remember the *Jeannie I!*" a man shouted.

"Avenge Tomasso Testaverde!"

"Retake Louisbourg!"

"What's Louisbourg?" asked Remo.

Sandy bit her lower lip. "Damned if I know."

Then the fleet passed them, rank upon rank of boats, making a path for them that closed up like a wound once it had passed the *Cayuga* by.

Finally they were out of the thickest part of the fleet.

Looking back at the scores of sterns with their colorful names and home ports from as far south as Virginia, Remo made a helpful comment. "Well, you *could* chase them."

"Fat lot of good that will do me. First I get captured. Then I run smack into this. It's back to the Alaska halibut patrol for me for sure."

"Before you pack, fetch me a cell phone. I'm going to check in."

"Maybe you can warn someone."

"First I gotta find out where Louisbourg is."

"Probably in Quebec."

"That's what I'm afraid of," muttered Remo, leaning on the one button, which set in motion automated relays that would connect him directly with Folcroft.

26

Dr. Harold W. Smith knew it could get worse. He just didn't know how much worse.

In the Pacific a Canadian submarine had breached in the middle of a U.S. salmon fleet. It was an unprovoked attack. Six boats had gone down. All crew had been pulled aboard alive and were in Canadian custody.

Smith had been about to reach for the red telephone when he heard a familiar ringing.

He experienced a momentary hesitation. It was the blue contact phone, not the dedicated line to the White House.

Smith lifted the blue handset and said, "Yes."

"Smitty, we're on the *Cayuga.*"

"Good. The rescue came off successfully?"

"We're in Canadian waters and had to sink a couple of Canadian cutters."

"It was unavoidable. Good work."

"There's just one problem."

"What is that?"

"We just passed the biggest concentration of boats since they assembled the Spanish Armada."

Smith's voice tightened like a violin string. "I am listening," he said.

"They're ours."

"Navy or Coast Guard?"

"Neither. Commercial fishing. And they're heading north with blood in their eyes."

"What is their intent?"

"To take what's theirs and sack Louisbourg, from what they're saying."

"Louisbourg?"

"Yeah. Ever heard of it?"

"Hold, please." Smith punched in the name and up came a short description, with maps.

Smith expanded the search, and what he read dried the saliva in his slack mouth.

"Remo, Louisbourg was the site of a pre-Revolutionary engagement between the Colonies and what was then New France. It was a fortress on Cape Breton Island in pre-Confederation Canada."

"So?"

"It was in part a battle over cod. Because no colonial navy existed, New England fishermen were convinced by the British politicians of that time to sail north and take the fortress from French hands. They battled the defending French fishermen."

"Looks like history is about to repeat itself."

"Remo, this is serious."

"You're telling me? Those fishermen are out to kick Canadian butt, and nobody's going to be able to stop them."

"Agreed. But there has also been an incident in the Pacific. A Canadian sub breached in the middle of a U.S. salmon fishing fleet. It is unclear if either strayed into the other's fisheries, but there are boats under the water and the Canadians took several prisoners.''

"You thinking what I'm thinking?" Remo asked.

"If you are thinking that Quebec is unlikely to be operating in the Pacific, you are correct."

"Then it isn't the French Canadians."

"Not exclusively."

"There's another thing, Smitty. I think the brogue or burr I heard is Newfoundland talk."

"Can you be certain?"

"No. But I got a good whiff of some half-potted fisherman's breath, and it smelled just as bad as the other guy."

"Breath?"

"Liquor."

"Screech," said Smith.

"Say again?"

"Screech. It is a kind of rotgut moonshine popular in that area. This ties the crew of the *Proud to be Frogs* to Newfoundland or Nova Scotia."

"So where is this going?"

"Unless I am wrong, it is going to Ottawa." Smith shook off his grim tone, and his voice sounded more energetic. "Remo, stand by. I must inform the President of these developments."

"He's going to be one unhappy camper," Remo warned.

THE PRESIDENT of the United States wasn't a happy camper at all. "Is this war?" he gulped.

"It is a kind of war. And as things are going, it will be unclear who the aggressor is."

"They are."

"We sunk their sub first. The Pacific action is a retaliation."

"What about the North Atlantic stuff?"

"The Canadians know we possess military superiority. They are attempting to stymie a U.S. response by opening up a second front."

"Second front?"

"Mr. President, this is now a two-ocean war."

"I don't want a war!"

"You have one now. And where it goes will depend upon the U.S. response."

"Maybe we should warn Louisbourg. Show good faith."

"It is a thought."

"I need deniability in this. Either that or get a battle group into the area."

"Naval action would be seen as a provocation, if not escalation of the conflict."

"I can't fight the entire Canadian navy with the Coast Guard."

"Actually you can. The U.S. Coast Guard constitutes the world's twelfth largest navy. We outnumber their coastal defense and Coast Guard handily. Not that I am suggesting engaging the Canadians militarily."

"What *do* you suggest, Smith?"

"Open up a third front."

"Where?"

"On the diplomatic front."

"Sounds relatively safe," the President said slowly.

"There is an old saying, Mr. President, to the effect that war is the pursuit of diplomatic affairs un-resolvable by less drastic means."

The presidential voice brightened. "That's good. I may use that as my first salvo."

"Feel free," said Harold Smith, who didn't bother to say goodbye before hanging up.

SMITH HAD NO SOONER replaced the red receiver than the blue contact phone rang once more. He snapped it up.

"What is it, Remo?"

"More trouble. That armada we just passed? It's opened up on someone."

"What is your position, Remo?"

"Search me. Hey, Sandy!"

"That's 'Lieutenant' to you," Sandy Heckman's salty voice rang out.

"Stow the attitude. My boss needs our position."

"Tell him we're thirty nautical miles due south-east of Halifax."

"You got that, Smitty?" Remo asked.

"I am on it."

"On what?"

"If we are fortunate," said Smith, "I may be able to access a real-time satellite overview of what is going on."

Smith's thin fingers depressed keys, which flared with each touch, functioning silently.

In a moment he had acquired a feed from an or-biting National Reconnaissance Office surveillance satellite.

The view was clear. Boats on the water in two giant V's, moving on one another, trailing dozens of wakes that in turn created a gigantic super-wake. Smith could see the puffs of gray smoke from the lead vessels. Small puffs from what he assumed was the U.S. fishing fleet. Larger puffs from other fleet. It was smaller, but the boats were all a uniform white.

"Canadian patrol boats," he breathed.

A puff from a cutter showed distinctly, and one of the ragtag fishing vessels actually flung off debris. A second later an orange glow flared from her superstructure.

Smith hugged the phone to his head. "Remo, I have Canadian Coast Guard vessels engaging the U.S. fishing fleet."

"You don't sound very happy about it."

"I am not," Smith said bitterly. "While we want to avoid the repercussions of U.S. commercial vessels attacking Louisbourg, we cannot allow the Canadians to attack U.S. ships."

"What can we do about this?"

"Remo, I am about to order our Coast Guard to counterattack. In the meantime the *Cayuga* will move to support the U.S. forces."

"Forces? We're not at war."

"We are now," said Harold Smith. "And U.S. prestige is on the line."

"It's your call," said Remo, "but I don't want to be the one to break this to Sandy."

"Break what to me? And for the last time, it's 'Lieutenant,'" Sandy's raw voice called out.

"I will handle this," said Smith. "Remain available for my calls."

Smith hung up. His long thin fingers spun the

rotary dial of the blue contact phone, and after only two transfers, he had the commanders of the nearest U.S. Coast Guard station to Halifax in a conference call.

Once Smith had filled them in, they were only too pleased to render assistance. For one thing Harold Smith outranked them both.

Or as one put it, ''Those goddamn Canucks have been throwing their weight around since that phony Turbot War. It's time to show them who rules the North Atlantic.''

27

Lieutenant Sandy Heckman had one eye trained on the north horizon where the relentless cannonading of small-arms fire was emanating and one ear tuned to Remo, whose last name she had completely forgotten.

"Our boss says we go to the ships' rescue," Remo was saying.

"Gladly. But I don't work for the National Marine Fisheries Service."

"Neither do we. We're really Naval Intelligence."

"He is naval. I am the intelligent one," Chiun said.

Sandy dragged her glasses down off her eyes and turned as her face assumed an assortment of expressions ranging from humor to stunned astonishment. She settled on an incredulous twist of her mouth.

"You don't expect me to believe that bilge, do you?"

"It's true. We've been investigating Canadian—"

"Subterfuge," said Chiun.

"The real reason the fish are missing," added Remo.

"Everyone knows why the area's fished out. It's not red tide, or algae blooms or the greenhouse effect or any of that fancy nonsense. It's fishermen. They scooped up all the prey fish. Now the predator fish that lived off them are dying off. All that's left are the scup and cusk and turbot."

"There's more to it than that," said Remo. "But it's—"

"I know. Classified." And presenting her back to them, she said, "Classify my sweet ass."

"Very well," squeaked Chiun. "It is fat."

Sandy whirled and gave Chiun a particularly bilious eye. "You can walk the plank for all I care."

And Sandy resumed her scanning of the horizon. "When I hear from my commander, we go into action. Not before."

"Wait for it," said Remo.

It wasn't long. Sparks came flying down from the bridge waving a yellow flimsy. "Orders," he huffed.

"Why are they written?" Sandy asked, snatching the flimsy.

Then she saw why. It was a sea-gram:

USGC *Cayuga* is hereby ordered into the seas off Halifax to succor U.S. fishing vessels under attack by Canadian Coast Guard cutters. Reinforcements steaming your way. Good luck and Godspeed.

Crumpling up the flimsy, Sandy Heckmen took in a deep, cold lungful of air and hollered, "Battle stations! Helmsman, hard about and full steam ahead. We're going into action!''

"Told you so," said Remo.

"Fine. Meanwhile you two landlubbers are confined to quarters. It's going to get too hot for you to be on deck."

"Make us," invited Chiun.

Under Sandy's direction a pair of seamen attempted just that. They were helped into the drink by the Master of Sinanju, and the *Cayuga* had to double back to pick them up. Another attempt led to a seaman climbing the radar mast to avoid the old Korean's needlelike fingernails. After that the crew of the *Cayuga* pointedly pretended that Remo and Chiun were simply not there. It made for smoother sailing that way.

At full speed, the *Cayuga* came around the edge of the battle, which was in full swing, and found a Canadian cutter whose port flank was exposed and undefended.

Sandy got on the UHF radio. "Attention Canadian Coast Cuard cutters *Angus Reid* and *Stan* and *Garnett Rogers*. This is the USCG *Cayuga*. Repeat, this is the United States Coast Guard cutter *Cayuga* ordering you to break off your attack or be fired upon."

The Canadian Coast Guard cutter captain was exceedingly polite when he came on the air. "This is Captain Fothergill of the *Stan Rogers*. Bugger off, please."

"That sinks it," Sandy roared. "Open fire!"

Seamen were spread out along the rails bearing

M-16 rifles. They lined up on the cutter and let loose. The Canadians returned fire.

The rattle and crack of automatic weapons grew more strident. Bullet holes began dotting the *Cayuga*'s complicated superstructure. The vicious *rip-squeak* of bullets chewing trim and combing became a near-constant sound.

Standing calmly in the heaving bow, Remo and Chiun watched.

Bullets whizzed around them. From time to time they bobbed their heads or ducked or simply stepped aside as casually as kids dodging spitballs. To them the flying lead was not much more than that.

"You two heroes lend a hand," Sandy howled at them over the din.

Remo shook his head. "We don't do guns."

"And we do not belong to your Navy," added Chiun.

"You're U.S. citizens. We're defending American lives."

"Insults will get you nowhere," Chiun retorted.

As the bullets flew, Chiun called out encouragement. "Smite the godless Canadians in the name of your emperor!"

"Maybe we should pitch in," said Remo, stepping back and twisting out of the way of a short burst of 9 mm bullets.

Chiun made a disapproving face. "The godless ones are losing."

"How can you tell?"

"They are outnumbered," Chiun sniffed.

"But the Canadians have bigger weapons."

"And they are fighting men who eat fish in prodigious quantities. They are outbrained."

"Good point. But maybe we should get in the water and sink a few cutters for Old Glory."

"You may if you wish."

"I don't wish."

"Then do not."

Remo frowned. "Could be I have a better idea."

Finding Sandy exhorting her crew between bursts, Remo said, "Get us close to one of those cutters. We can board them."

"We'd get our white sterns shot off." She had a Glock in hand and laid its sights on a Canadian seaman who was swinging his rifle around for a clean shot. Taking her tongue between her teeth, she squeezed the trigger.

The seaman with the rifle threw it up into the air and grabbed at his side. The rifle made two complete turns, and the heavy butt slammed him on the head. He fell over and into the water, where he sank from sight.

"Nice shooting," said Remo conversationally.

"For practice I pop the heads off gulls and Mother Carey's chickens," Sandy said, reloading.

"Why don't you just fire to sink?"

"No fun in that."

"Guess not," said Remo, who decided that he'd probably have to go into the water after all.

That was when the first Coast Guard Falcon jet came barreling down out of the gunpowder gray sky.

"They armed?" Remo asked Sandy.

Sandy looked up from winging a Canadian chief

petty officer and said, "No. But the Canucks don't know that."

The jets screeched down low and made a single pass. The Canadian cutters took instant notice. A fusillade of fire was aimed at the fast-moving planes. It was pure reflex. By the time the bullets left their barrels, the jets had screamed by and were a distant, fading thunder.

As things turned out, it was enough of a distraction to turn the tide.

Their attention on the cold, gray skies, fearful of a second pass, the Canadians were sitting ducks to the rifles of the ragtag fishing armada.

"Slay the fishmongers!" Chiun exhorted, shaking a raging fist in the air.

U.S. seamen scrambled up their masts and fired down from crow's nests. That gave them the high ground, and Canadian seamen began succumbing to the withering fire. Others leaped up from below-decks to take up their fallen weapons, but they, too, were easily picked off.

"We're winning! We're winning!" Sandy crowed.

"You mean *they're* winning," Remo corrected.

"Us. Them. We're all Americans, aren't we?"

In the end the Canadian cutter captains were forced to raise the white flag.

Seeing this, Chiun cried, "Now. Finish off the murderous fishmongers!"

"That's the white flag of surrender," Remo corrected.

Chiun shook his grim head slowly, "No. That is

the pale flag of death. For he who surrenders deserves death.''

Sandy was on the horn saying, ''Attention! All vessels within the sound of my voice. This is the USCG *Cayuga*. I am instructing the Canadian Coast Guard vessels to lay down their arms and prepare to be boarded. All you others, hold your fire and stand back. This is a Coast Guard operation.''

A gravelly voice called back. ''This is Captain Sirio Testaverde of the *Sicilian Vengeance. I* say who does what. And I say these damn Canucks are my prisoners.''

''Then you are all Coast Guard prisoners,'' Sandy countered.

Silence filled the air.

''I tell you what. You may have these spineless ones. We will sail north to avenge Tomasso.''

''Who's Tomasso?'' Remo wanted to know.

Sandy shrugged. ''I forbid you to further penetrate Canadian territorial waters,'' Sandy yelled loudly enough that the Master of Sinanju covered his delicate ears with his hands.

''Forbid your mother. We are going.''

And with that the fishing fleet dispersed in all directions. They moved away from the center of battle, leaving the Canadian cutters sitting exposed. One cutter tried to slip away with the fleet, but a shot fired across its bows from three directions cooled the ardor for flight.

Sandy scanned the surrounding seas. ''Damn! Where are our reinforcements?''

At that moment the Falcons made another noisy, impotent pass.

"Don't look now, but I think that's them," Remo said glumly.

THE *CAYUGA* CIRCLED the three Canadian cutters for nearly an hour until the U.S. cutters *Presque Isle* and *Miskatonic* put in an appearance.

With the opposing forces at parity, the Canadian vessels were boarded, and the prisoners were clapped in irons. Technically there weren't enough irons to go around, so they improvised with spring lines and other types of cord.

The Master of Sinanju used his fingernails to inflict a temporary spinal paralysis upon the remaining unfettered Canadian seamen.

When the operation was over, the *Cayuga* had the pleasure of leading the flotilla of cutters, both captors and captured.

Sandy Heckman stood on the bow, the wind in her hair, her hand on her holstered side arm.

"This," she said, "is why I first set out to sea."

"To shoot up other boats?" asked Remo.

"No, to get my blood racing."

In a while they put in at the Coast Guard station at Machias. The commander was there to greet them. He shook Lieutenant Heckman's hand as she came off the gangplank. "Great work, Lieutenant!"

"We helped," Remo said laconically.

The commander bestowed upon Remo and Chiun a very fishy eye. "Who are these two?"

"They claim to be out of Naval Intelligence," Sandy said quickly.

"We rescued her from the vicious Canadians," Remo said dryly.

"You two?"

"Before that," Sandy added, "they said they were with the National Marine Fisheries Service, looking into the fishing crisis."

The commander walked up to Remo and assumed a skeptical demeanor.

"What would be the Navy's interest be in the fishing crisis?"

"That's classified."

"They say that a lot," Sandy remarked dryly. She had her hands on her wide hips and a look in her eye that said that she thought she had the upper hand.

"Out with it," the commander demanded.

"Do not pry further under pain of extreme death," Chiun said thinly.

The commander half suppressed a grin. "Extreme death. What's that?"

The Master of Sinanju floated up to the Coast Guard commander. The commander loomed over the aged Korean. Chiun looked up into his face. The commander looked down.

"Chiun," Remo warned, "he's on our side."

Without taking his eyes off the Coast Guard officer, Chiun said, "He has requested wisdom."

"Okay. But remember, if you must crush a testicle, do only one. He can sue for two crushed testicles, but not one. One is simple assault. Two costs him future children. That's a sueable offense."

Turning white, the commander suddenly crossed his hands in front of his crotch and hopped back like a frightened frog.

"We need a private minute to talk to our boss,"

Remo said, sensing the trend of the confrontation going their way.

"Done," said the commander, stepping hastily aside.

Remo led Chiun to a secluded spot and called Smith from the cell phone.

Harold Smith's lemony voice was harried when it answered. "Remo, I am aware of your situation."

"Good. What's going on?"

"There is a gigantic naval engagement going on off Halifax, Nova Scotia."

"Who's winning?"

"It is impossible to say. All fishing vessels look alike from the air."

"Huh?"

"The U.S. flotilla has run smack into fishing boats out of Nova Scotia and Newfoundland. They are in pitched battle."

"Over what?"

"Over the right to take cod from whatever waters suit them."

"But the cod is practically extinct around here."

"Which is exactly why it is so deadly important to both sides," Harold Smith said earnestly.

"So we've got three Canadian cutters here. Are we at war?"

"If not at war, very close to it. The President is attempting to work through the diplomatic channels. But the Canadian government is stonewalling him."

"If the Canadians won't listen to him, then who will they listen to?"

"That is an excellent question," said Harold Smith in a hopeless voice.

28

The President of the United States had put in a call to the prime minister of Canada.

The call was not returned.

He tried the premier of Quebec.

The premier returned the call but insisted on speaking French. Since the President's command of French was limited to three words, two of them curse words, he found the conversation short and unhelpful.

In desperation he put in a call to the Secretary-General of the United Nations.

"Mr. President," purred Anwar Anwar-Sadat, "I am very distressed by the friction between your nation and the Canadians."

"I could use your help."

"It is a consequence I think of the extension of the two-hundred-mile limits and the fierce quest for diminishing fish. As the leader of the former free world, I must ask you to reconsider your two-hundred-mile limit."

"Reconsider it how?" the President asked in a guarded tone.

"Roll it back. Unilaterally. If you make this gesture, other nations may follow your lead. Then the international waters will be truly free again.''

''That means anyone can loot them.''

''Not at all. I foresee a time when UN patrol boats, neutral and unallied, will ply the blue seas, monitoring shipping traffic and fishing both. It will usher in a new era of international cooperation and make the UN the truly global organization its wise founders wished it to be.''

''I don't see it that way,'' the President said stiffly.

The Secretary-General didn't skip a beat. ''Possibly you desire to think on it,'' he said. ''While you are doing this, I wish to call your attention to the frightful arrearage of the United States in the matter of its UN dues. It is a question of some—ah, here is the file—1.3 billions of dollars. When may I expect a check, Mr. President?''

''When the United Nations earns its subsidies,'' the President said bitterly, hanging up.

An hour later he was staring out a window in the White House top floor wondering whom to turn to when his chief of staff came in waving a report.

''The Canadian fisheries minister has given a speech, Mr. President.''

''So?''

''Remember the last fisheries minister? The one who launched the Turbot War? Well, this one looks like he's bent on a salmon war.''

''Salmon?''

The chief of staff lifted a sheet of paper. ''I quote—'The plundering piratical policies of the pharisees to the south show they are bent upon a course of Malthusian overfishing that will ruin us all.'''

"Pharisees?"

"He means us, sir."

"But pharisees?"

"The Spaniards were philistines last time." The chief of staff went on. "'I pledge for as long as I am minister of fisheries and oceans that I will protect the tiny little salmon so they can go to sea. God help any nation or navy who gets between our smolts and the Pacific.'''

"What are smolts?"

"I have no idea. But it sounds like smelts."

"Must be a typo."

"The fisheries minister has imposed a transit tax on U.S. salmon trawlers from Seattle to Cape Suckling, Alaska."

"They can't do that! We own Alaska."

"Here's the problem, Mr. President. We own Washington State and Alaska, but there's a slice of coastline standing between them called the Alaska Panhandle. That's ours, too. But we don't own the entire coastline. There is a kind of buffer zone called British Columbia. Running parallel to that is an ocean current called the Alaskan Gyre. The salmon ride this current to their spawning streams, mostly rivers in British Columbia."

"Is that in our waters or theirs?"

"The gyre flows within our two-hundred-mile limit until it hits British Columbia, then resumes in U.S. waters."

The presidential brow furrowed in confusion.

"Do you have a map? I think I need to look at a map."

"I'm sure there's one somewhere."

They found a map in the situation room. A big wall map. The President and his chief of staff put their heads together just below Alaska.

"I see what you mean," the President said unhappily.

"In order to reach the Gulf of Alaska, our fishermen travel along the coast of B.C. until they reach Alaskan waters. But with the transit tax, they are subject to seizure or must go outside the two-hundred-mile limit we have in common with Canada. That's a big jump, and can hurt them economically. And there's this—the Alaska fishery is our last healthy fishing ground. We need it more than ever."

"You know, maybe the UN Secretary-General had a good idea."

"Since when?" the chief of staff asked skeptically.

"Excuse me."

The President went to the Lincoln Bedroom, where he took up the red telephone that connected to Harold W. Smith at an office that, for all the President knew, was across the street in the Treasury Building.

"Smith, have you heard the Canadian fisheries minister's speech?"

"I am reading a wire-service transcript," answered Smith.

"What do you make of it?"

"It may be tit for tat. A bargaining chip to ransom the Canadian patrol craft captured today."

"I hear an 'or' in your voice."

"Or it may be the next phase in a plan that is still unfolding."

"These Canadian fishing ministers like to throw their weight around, don't they?"

"The last one parlayed his portfolio into the premiership of Newfoundland. This one may have similar ambitions."

"Maybe he'll take my call."

"It is worth a chance," said Smith. "The prime minister has issued a statement saying he had full confidence in his fisheries minister."

"That sounds like he'll cut the guy off at the knees if things go bad for Canada."

"I could send my people to pay him an unofficial call," Smith offered.

"Wait a minute. I don't want him killed."

"They are capable of applying pressure without terminating him."

"I wish someone would do that to the Secretary-General of the UN. He tried to hold me up for back dues before he would stick his oar into the water."

"I will instruct my people to fly to Ottawa."

And the line went silent.

The President picked his coat off the bedpost and drew it on. Of all the perils that had loomed on the international horizon—a fractured Russia and an increasingly belligerent China—this was the one he never saw coming.

It was a good thing no one knew he had a hand in creating it.

29

In his office on the thirty-eighth floor of the United Nations Building overlooking the East River, Secretary-General Anwar Anwar-Sadat was fielding telephone calls.

Strange things were happening in the world. The call to roll back the two-hundred-mile limit seemed to be resonating in certain world capitals.

From Argentina a thickly accented voice was telling him that his was the first sane voice heard on the subject in decades.

From South Korea there were plaudits. Japan appeared interested. Of course, they would be. Their fleets plied the seven seas voraciously, often encountering resistance and sanctions.

From other quarters, of course, came dark threats. Russia had been claiming dubious management rights over disputed waters, and Moscow was irate. Likewise Burma, or whatever the current name was, engaged in raffling off their coastal fishing rights, was being unpleasant.

The U.S. ambassador to the United Nations was particularly upset, if her telephonic screeches were any indicator.

Anwar Anwar-Sadat excused himself in the middle of her unrelenting vitriol and stood up.

It was the turning point, but it was very strange. All he had done was make a speech. It wasn't even a very good speech, although it was delivered with conviction. With force. Obviously that was why it had resonated so.

His chief aide buzzed him very soon after the first wave of calls to inform him, "A Miss Calley to speak with you."

Anwar Anwar-Sadat perked up. "Really?"

"Yes. She is not on the list, but she sounded so sure of herself, I said I would see if you were in."

"I will take the call," Anwar Anwar-Sadat said eagerly.

Taking his chair, he cleared his throat twice very noisily because he seemed to have raised a bothersome frog, then took up the receiver. "This is Secretary-General Anwar Anwar-Sadat speaking," he said, his voice a quavering purr.

"Good of you to take my call, my Anwar," a cool female voice said crisply.

He all but gasped. "It is you?"

"It is I."

"I have longed for this moment."

"And for another moment, nearing soon."

"You are in New York?" he said joyously.

"No. But you are coming here."

"I look forward to our first meeting. I must say that I very much admire your voice."

"And I yours."

"It is—how shall I put it?—uplifting." He tittered.

"I will accept that as the compliment of a gentleman, and keep my innuendo to myself."

She was charming. Her voice was a husky contralto. Sexy, yes, but not sluttish. It did not quite go with his mental image of a blond goddess, but in fact, it was an improvement. It was a very capable voice.

"I am very excited about the reception to my speech," he said.

"The world's ears are turned in your direction, my Anwar."

"Although my duty calls for me to be here, I will come to your city wherever it may be."

"Ottawa. Come tonight."

"We will laugh, we will dance and we will dine on one another's charms," Anwar Anwar-Sadat tittered.

"And we will confer with the Canadian minister of fisheries," said Mistress Kali.

Anwar-Sadat's face quirked as if bee-stung.

"That does not sound very...romantic."

"We will have our little romance, you and I. But your words have struck a chord. The minister of fisheries has struck a like chord in his own nation. I thought you two should meet."

"Whatever for?"

"To plot your dual strategy."

"I do not have dual strategy."

"No. You have a unified strategy. *My* strategy."

"And after this meeting, what shall I look forward to?"

"What would please you, my Anwar?"

"Something new. Something extraordinary."

"I am adept in many arts. Both subtle and sensual. I will conjure up something appropriate for the occasion of our first meeting."

"It is done."

"A car will meet you at the Ottawa airport. Please hurry. Events are overtaking the globe. We must move to control them, if we are to profit by them."

"Until tonight," purred Anwar Anwar-Sadat, who blew a kiss into the receiver and was rewarded with a breathy return peck.

Hanging up reluctantly, he came to his feet and called out. "Christos! Book me on the earliest flight to Ottawa."

Christos came into the room and noticed the unseemly bulge in Anwar Anwar-Sadat's well-tailored crotch and averted his eyes with red-faced embarrassment.

"At once, my General," he said, saluting crisply.

CANADIAN FISHERIES Minister Gilbert Houghton was giving a follow-up speech where the Fraser River emptied out into the Strait of Georgia among the coastal pines of British Columbia. Vancouver's sparkling towers formed an impressive backdrop.

The Canadian Broadcasting Corporation was there. As were foreign press, including a solitary representative from the U.S. ABC, of course. Their chief anchor was Canadian. A good man to have in New York when the Canadian view needed putting forth.

The cold winds were out of the Pacific. They ran chilly fingers through Houghton's crisp hair. Opening his mouth, he inhaled a bracing charge of the purest air in Mother Nature.

"I have come here to our fifth province to make a firm stand against piracy and environmental pillaging."

From a packet he took up a dead fish. It lay limp in his hand.

"This is a green sturgeon. A brave, mighty and tasty fish. Here in the Fraser, green sturgeon are all but extinct." He lifted up another fish, this one white. "If something is not done, his brother, white sturgeon, will go the way of all fish. My friends, we are expecting here in B.C. a die-off of fish unprecedented in modern history. Just as the dodo is extinct, just as the whale was hunted to near-extinction, we are about to lose our sturgeon and salmon. It must not be allowed to come to pass.

"It is no secret that one of the chief causes of this die-off is overfishing. In that, we Canadians must assume our rightful share of blame."

From the crowd there were boos—fishermen, many of whom were restricted from fishing in their own waters. Among these men the name of Gilbert Houghton was something to expectorate from the mouth.

"Some blame logging for injuring the habitats. Others say El Nino's warmer waters are responsible for diminishing salmon returns. While these events may have their individual impacts, there is a greater menace. Salmon return to the Fraser and other B.C. rivers to spawn. If they do not return, they cannot spawn. It is no secret that virtually all the salmon runs in this part of the world belong to British Columbia. Nor it is any secret that the salmon do not return to the Fraser and other coastal streams as they have because they are *intercepted*.''

He let the word hang in the cold air, bitter as castor oil.

''U.S. fishermen operating in the shared waterways off B.C. are capturing salmon in record numbers. In doing so, they are confiscating the next generation of salmon before they can hatch. Confiscating our food, our livelihood and our very futures!''

''The bloody bastards!'' a man cried out.

Gilbert Houghton looked out. It was a typical B.C. fisherman. But his face was painted white, and smack in the middle, resembling a blotch of fresh blood, was the red maple leaf of Canada.

Houghton suppressed a smile. A plant. There were others. They were salted throughout the crowd for the benefit of the camera.

''In the Atlantic my predecessor stepped in to arrest the Maritime cod crisis. He was a good man, but he acted too late. I have taken steps to halt the salmon crisis. For this I have been roundly and unfairly criticized.''

There were boos but a few cheers, too. These came from the white-faced maple-leafers.

''What is the point of protecting the salmon spawning streams of British Columbia if the fish who seek them are captured, gutted and eaten on their way home? These fish are born in B.C. They return to B.C. These are not Pacific fish. They are B.C. fish. They are Canadian fish. And as Canadian fish, they deserve—no, they cry out for protection.''

This got a rousing cheer even from the disgruntled lot waving a placard that read United Fishermen's And Allied Workers' Union Against Federal Interventions.

"From this day, I pledge the full might and protection of my office to the rescue of the beleaguered salmon. It may be too late to succor the sturgeon. But the salmon can and will be saved. My vow to all Canadians—victory will be ours! Victory by Victoria Day!"

The crowd ignited. It roared. The boos, so loud before, were drowned out. And while there were still catcalls and hoots directed at him, the TV sound equipment would register only the roars of acclaim for Minister of Fisheries Gilbert Houghton, future prime minister of Canada.

"Victory by Victoria Day! Victory by Victoria Day!"

As he stepped down from the makeshift podium to the thunderous applause of his fellow countrymen, Gil Houghton was met by an aide clutching a cellular telephone.

"It's for you, sir."

"Not now," Houghton snapped. "I am rebounding in popularity."

"She says you will take the call."

"*She?* Not my wife, I hope?"

"No. *Definitely* not your wife," said the aide.

Pressing one ear shut with a cool palm, Gil Houghton returned to his waiting Bentley and, ensconced inside, took the call.

"I must see you," said the crisp contralto voice that took the breath from his lungs.

"This is awkward timing. I'm in B.C."

"I know. I saw it all."

"And you approve?"

"I require your presence, you miserable piece of bait."

"Yes, Mistress," said Gilbert Houghton, his face contorting between misery and pleasure—both equally enjoyable sensations.

Oh, how that woman could make him squirm with delight and desire.

"I will be there directly, Mistress," he said.

When he hung up, he discovered he had his hands in his pants like a naughty little boy.

30

The stewardesses on the Air Canada flight to Ottawa were not only indifferent, but they were openly hostile.

"You must sit in the rear of the aircraft," one told Remo, ripping up his boarding pass for a window seat.

"Why?"

"Because you are a Yank."

"I'm an American," Remo protested. "Proud of it, too."

"You Yanks are so full of yourselves. Shook yourself free of the British Empire and have looked down your short noses at us ever since."

"Hey, didn't we pull the British Empire's chestnuts out of two world wars?"

"That is another thing," a second stewardess put in, "you act as if you won them single-handedly. You came in late, you did, and hogged all the credit."

"That is true!" the first stewardess snapped.

"Yankee come lately!" various passengers shouted as Remo made his way down the aisle. A few cursed American beer and television as inferior and insidious influences upon all good Canadians.

Remo wasn't sure which was insidious and which inferior and he didn't care.

When he came to the Master of Sinanju seated over the starboard wing, Remo mouthed, "I'm stuck sitting in back."

"Yankee poodle dandy," hissed Chiun.

"Not you, too."

"War hog."

"What happened to smiting the fishmongering Canadians?"

"I intend to keep a still tongue until this ungainly bird is safely on the ground once more," Chiun undertoned, "and I suggest you do the same."

"Fine," said Remo, taking his seat.

After the plane was in the air, Remo buried himself in a magazine. It was something called *Maclean's* and it read as if edited by stuffy old goats with leather patches on their tweedy elbows.

He wasn't offered a drink or a complimentary meal.

When the stewardess in charge of his end of the plane rolled the serving cart back to the front without offering him anything, Remo called after her.

"I read that Air Canada has the worst service record of any major carrier."

"That may be true," his stewardess called without looking back, "but that is only when dealing with pharisees."

"Pharisees?"

"That is what Fisheries Minister Houghton calls your kind."

Remo tried to think of a comeback, but decided it would be wasted on a stupid Canuck.

To kill time he inserted his credit card into the sky-phone slot and called Harold Smith at Folcroft.

"What's the latest?" he asked when Smith answered.

"We have open war in the Pacific."

"How did the Atlantic battle end?"

"In a draw. Approximately forty boats have been sunk or burned to the waterline. The two sides have withdrawn to neutral waters. But this was only the first skirmish. Tensions are running very high."

"What's the Canadian Coast Guard doing?"

"At the moment, nothing. I suspect they will let the fishing fleets fight it out."

"Why?"

"Our Coast Guard can beat theirs. But in a fight between commercial fishermen, it could go either way. Also this gives both sides maneuvering room for a ceasefire or diplomatic solution."

Remo grunted.

"Remo, this conflict is spreading to other waters," Smith said.

"Like the Gulf of Mexico?"

"Farther. You recall the Falklands War in '82?"

"Yeah. The British and the Argentinians were fighting over a bunch of islands down in the South Atlantic."

"Not just islands, but valuable fishing territories. It is toothfish season down there, and the two nations have been at odds over fishing rights in the South Atlantic. The Argentinians resist having to pay the British for licenses to fish in waters they see as theirs. Citing the UN Secretary-General's calls to free the seas, Argentinian fishing boats are fishing freely. The British are sending the destroyer *North-umberland* to the scene. It looks like a repeat of the Falklands crisis.''

''Does it matter to us?''

''There is more. Tensions between Turkey and Greece over the two disputed islets in the Aegean have flared up again.''

''I thought that was settled.''

''So did the International Court of Justice at the Hague. There is more. Russia and Japan are squabbling over the South Kurile islands, and in the Pacific, Korea and Japan are renewing their feud over the Dok-to Islands.''

''Never heard of them.''

''They are a handful of rocks projecting from the sea. Too small for more than standing on, but enough to fight over.''

''Has everyone gone crazy?'' Remo exploded. He was shushed by other passengers, including Chiun.

''Certain governments see opportunities, and they will grab them if the lid is not put back on. Remo, the Secretary-General of the UN is becoming an international troublemaker.''

''Who do you want talked to first, the fisheries minister or old Anwar-Anwar?''

''I want international tensions cooled as quickly as possible.''

''Trust me. It's in the bag. After the way I've been treated, there's nothing more I'd rather do than strangle a Canadian.''

''Do not get carried away. The object of this mission is to defuse the situation.''

On the ground Remo's passport got him through customs. But not before he got a good talking-to.

"While in this country you must observe certain rules of decorum," a stern customs Mountie recited.

"No problem," said Remo in a bored voice.

"Do not spit on the walkways, scratch yourself in a place not normally discovered, and when spoken to, reply in the language in which you are addressed."

"You *are* bilingual, aren't you?" a second Mountie inquired.

"Sure. I speak English and Korean."

"I will take your word on the latter," the Mountie said frostily. "But in the former you are seriously deficient."

"Thanks," said Remo. "Is your red suit at the cleaner's today?"

"The red serge is strictly ceremonial," the first Mountie said stiffly.

"Really? I didn't know that."

"Tell your damn friends," both Mounties called after him.

In the lobby Remo met the Master of Sinanju, who was wearing a placid expression.

"Have any trouble?" Remo asked.

"I was well treated."

"You must have used your Korean passport."

"Of course. I would not wish to be mistaken for a fish-stealing pharisee."

"Cut it out."

They grabbed a cab, and the driver accepted them on the proviso that they pay in advance, which Remo did because strangling this cabdriver would only mean having to find another who might be even more insufferable.

Other than the bilingual French-English signs and the profusion of green copper roofs on Parliament Hill, Ottawa might have been any American city. On the way into the city, Remo noticed the only thing that was unusual.

"Check it out, Chiun. The squirrels are black."

Chiun spied a squirrel sitting on a snowy branch of an oak.

"I have never seen a more sinister rodent. No doubt he is a fish hoarder."

"Doubt it. Squirrels are strictly nuts. Like Canadians."

Chiun peered out his window at the snow-covered buildings that marched by. As they got closer to the heart of the city, it looked more and more European, like a theme park of stone and green copper roofs.

"Ottumwa lies fat under its snows. Fat and easily sacked," intoned Chiun.

"It's Ottawa, not Ottumwa, and we're not in the sacking business," said Remo.

The cab let them off in front of the Château Laurier, and Remo handed the driver twenty dollars for a fifteen-dollar fare.

"Thank you," said the driver, pocketing the bill.

"Hold up. What about my change?" Remo demanded.

"What about my tip?"

"I like to tip from my change."

"Your change is my tip," the driver countered.

"Normally I'm the judge of that."

"Normally you tip American taxi drivers. You are

in Canada, and we like to take our gratuity this way, owing to the muddled manner in which Americans confuse U.S. and Canadian dollars.''

"I'm not confused.''

"Very well.''

Back came a handful of coins.

"What are these?'' asked Remo, staring at the one gold and two silver coins.

"Coins. They constitute your change.''

"I want bills.''

"They are legal tender, out of which I expect a generous tip.''

"Here's a tip,'' said Remo. "Don't tick off a paying fare.''

And Remo took the silver coins between the thumb and forefinger of each hand. He performed a double squeeze, and the coins went *scrunk.* Remo returned them in the form of silver Tootsie Roll bits.

"What is this?'' demanded the cabbie.

"Four bucks' worth of warning,'' said Remo, getting out.

The driver started to protest, but the rear passenger door slammed shut in a way that shook the car on its springs. It bounced so badly that the driver got out, thinking it was an earthquake.

By that time the two peculiar passengers had vanished into the hotel.

INSIDE, REMO DECIDED on the direct approach.

Walking up to the front desk, he asked a supercilious-looking desk clerk, "We understand the Secretary-General of the UN is staying here.''

The clerk looked up, frowned at Remo's casual,

out-of-season dress and sneered, "You understand imperfectly."

"Oh, but I beg to differ," said Remo, adopting a similar tone.

"Sir, you are mistaken."

Remo was about to take the clerk by the tail of his tie, the better to yank him out of his polished shoes and equally polished attitude, when the Master of Sinanju squeaked, "Remo, behold!"

Remo turned.

A stone-faced man of sprightly sixty years floated past, wearing a gardenia in his lapel and trailing a vaguely effette after-shave scent. He went through the revolving door and stepped into a waiting car.

Remo turned to the desk clerk, saying, "Caught you fibbing."

"You are mistaken. That was an untruth."

Remo gave the man's reservation terminal a friendly pat, knowing from past experience that the screen display would turn to an unreadable electronic jigsaw puzzle. From the horrified look that came over the man's face, it did exactly that.

The car was pulling away when Remo and Chiun reached the street.

As it happened, the cab that had brought them to the hotel was still bouncing on its springs, the cabbie looking on with vaguely fearful eyes.

Beside it a rainbow-striped white car with a blue horseman symbol on its rear fender was pulling up. A man in a crisp uniform stepped out.

"If you don't mind, we're going to borrow your cab," Remo said, brushing past the man and taking the wheel.

"I mind very much," the man said.

So the Master of Sinanju seized him and flung him into the back seat, there to join him.

"I won't stand for being kidnapped," the driver demanded as the cab left the curb. "This is Ottawa. And this happens to be an official RCMP vehicle, not a taxicab."

"My mistake," said Remo. "How do you feel about riding in the trunk?"

"In that case, I will do my best to persevere," the Mountie said.

Remo fell in behind the car carrying the UN Secretary-General. They could see the back of the man's iron gray head through the back window. He was primping like an old maid.

The two cars moved through Ottawa traffic, leaving the historical heart of the city and entering a neighborhood where old snow lay in the gutters, dirty and unplowed.

"This is not a good area," the Mountie warned.

"What is wrong with it?" Chiun probed.

"The snow is dirty."

"Is it dangerous?"

The Mountie scoffed. "This is Canada. We do not have violence here."

"That's about to change," Remo growled.

"Are you gentlemen assassins?"

"No," said Remo.

"Yes," said Chiun in an overlapping voice.

"Well, which is it?" the Mountie asked in subdued horror.

"We're assassins, but we're on vacation," Remo told him. "We're not here to waste anyone."

"Then why are you following that vehicle?"

"You take it, Little Father," Remo said to Chiun.

"To see where it goes," answered the Master of Sinanju.

The cab carrying the UN Secretary-General took them to what looked to have once been an electrical substation or power-generating plant on the fringes of the Canadian capital. It was a grimy brick box, and over the main door was a faded sign that at one time said Ottawa Electric, but now said, Otta a Tric. A single red light bulb made the front door smolder.

The taxi pulled up before it, and the UN Secretary-General stepped out and paid the fare with a stiff bow. Adjusting his tie, he walked up to the main entrance and smoothed his waistcoat before pressing the doorbell.

The door opened inward, and he vanished inside.

"We're going to stop here," said Remo, "but we may need the car later."

"I do not object," said the cowering Mountie. "Simply call dispatch when you are ready."

"We'd rather you wait."

"In that case, kindly turn off the engine."

"No problem," said Remo, who left the engine off and the Mountie curled up in the locked trunk while he and Chiun went to the building entrance.

Remo looked around. "Looks like the kind of place where a UN official would meet up with a Canadian minister when they don't want witnesses."

"Possibly," said Chiun.

"This should be a piece of cake."

"Do not count your salmon before they spawn," warned the Master of Sinanju darkly.

"What could happen? We're in Canada. Even the Mounties don't put up a fight."

31

Canadian Fisheries Minister Gil Houghton practically floated off the Air Canada air-stairs and bounced into his waiting Bentley.

He sent the gleaming silver vehicle spinning into Ottawa's sedate traffic. His foot pressed the accelerator with too much eagerness, and he found himself speeding. It was something he never did. Speed.

He sped now. Just this once. His official license plates would purchase him indulgence from the traffic police.

His drive to the Temple of Kali was a whirl of inchoate thoughts. Gil Houghton hoped Mistress Kali would find time for him before the meeting. If not, after. Either would suit him.

The building looked dark when he pulled up before it twenty minutes later. But then, it always looked dark. Only the red light bulb burning in its cage over the entrance door gave any hint that the old generating station was not deserted.

Parking on a side street, he walked briskly and officiously to that ruby light. The bell vibrated at his touch, and he was buzzed in.

In the anteroom with its erotic statuary he declined to doff his clothes. Better not. What if the

UN Secretary-General were present? It was true that Mistress Kali's rules were severe and inflexible. One didn't enter her presence except in the state one came into the world.

But this was different. He was not here as a supplicant, but as the minister of fisheries and oceans.

And if he erred, well, he wouldn't mind a taste of the whip as a reward for his roguish incorrigibility.

Presenting himself before the mirrored door, he raised his voice. "Permission to enter the awful presence."

"Enter," a cold-as-steel voice snapped.

She sounded delightfully impatient, Gil Houghton thought, stepping forward.

The doors rolled apart, and he froze.

Mistress Kali stood, hands on hips, arms akimbo, her domino-masked face lowered so that her changeable eyes regarded him with an emerald green blazing up-from-under glare.

Then they were like blue diamonds, icy and fiery, and they made the pit of his stomach clench.

"I trust I am not late for the meeting," he remarked.

"You are early."

"Good."

"I *despise* earliness."

Houghton swallowed. His tongue turned to dry rubber.

"I—I can come back if you'd rather."

At that moment he noticed the long-stemmed scarlet rose tucked into the loop of chain draping her lyrelike hips. With a quick gesture she plucked it into the air.

Turning so that her body showed in full profile, the uplifted breasts and the stunning ice-princess profile, she lifted the rose to the light. Red mouth compressing, she began snapping off the thorns one by one.

"Approach," she invited.

Cautiously he stepped forward. Her nimble fingers snapped off thorn after thorn. They dropped to the black glassy floor with dry tiny sounds like cat claws clicking on porcelain.

"Unzip!" she commanded.

"Whatever for?"

"Obey!" Mistress Kali snapped.

Slowly, because his heart was pounding, he drew down his trouser's zipper as Mistress Kali stripped the stem of its thorns. When the last was on the floor, he stood there tumescent and quivering.

"Whatever are you—?"

"What was it you said the other day?" she said thinly.

"That you never touch me."

"What else?"

"That we never do anything new anymore," he admitted, his voice a bleat.

"So you want to try something new, do you?" she asked in an arch voice. She wasn't looking at him. He felt almost beneath her notice. His quivering member stiffened further.

"I do," he said, bowing his head, "very much."

"Very much what!"

"Very much, Mistress Kali. I want to try something new very much, Mistress Kali," he said hastily.

A faint smile touched her scarlet lips. From somewhere about her person she palmed a long vial of massage lotion. She snapped the cap with her black-nailed thumb and dipped the stem to its full length. A faint fishy scent came to his nose. Cod-liver oil. His favorite. He tingled down to his curled-in-anticipation toes.

"What are you doing?"

"Something new," she said, drawing the stripped stem from the bottle. It dripped viscously.

He licked his lips. "Really?"

Her voice dropped several degrees. "Yes, really."

And whirling, she took his member in one hand and with the other inserted the lubricated rose stem deep into his urethra, jerking it in and out, in and out until he screamed in the exquisite pain and pleasure of a sensation he had never in his wildest imaginings imagined.

The pain brought him to his knees. He knelt there, gasping and clutching himself, a fresh spill like fish milk and dark red raspberry juice forming under his agony.

Her voice cut through his agony like a steel needle. "Never again complain that I won't try anything new...."

32

United Nations Secretary-General Anwar Anwar-Sadat stepped through the buzzing door into an anteroom that was surprisingly sumptuous.

The walls were some pink-veined marble that brought to mind the delicate flesh of a concubine. At least that was how his romantic eyes perceived the cold marble.

There were statuary. A black-skinned woman with more than her natural provision of arms. They were held in an attitude that was both provocative and inviting.

Kali, of course. The Hindu goddess of death. How appropriate for a woman whose cyber-pseudonym was Mistress Kali. The eyes of the statue looked down upon him, two blind blanks.

He noticed that her proportions were generous to the point of ripeness. He took this as a promising sign. Anwar Anwar-Sadat liked his women on the voluptuous side.

On the other side of the door, another statue. This one not of basalt, but porphyry. He did not recognize the god depicted but decided it could only be Shiva, consort of Kali. Shiva clutched in his four arms various devices both arcane and doubtful of purpose.

Clearing his throat, he raised his voice. "Hello?"

"Do you desire to enter into the presence of Mistress Kali?" a very firm voice returned.

"I do. Are you she?"

"Silence!" the voice cracked out.

In spite of himself and his position in the world, Anwar Anwar-Sadat felt a cool hush descend over his soul. "Allow me to gaze upon you," he asked.

The voice was coming from the mirrored area between the two statues. It was at once evident that these were mirrored doors. He was being studied. Assuming a rakish pose, he allowed this.

"Anwar Anwar-Sadat, are you brave enough to enter into the domain of Kali?"

"I am," he said in a voice that cracked with anticipation.

"Very well. Steel yourself."

"I am steeled."

"For those who enter into my terrible presence are forevermore changed."

For a dark moment Anwar Anwar-Sadat quailed inwardly. He did not wish to be changed. He only wished to meet this creature who had so bewitched him sight unseen, voice unheard, until this pregnant hour.

He swallowed. And then the doors parted.

Mistress Kali was all that he had imagined, Anwar Anwar-Sadat saw at once.

She was tall and statuesque and as blond as sunlight on pure gold. Her features were classic, ethereal yet chiseled. The domino mask of golden silk framing her Nile green eyes added a touch of mystery that was perfection itself.

Her body was a black flame, and as she shifted her weight from one generous hip to the other, it shimmered. Leather. She wore leather. He had not expected leather.

His eyes followed the shimmer to pick out the enchanting details. The silver chains, the vampiric black nails and ivory skull set in her navel like a barbaric ornament.

She held a whip in one hand. The other clutched a dog's leash.

Anwar-Sadat's eyes followed the leash to the floor and his heart jumped quick and hot in his chest.

On the floor at her side crouched a man on all fours. He was naked except for a spiky dog collar banding his throat. He clutched a scarlet rose between his teeth like an obedient dog holding a bone. It dripped crimson droplets on the floor.

His eyes were on the floor. Mistress Kali gave the leash a sharp tug, and he raised his head.

"Allow me to present the minister of fisheries and oceans, Gilbert Houghton," said Mistress Kali in a voice that mocked the two dignitaries.

"Er, pleased," gulped Anwar Anwar-Sadat.

Through the clenched rose, the Canadian official growled low in his throat.

This was *not* going as expected....

33

At Folcroft, Harold Smith was watching the global conflict unfold.

"This is unbelievable," he said to himself. "It is as if the entire seafaring community has descended into a feeding frenzy."

In the North Atlantic the renegade U.S. fishing fleet had retreated to a closed fishery called the Flemish Cap, where they were taking Canadian cod and yellowtail in a feeding frenzy that defied fishing regulations of both nations. Coast Guard cutters were moving to rendezvous with them in an effort to persuade them to abandon Canadian fishing waters.

In the Pacific the U.S. destroyer *Arkham* was prowling the waters between Alaska and Washington in search of the Canadian submarine *Yellowknife/Couteaujaune* before it could surface in the midst of American salmon-fishing craft.

Meanwhile Canadian coastal-defense vessels were trying to collect transit taxes and taking small-arms fire from disgruntled U.S. salmon fishermen.

From Ottawa there was silence both official and unofficial. But from Quebec emanated semiofficial rumors that in the U.S.-Canadian fishing war, Quebec intended to side with Washington.

And so Harold Smith saw the first seeds of Canadian civil war. The choosing of sides.

Already in the U.S. media, old memories were being dredged up. The depredations of one French and Indian war. The Deerfield raids. Louisbourg. How during the War of 1812, Canadian and British forces had burned the White House to the ground.

In Oregon a paramilitary force called the Unconstituted Oregon Militia had slipped across the Forty-fifth Parallel and hung three Mounties from fir trees and called for the repeal of the treaty that had given much of the original Oregon territory to Canada.

Along the Vermont-Canadian border, tensions were running extremely high. It appeared there was a library that straddled the border in a town that existed half in Canada and half in the U.S. Hotheads on both sides of the border had begun to lay concertina wire straight down the middle of the humanities reference aisle, and the library was being hotly contested, chiefly with thrown encyclopedias. It was only a matter of time before the first shot was fired.

In Lake Champlain a long-simmering controversy over the spread of a thumbnail-sized mollusk, the zebra mussel, from U.S. waters into Canadian territory was flaring up again.

Tiger-striped Canadian air-force F-16s were patrolling the Alcan Highway, which had been sealed off at Alaska's border with Canada. All U.S. traffic was being turned back. Alaska had been cut off from the continental U.S. except by air.

From Parliament Hill came threats of withdrawal from NORAD and other mutually beneficial treaties.

On Capitol Hill the provisions of the Treaty of Ghent, which ended the War of 1812, were examined for loopholes and unfinished business.

In the meantime the President of the United States and his advisers were making the Sunday-morning talk-show circuit trying to placate all sides and cool the growing war fever.

Smith knew that open warfare was but hours away. If it erupted and Quebec sided with Washington, a rift deeper than any would develop. And U.S.-Canadian relations would be poisoned for a century to come.

And all because Man needed more and more fish to live.

34

Remo rang the bell. His supersensitive fingers sensed the electric current so he knew it was wired up.

There was no answering buzzer.

Remo rang it again.

"You know," he said to Chiun while they waited, "in the old days a red light like this meant a house of ill repute."

"All houses are of ill repute. Besides our own," Chiun intoned.

"You have a point there," said Remo, leaning on the bell. It was an old push bell, a small black nub in a rusty brass bell.

Whoever was inside refused to buzz them in.

"Guess we do this the hard way. Wanna split up or go in together?"

"We will go in together, for what danger would a house of such ill repute have for two fish-eating Masters of Sinanju such as we?"

"Good point," said Remo, stepping back to lift one Italian loafer. The fine leather gleamed under the lurid light for a moment. Remo kicked once, hard.

The door was painted steel, but it caved in as if

it were tin. The panel bent in the middle from the kick, but actually gave at the hinges.

Remo jumped in and caught the thick slab of steel before it hit the floor. Pivoting, he directed the downward impetus to one side and set the door in one corner. He gave it a spin. It twirled in place like a square top, wobbled then gyrated as if possessing a waking mind, and leaned itself obediently against one wall, making no more sound than a basket settling.

"Pretty slick, huh?"

"Hush," said Chiun, lifting a quelling hand.

Remo listened. Under his feet he sensed a vibration. It was familiar. Vaguely electric, but not electric in the man-made sense. It was the electricity of something living.

He looked down. Chiun was regarding the floor at their feet.

It was black. Not ebony black or obsidian black, but a shiny black that was like a mirror. The floor looked as if it were possible to see through it. Their eyes narrowed.

"I never saw a floor like this," Remo muttered.

"Nor I," said Chiun.

"It's like I should be able to see through it, but I can't somehow."

"It is black. One cannot look through something that is so black."

"So why do I think I can?" Remo pressed.

"I do not know, but I feel the same way as you, Remo."

From under their feet a sudden sound came unbidden. A gurgle, followed by a noisy splash. Other smaller splashes sounded.

"Sounds like a sewer pipe down there," Remo said.

"If that is so," said Chiun, "in the sewer dwell living things."

"Not our problem. Let's go where this takes us."

They advanced in the dim back-glow of the red entrance light.

The walls were marble, but broken by a mirrored section. The mirror shone of quicksilver.

And on either side two shadowy statues stood sentinel.

Chiun's quick intake of breath made Remo freeze in place. "What is it?" he hissed.

"Behold."

"Behold what?" said Remo, peering behind the statues for hiding enemies.

"The figures on either side of the door, Remo."

"I see them. Statues. So what?"

"How many arms does the statue on the right possess, my son?"

Remo's eyes dispelled the clotting shadows. "Four."

"And the statue on the left?"

"Four."

"They are no mere statues, but Shiva and Kali, the Red One and the Black One."

"Big deal. Two statues."

"Remo, why are they here in pagan Canada?"

"Decoration." And Remo advanced.

With a flutter of silken skirts, Chiun got in his way. Two hands came up and pressed themselves into Remo's chest. The Master of Sinanju's hazel eyes were pleading. "I do not like this. Why would such Eastern gods guard this Western place?"

"They look pretty naked. Maybe this *is* a cathouse."

"Remo, you may remain here. I will go in. Do not follow."

"Cut it out, Chiun."

"What if *she* is here?"

"She who?"

"Do not trifle with me, Remo Williams."

Remo sighed. His mind went back to other times.

He couldn't recall the year, but it had started with a statue of the Hindu goddess Kali, patron demon of the cult of Thugee, who strangled travelers for their money. When airline passengers started popping up throttled by yellow silk scarves, Harold Smith had sent Chiun and Remo to look into it. They found more than they'd bargained for. The modern-day Thugs were controlled by an ancient statue that held the power to exert an evil influence upon its followers—and upon Remo, who was, according to Sinanju legend, the dead white tiger destined to be the avatar of Shiva on Earth.

Remo had shattered the statue supposed to be the vessel of Kali's evil spirit, but the spirit later returned in another form. This time as a four-armed call girl who had lured Remo into the cauldron that had been the Gulf War. He was alone then. Chiun hadn't been there to guide him. Somehow, using yellow silk strangling scarves as a symbol of the U.S. hostages in the Middle East, Kali had ignited the Gulf War.

Something terrible had happened to Remo then. He had no memory of it. Later Chiun claimed Kali had broken Remo's neck and caused Shiva to possess his body to keep it animated. Somehow Chiun had defeated Kali, cast out Shiva and reclaimed Remo as his son in Sinanju. All Remo remembered was waking up with a weird bump the size of a pigeon egg in the middle of his forehead that had to be surgically removed. Chiun claimed it was Shiva's third eye. Remo called it the goose egg that wouldn't go away.

Remo shook off the disturbing memories. "Look," he told Chiun. "That statue was wrecked. If Kali's spirit were anywhere around here, I'd smell that sex scent of hers. I'd sense something."

"Perhaps..."

"I don't. So that means they're just statues. Watch."

And deftly slipping around the Master of Sinanju, Remo floated up to the towering Kali statue.

Reaching up, he took a wrist and snapped it. The hand broke off with a splintery snap. Remo tossed it over his shoulder. It struck the glassy black floor with a clattery clunk. With a casual upward slap Remo shattered the fingers of another hand. A downward slap defingered another.

A stamp of his foot powdered the hand that fell at his feet.

Finally, with a tight fist, he cracked the statue at the exposed belly. The torso wobbled, then toppled forward.

Remo caught it, half turned and let fly.

The top of the statue went zinging out the open

door to land in the street, and bounced apart into a dozen pieces of various sizes.

Remo faced Chiun. "See? No evil Kali statue. This is just some goofball cathouse or something."

Chiun padded up to the Shiva statue and looked into its austere countenance. "I detect a faint resemblance," he said, thin of voice.

"Yeah. It has two eyes, one nose and a mouth with thirty-two teeth. Same as me. That's where the resemblance begins and ends."

"There are things you do not remember," Chiun warned.

"If I don't, it's probably for good reasons," returned Remo.

"Shiva has possessed your corporeal body before."

"If you say so..."

"Several times."

"Fine. I channel Shiva on my off days. I don't feel an off day coming on."

"The last time, he promised me that he would claim you, his avatar, when the time was ripe, and not before."

"Let me know if that day ever comes," said Remo. "Now do you want to go first or should I?"

Chiun regarded Remo thinly. "You are the brave one. You may go first."

"Since when are you afraid?" asked Remo, genuinely surprised.

"When I saw those two statues in this very room," returned Chiun, his wrinkled visage darkening with shadows.

"Fine. Try not inhale too much of my dust...."

And turning, Remo faced the mirrored double door and smacked it with one palm.

It shattered into a thousand fragments that hung in space for a long breath until the pieces recognized that they no longer belonged to a whole. Then they fell like a metallic rain.

ANWAR ANWAR-SADAT LOOKED down at the fisheries minister of Canada, Gilbert Houghton.

The man spit out his bloody rose. His hello was grudging.

"I—I—" Anwar-Sadat swallowed "—I thought we—" he cleared his throat "—I mean—"

"You thought that you were the only one upon whom I bestow the favor of my wrath?" Mistress Kali said in a metallic voice.

"That is one way to put it," Anwar-Sadat said. He averted his eyes from the lurid spectacle of the fisheries minister. This was not Anwar-Sadat's scene. Not his scene at all. What had he walked into? he wondered.

"I thought it was time my two puppets met."

"I am not your puppet," Anwar Anwar-Sadat insisted.

Gilbert Houghton spit out a sticky tendril of blood and said, "But I am. Am I your only puppet, Mistress?"

"Of course not," Mistress Kali sneered.

"But I *am* your most important puppet."

"You are my most *useful* puppet," said Mistress Kali.

The fisheries minister smiled sickly. He beamed.

Then Mistress Kali's Nile green eyes fell on Anwar Anwar-Sadat's stone features.

"Until this hour," she added coldly. "Kneel, Man who would be Pharaoh."

Anwar-Sadat stiffened his spine. "I will not. I am a UN diplomat."

"And I am the woman who baited her hook with your miserable penis and reeled you in like a fish. Kneel or be flayed!"

"You would not dare."

"Kiss my feet and I will spare your hide of a splitting."

"Resist," Gilbert Houghton hissed.

"Should I?"

"Yes. I want to hear the crack of the whip on your recalcitrant ass. It will make me hard as a bone."

On reconsideration, Anwar Anwar-Sadat said, "I will kneel."

And lifting his trouser legs so the knees did not bag, he got down on one knee, like a knight before his queen.

"Both knees," Mistress Kali insisted.

"Very well." The second knee fell to the floor.

"Now prostrate yourself before my magnificence."

"Prostrate? Do you mean—?"

A gloved hand reached down, seized his hair and pushed his head down violently.

Anwar Anwar-Sadat's forehead banged the floor. A spiked heel pressed into the back of his neck, then withdrew.

A very pointed toe slipped under his downcast face.

"Kiss it and be mine."

Anwar Anwar-Sadat hesitated. But only for a moment. The stiletto heel returned into his neck vertebrae, and he planted his dry lips to the black vinyl. A peck. He hoped there were no hidden cameras.

The heel came off his neck.

With a tug of her leash, Mistress Kali brought the fisheries minister closer. They faced one another, two dogs at the heel of their mistress.

"This one," she said, giving the leash a head-jerking tug, "is ambitious. He seeks to be prime minister. He believes that he can accomplish this by strutting his balls on the global stage and facing down the United States while blaming Quebec for the conflict we engineered."

"Is this true? Is this your plan?" Anwar-Sadat demanded.

"It would have worked, but someone sunk my sub," Gilbert Houghton said dolefully.

"It is a very intriguing plan," Anwar Anwar-Sadat admitted.

"Thank you," said Gilbert Houghton. "But I must kindly ask you to stay away from my mistress."

"She is *my* mistress."

"You think a slavish peck on her boot will make her yours? I have tasted her lash. I have licked her in places you will never see. Have *you?*"

"I hope not to," Anwar Anwar-Sadat said truthfully.

And he felt the boot heel press into his neck again.

"Now, this one," Mistress Kali said, "seeks global power." Her voice dripped with scorn and contempt. "He has failed to bring the world into his orbit, so now he seeks control of the seas as a way to control nations."

"It was your idea," Anwar-Sadat reminded. "This control of the sea."

"Interesting concept," said Gilbert Houghton.

"I have not yet begun."

Mistress Kali interrupted. "Both schemes are mine. Now they are one. You have both worked my will in the world. Now you will work together."

"I will consider this," said Anwar Anwar-Sadat. "Now, about our dinner engagement..."

"I will dine upon the hams of your rump if you fail to achieve my goals," Mistress Kali spit.

"What exactly *are* your goals?" Anwar Anwar-Sadat asked.

"To plunge the world into the Red Abyss."

"I am not familiar with the Red Abyss, is it near the Black Hole of Calcutta?"

The answer never came. There came a sound like shattering glass, followed by the gritty settling of a particles.

It froze time. Anwar Anwar-Sadat started to look up, but his gaze never reached his mistress's masked face. With a savage gesture she kicked Anwar-Sadat and the fisheries minister aside and stepped past them, snarling, "Avert your eyes, supplicants."

Like a black snake uncoiling, her whip slithered to the floor. She snapped it up and demanded in a harsh, shrill voice, "Who is this who invades my domain?"

A squeaky voice returned, "Who is this who demands such answers of us?"

"I am Mistress Kali."

"If you are Mistress Kali," returned the squeaky voice, "then you will recognize my companion, who is sometimes called Shiva the Destroyer."

Hearing that interesting comment, Anwar Anwar-Sadat couldn't help but peek. He turned his head.

35

Lieutenant Sandy Heckman had interdiction patrol. They were calling her the heroine of the Battle of Sable Island Banks. There was talk of a promotion.

Now she was in the waters west of the Grand Banks' infamous Nose trying to protect U.S. fishermen as they plundered cod from Canadian waters.

Not that there would be any stopping them.

It would have been simple in the past. Show up in force and seize their vessels. But these fishermen had tasted combat. They had defeated the Canadian Coast Guard. They would not be denied. They wanted to fish, so the orders from Cape Cod were to let them fish. It was, politically speaking, a way to pressure Ottawa into capitulating.

Sandy didn't care about Ottawa. After the skirmish was over, there would be even less fish in the North Atlantic, pushing the stock-rebounding process further into the next century.

The trouble was, the U.S. fishing fleet was firing warning shots at its own Coast Guard.

Keeping a respectful distance, watching the sonar scope because there was nothing more constructive to do, Sandy spotted a familiar metallic underwater contact.

It was chasing a school of flatfish that looked like tilapia, one of the underutilized species that used to be by-catch but was reclassified as edible now.

"Helmsman, stay with this contact."

"Aye, sir."

The *Cayuga* moved smartly to a southwesterly heading.

Sandy jammed her pugnacious nose to the greenish scope. "It's got to be one of those damn torpedoes again. I want to see what it does and where it goes."

The *Cayuga* slammed through the heaving swells like a flashing white terrier.

36

Remo Williams folded his arms as the Master of Sinanju asked the blond woman in the dominatrix rig if she recognized him.

"I do not," she said, continuing her advance. Snapping her whip back, she let fly.

The whip snaked up and out.

Remo read it coming. To his trained eyes, it wasn't even a blur, just a sluggish, uncoiling serpent of gleaming black leather. It snapped at a lock of his hair. Remo tilted his head. The lock escaped chopping.

The whip came back, and this time she swung it broadside.

Remo stepped in, met the black tentacle halfway and took hold of it. He spun. The whip, still traveling in his grasp, came flying out of its owner's grasp.

Mistress Kali stepped back in shock, looked at his empty hands and his pale features, then she turned a smoldering red under her yellow silk domino mask.

"You dare!"

"We dare all the time," said Remo casually.

"I am Mistress Kali!"

"Like the cat says, 'Big hairy deal.'"

"Defier! I slay you with my scorn."

Kali lunged. Remo reached out and took her by the throat. He squeezed. At once her face reddened, then purpled. Her black-nailed fingers clawed for his face. Remo held her off at arm's length.

"What do you say now, Little Father?" he asked Chiun as Kali tried in vain to claw the skin from his face.

Chiun frowned. "Her strength is only the strength of an ordinary person," he said quietly. "And she possessed but two arms."

"Right. That means she's not Kali."

"I *am* Kali!" Mistress Kali snapped, taking another swipe at Remo's eyes.

"Butt out. We're talking about another Kali," said Remo.

"I am she! I am the Black One. I am the Mother of all. He who eats, eats by me."

Chiun frowned. "She speaks the words of Kali."

"She's a high-priced hooker. That's all."

Chiun walked around the dominatrix whose shiny black body shook with impotent rage and hate.

"You do not recognize my son Remo?" he asked Mistress Kali.

Kali glared venomously at the Master of Sinanju.

"Look closer, shrieking one. Are his features known to you, you who call yourself by the hated name?" demanded Chiun.

Kali spit at the Master of Sinanju. Chiun evaded the expectoration with a graceful pirouette.

Reaching up, Chiun took her head in one hand and inexorably turned the eyes of Mistress Kali to face Remo. "Look deep. What do you see?" he commanded.

"I see a dead man!" Kali hissed. "Kneel before me or I will gnaw the skin from your bones."

Chiun shook her head. "You do not know my son?"

Kali glared more fiercely. But somewhere deep in her icy blue eyes flickered a different light. "I know..."

"Know what?" asked Remo.

"You..."

"Well, I don't know you," Remo returned.

"Are you certain, Remo?" demanded Chiun.

"Yeah. I'm—" Then Remo looked closer. He realized he wasn't looking at her face, but at the silk and the eyes they framed. Now he looked deeper. "Her eyes. There's something familiar about her eyes."

Chiun's voice grew sharp. "Are you certain?"

"Yeah. The eyes look familiar. But I can't place them."

"Your essence is remembering, not your brain. She is Kali. You must slay her, Remo."

"Let's see her face first," said Remo, releasing her neck. His fingers plucked at the yellow domino mask.

Mistress Kali turned into a tiger. She twisted, squirming, and one hand reached into small of her back.

It came back trailing a long scarf of pure golden silk.

"Remo!" Chiun cried. "Beware her strangling scarf!"

Remo, as usual, was too slow. Swift as he was, he was too slow. His mind was on her face and the mask over it.

The Master of Sinanju, ever vigilant, shook off his jade fingernail protector and plunged the gleaming nail beneath into Mistress Kali's unprotected throat. It sank in to the tip of the finger and withdrew before anyone could absorb the movement.

Mistress Kali shuddered on her feet. A gasp came from her open harridan mouth. Her eyes flew wide with shock.

She spoke a single breathy, incredulous word. "Remo?"

Then, eyes rolling to whites, she collapsed at their feet.

Remo was holding the domino mask in one hand. For a frozen moment, he stood there, not inhaling, not exhaling. His eyes, dark as the hollows of a skull, went sick.

"What happened? I never touched her," he said.

"I did," said Chiun, who held up the golden tail of silk. "Behold, for she was about to wrap her silken wiles about you."

"Chiun."

"What?"

"Tell me you didn't…"

"I did."

"You killed her," Remo said. His voice shrank with each utterance.

"She was a harlot and a demon in the flesh of a woman."

Remo swallowed. Only then did Chiun see the bone white aspect of his face. With his hollow eyes

and his high cheekbones, Remo's face looked like a
skull with a paper-thin coating of skin.

"She..."

"What is it, Remo?"

"She..." Remo swallowed hard. He knelt.

Mistress Kali lay in a crumpled heap. Her head
rested on one pale, outflung arm, the golden hair
covering her face like a feathery broken wing.

Carefully Remo raised the hair, brushing it back.

Chiun looked down, eyes narrowing.

The features showed in profile, showed in death.
They were chiseled and firm. One eye lay open in
shock. The black lips were parted to show the dead
white teeth.

Remo stared at her profile for the longest minute
of eternity.

Then, face twisting in pain, Remo looked up.
Looked up at the Master of Sinanju. Bitter tears
started from his eyes. His voice was a shocked
croak. "Chiun. You killed her. You killed Jilda. You
killed the mother of my little girl."

And the Master of Sinanju, the force of the truth
striking him fully, stepped back as if he'd been dealt
a physical blow.

37

The sonar's metallic contact led the *Cayuga* to Stellwagon Bank, a closed fishing area off Massachusetts.

"If that's a torpedo, I'm Davy Jones's favorite hooker," Sandy said grimly. "It's herding those fish. Every time they veer south, it changes course and chases them north. Someone's controlling it."

After an hour of cat and mouse, Sandy got an inkling what that someone was.

A big gray factory ship. It lumbered along on a course generally parallel to their own.

She went up to the flying bridge and used her binoculars.

"Circle that tub," she ordered.

The *Cayuga* circled the wallowing factory ship until the name appeared on the bow.

Hareng Saur
MONTREAL

"Sparks, inform Cape Cod we have a French-Canadian factory ship in our waters and ask what should be done about it."

"Aye, sir."

As she waited for a reply, Sandy saw something that seemed incredible.

The *Cayuga* was still in pursuit of the mysterious torpedo.

Suddenly the torpedo accelerated, surfaced and began to home in on the *Hareng Saur.*

"Looks like our next course of action will be decided for us," she said.

The torpedo, trailing a foamy wake, closed with the gray ship.

Sandy had her glasses trained on the probable point of impact. Amidships of the big boat.

She saw the wake close in. There was no way to avoid a direct hit. The *Hareng Saur* seemed completely oblivious to the threat. The tiny white figures on her deck were going about their business in a brisk but unpanicked fashion.

At the last possible minute, a panel opened just at the waterline as if to devour the incoming device.

The torpedo struck. Sandy flinched inwardly. But there was no explosion. The torpedo just scooted into the black aperture.

The black port closed up, and all was quiet except for the sudden heaving of fish nets overboard.

"What the hell happened?" the helmsman wondered aloud, coming out of his protective crouch.

"The torpedo herded the fish to the ship," she said. "Damn it. They're chasing our fish into their waters and stealing them. This is environmental piracy on the open seas!"

38

Remo stood up. He was trying to compose his features. His shoulders shook. His fists made two mallets of bone.

"Chiun..." His voice was soft, not accusing, but numb with shock. "Chiun, it's Jilda. Jilda's dead."

"I know," said the Master of Sinanju, eyes round and wide.

Remo looked around the room. "If Jilda's here, where's Freya?"

"I do not know. But I vow that I will find for you your daughter, Remo. I will atone for this grave error I have committed."

"That's why I recognized her. It was Jilda. Jilda..."

Remo looked back at the dead woman he had loved many years ago. His eyes seemed to retreat into his skull-like countenance. Then he asked a question. "What was she doing here? Why was she dressed like that?"

The Master of Sinanju surveyed the room. His eyes fell upon two kneeling men, one nude and one not. "They will know," he intoned.

With determined steps Chiun strode up to the

cowering pair. "Speak! Why did you kneel before that woman?"

"She was Mistress Kali," Gilbert Houghton said, as if that explained everything.

"I loved her, although to speak the unvarnished truth I only met her just this day," Anwar Anwar-Sadat admitted. "Is she truly...dead?"

"She is no more, popinjay," Chiun said severely.

Remo had joined them. Reaching down, he seized the Egyptian by his collar and dragged him to his feet. His eyes were hot. His voice hotter.

"We're looking for a little girl. Blond. About twelve."

"Thirteen," Chiun corrected. "Golden of hair and blue of eye. Like her mother, who lies here dead. Where is she?"

"I know nothing of any little girl," the Secretary-General of the UN protested.

Remo found the leash with his toe, dug under it and snapped his foot. The free end of the leash whipped into his waiting hand. He tugged hard.

Fisheries Minister Gilbert Houghton was yanked off his hands. "Urrkk," he said.

"What about you?"

"I have seen no little girl and I have been Mistress Kali's slave for many weeks now."

"I am crushed, desolated," said Anwar Anwar-Sadat. "I thought she loved only me. And now she is dead."

"She never loved you. But she scorned me. I was the object of her scorn," Houghton snarled.

"Both of you shut up," Remo ordered. Turning

to Chiun, he said, "I'm going to find Freya if I have to tear this place apart brick by brick."

"And I will help," vowed Chiun, girding his skirts.

"But first we deal with these two."

"We are instructed to intimidate, not dispatch these two."

"Accidents happen," Remo growled. "You got that one. I'll take the other."

Remo stood the Canadian fisheries minister up against a wall while Chiun immobilized the UN Secretary-General with a painful twist of the Egyptian's ear.

"You're behind all this?" Remo accused Gilbert Houghton.

"I admit nothing."

"And this is about fish?"

"No comment."

"That's your answer? No comment?"

Gil Houghton gulped like a goldfish. "No comment."

Sweeping his hands out, Remo brought them together with a sudden loud clap. Gilbert Houghton's head happened to be caught between his palms in the thunderous instant Remo's palms came together.

When Remo stepped back, hands returning to his sides, Gil Houghton's head sat on his neck like a sunfish's. Flat with eyes set on opposite sides of what had been a round mammalian skull.

The surprised whites filled with blood, and the pursed lips seemed to be kissing empty air—then he pitched forward, dead.

Remo turned.

The Master of Sinanju had one sandal on the Egyptian's heaving chest. Anwar Anwar-Sadat attempted a protest. Chiun quieted it with a sudden pressure of his foot.

While Anwar Anwar-Sadat unwittingly watched his last breath leave his dry, open mouth, Chiun calmly took hold of his dusky mandibles and lifted his head off his spinal cord.

It came off with a popping suck of a sound like a head off a plastic doll. As simply as that.

Tossing the head in a corner, the Master of Sinanju faced his pupil in expectant silence. His chin lifted.

"It wasn't your fault," Remo said.

Chiun bowed his aged head. "I accept responsibility for my rash actions."

"You were just trying to protect me," Remo said distractedly.

"And I have wounded you deeply, for which I am deeply regretful."

"If we find Freya okay, it will be all right. Let's find Freya. Just find Freya and everything will be forgiven."

Remo's cracking voice told the Master of Sinanju that their future together hinged on finding alive the daughter Remo had lost once and could not bear to lose again.

"I will not fail you, my son," Chiun vowed.

Carefully Remo went over to the splayed body of Jilda of Lakluun and carried it to a stone shelf that ran along one wall. He laid it on the ledge, arranged the leather-clad limbs modestly and touched her gleaming hair briefly.

Then they went in opposite directions.

Under their feet the gurgle and splash of troubled waters came intermittently. The flooring was a continuation of the anteroom floor. It was like a hard black mirror that reflected everything above it, yet it seemed ready to pull them down into an abyss blacker than universal night.

Remo's sensitive ears turned this way and that, hunting sounds.

Somewhere deep in the building he heard a constant clicking. It came in bursts and spurts, yet was steady as a dry hail.

"This way," Remo said, looking for a door.

He found not a door but a narrow niche in a wall behind a heavy wall hanging.

"What do you make of this?" Remo asked, snapping off the hanging.

Chiun examined it. "A passage."

"Too small for a grown-up."

"Perhaps it is meant for a dwarf. Or a child. This was constructed for the use of one who wishes to remain undisturbed."

Remo felt the edge of the stone. "We can chop through this easy."

Chiun indicated the arch over them. "Look, Remo. A keystone. If you break the sides, it will all coming tumbling down."

Remo sniffed the cool air coming from the niche.

"I smell someone in there."

Chiun said, "I, too."

Setting himself, Remo inserted his shoulder into the niche. He drew in his breath, then let it out very deeply until his rib cage all but collapsed. It was still too thick. He blew out more air until his lungs were like two empty balloons.

Then, with infinite care so he didn't break any ribs or crush his own internal organs, Remo insinuated himself into the niche. It was a slow, careful task. His cartilage crackled under the stress. Like a snake he slithered through, getting halfway and concentrating to keep the air from rushing back into his hungry lungs.

Chiun called soft encouragement. "You will succeed because failure is too bitter to taste, my son."

Halfway in, Remo paused, then with a jerk, he threw himself all the way in. He disappeared into the gloom.

Chiun called softly, "Wait!"

But there was no answer.

Quickly the Master of Sinanju expelled all the air from his own lungs and attempted to duplicate the feat of his pupil, whom he had taught many things but not the dangerous technique he had just witnessed.

The best Masters are those who devise their own skills, Chiun thought with a bitter pride.

THE CORRIDOR WASN'T as narrow as the niche entrance, but it wasn't comfortably wide. Remo negotiated it by walking sideways. That put him at a disadvantage if there were traps or snares lying in wait.

Under his feet he sensed vague electrical disturbances. Water purled. But the ebony floor seemed solid.

Abruptly the stone corridor right-angled, and

Remo went with it. It opened farther and the ticking, like incessant hail, came more clearly.

For all the world it sounded like someone keying a computer. On second thought Remo decided it sounded like two people at two keyboards.

Well, whoever they were, they had better have some answers to the only important question in his universe....

39

Harold Smith got the word from Cape Cod air station as soon as it was received.

The *Cayuga* had made contact with a Canadian factory ship, *Hareng Saur*.

Smith read the name and blinked. He spoke passable French, a relic of his OSS days in France.

Hareng Saur sounded vaguely familiar to him. He input the name into his computer and accessed the automatic French-language-conversion program.

Up came the name *Red Herring* and an etymology of the phrase.

Suspicion flickered across Smith's patrician face. There was no such fish as a red herring. It was a figure of speech. One that was exclusive to English, he saw. There were no red herrings in the French language, real or figurative. Thus, no French-named vessel would be called the *Red Herring* any more than a French submarine would be christened *Proud to be Frogs*.

Smith got on the phone with Coast Guard Station Cape Cod just in time to hear a follow-up report straight from the commander there.

"My people say it's releasing some kind of fish-chasing torpedo. This is definitely a hostile act,'' the base commander said.

"I am ordering the *Hareng Saur* be boarded, detained and searched,'' said Smith.

"Will do, sir,'' said the commander, who thought he was talking to Coast Guard area headquarters in Boston.

Smith hung up and returned to his system. A torpedo that herded fish. If such a device existed, perhaps he could discover it on the World Wide Web.

WHEN LIEUTENANT HECKMAN received her orders she said, "What the hell? We can't board a boat that size. They've got us outcrewed. Probably ten to one.''

"Maybe we can fake them out,'' suggested her helmsman.

"How's that?''

"Call in a Coast Guard air strike.''

"CG doesn't have air-strike capability.''

"Maybe they don't know that.''

"Good thinking.'' Taking up the mike, Sandy began chanting, "Attention, *Hareng Saur*. This is the CGC *Cayuga*. You are in violation of the Magnunson Act and are ordered to heave to and submit to boarding or be sunk.''

There was no answer from the *Hareng Saur*.

Then the factory ship launched a torpedo.

"What are the chances that a fish-chasing torpedo has a warhead?'' Sandy wondered aloud, her eyes on the incoming wake.

"The last one blew up on command,'' her helmsman reminded.

"That was only a self-destruct charge."

"TNT is TNT."

"Evasive!" Sandy ordered, then grabbed something solid.

The *Cayuga* went into extreme evasive maneuvers, and the torpedo ran after it like a hungry dog.

"It's gaining!" the helmsman roared.

"Then turn about and ride into its teeth," Sandy flung back.

"Are you crazy? Sir!"

"Do it!"

As the *Cayuga* heeled into the teeth of the torpedo, Sandy Heckman manned the sixteen-inch gun mounted on the foredeck and zeroed in on its bubbling nose.

Shells began heaving. The first one sent up a chopping uprush of water. That gave her the range. Her second shot struck just ahead, and the torpedo flashed through the turbulent water unscathed.

"Third time's the charm," muttered Sandy, who fired with careful precision, one eye shut, her pink tongue nipped between her neat white teeth.

The torpedo blew up with a force and a roar that settled the question once and for all. It was an antiship torpedo.

No more torpedoes came out of the *Hareng Saur*.

Twenty minutes later the skies were full of screaming white Falcon jets.

"Last chance, *Hareng Saur!*" Sandy warned. "Surrender or sink and swim for it. Last I heard, the water temperature was a relaxing thirty-one degrees."

The white flag was run up, and the rails became packed with sailors with lifted hands and blue faces.

"I'll bet my sea legs those are fleurs-de-lis on their damn faces," Sandy murmured as the *Cayuga* came alongside the towering gray factory ship.

40

Remo came to a door. It was like a frozen sheet of turquoise water. The clicking was coming from the other side. He looked back. No sign of Chiun. But he couldn't wait. The soft pad of sandals came. Chiun was not far behind. Fine. He could catch up.

Remo moved to the door. He saw it was split down the center.

Touching it, he had expected the two panels to part for him like an electric door. There were no handles or buttons. It had to be electrically operated.

But the doors remained firmly shut.

Remo pressed both hands to the panels. He tried to peer in. There was something or someone on the other side. He could hear the unbroken keying.

Using his fingertips, he dug into the seam between the two door halves. He found purchase, and exerted opposing pressure.

The doors came apart like stiff curtains. Remo jammed them into their wall grooves and stepped in before whoever was on the other side could react.

The room was square with brick walls. There was a table. On the table sat two computer monitors side by side. Nearby were other monitors, their screens glowing.

Seated before them, her back to him, was a young woman whose visible hair was a cloud of golden filaments.

Remo froze.

Whoever she was, she seemed oblivious to him. He could see her arms spread out on either side of the oversize chair back. One went to a keyboard attached to the right-hand monitor. The other expertly worked the keyboard of the left-hand monitor.

Two monitors were being worked simultaneously.

Remo could read them both.

The left hand was typing in French.

The right typed something completely different in Cyrillic Russian. Two hands, one mind, simultaneously typing in two languages. Remo felt the hair on his suddenly chilly forearms lift.

Then he noticed the great mound of clay that sat on the desk, looming over the seated figure like a spider weaving a web. It looked like a statue of Kali, but the arms were many and malformed. Some tiny as a baby's arms, others adult sized. Some fingerless. Others fisted in defiance. It gazed down with a heavy face that was twisted and evil.

And with a sick feeling in the pit of his stomach, Remo asked, "Freya, is that you?"

Both pairs of fingers froze in midword. Leaving off their work, they withdrew, and slowly the sunny-haired figure in the chair rotated to face him.

Remo's eyes stayed on the crown of hair, then the profile as it came around. As the full features revealed themselves, Remo was caught on the deep brown eyes he had not seen in what seemed like decades.

He swallowed. "Freya?"

She smiled. Her smile was as sunny as her hair.

"Hello, Daddy. You found me."

Dropping to one knee, Remo said, "Freya?"

And two hands met his. Their fingers entwined. Remo felt their warmth. Then they constricted like talons of slim, hard bone, and another pair of hands came up from her lap to snap a yellow silk scarf over his head and around his neck.

"You killed my mother!" she shrieked. And the silk scarf jerked left with irresistible force....

41

Harold Smith received the report that the *Hareng Saur* had been boarded without incident as he was reading through a web site of a Russian company that was offering a device called the Acoustic Fish Concentrator on the international market.

After searching the World Wide Web for everything from ''Fish'' to ''Fisheries'' without success, in frustration he had typed in ''Torpedo,'' and it just popped up as if by magic.

Based on old Soviet antisubmarine-warfare technology, and operating by sonic waves, the AFC was alleged to drive fish of some thirty-seven varieties into or from any waters the operator desired. Radio controlled, it was equipped with remote TV cameras to allow for remote control and operations.

In that simple discovery Harold Smith understood perhaps ninety percent of the activities of the *Hareng Saur* and the *Fier D'Être des Grenouilles*. The Canadians were herding food fish from international waters and into their own. From the *Santo Fado* to the *Ingo Pungo,* the sinkings of ships were designed to conceal their operation and discourage competition for those same fish. And the blame was to be laid squarely on Quebec.

The whys and hows were clear. Now all that remained was the settling of the whos behind it.

42

The Master of Sinanju felt his rib cage pressing against his beating heart and willed his heart to be still.

It was difficult, for it raced. Even with his confidence in his pupil, Remo, it raced.

The sides of the stone niche were like a vise that constrained lungs and heart both from performing their proper functions.

But Remo had shown the Master of Sinanju the way, and as Reigning Master, Chiun could not be defeated by so crude a barrier. Especially when Remo was burdened with the gross rib cage of a Westerner.

But it was not a question of holding the breath or constricting the ribs. His kimono silks were delicate. To rip them was to lose the precious garment. It would be unseemly. So the Master of Sinanju insinuated himself delicately, knowing that once he achieved the other side, there would be no stopping him.

Down the dank corridor came a cry. It was high and shrill. The words, twisted and echoing, were difficult to make out.

The voice was not Remo's voice. A female. A harridan voice, ugly and biting.

Nearly all the way through, Chiun lifted up on his sandaled toes. This straightened his spine, and the elastic cartilage contracted.

Thus straight, he skinned the last few inches inward, preserving his silks and his dignity.

On the other side Chiun drew in a recharging breath. One would be all that was needed, then on fleet feet, he moved down the stone passage, taking the turn when he came to it.

Under his feet he sensed strange charges and disturbances. He paid them no mind. The floor here was solid stone.

After the last turn, his hazel eyes fell upon a brick-walled room illuminated by twin computer terminals of amber.

Remo stood there, his back straight. He was facing a seated person.

With an sharp intake of breath, the Master of Sinanju saw the weaving delicate hands with their banana yellow nails.

And he saw the scarf of yellow silk that was pressed tight to the back of Remo's head.

"No!" he cried, leaping ahead.

His long nails slipped up, under the silk, and with a snap and a snarl it parted.

Remo staggered back. Chiun took fistfuls of his T-shirt and spun him out of the way. Strangely Remo didn't resist. He seemed without will.

"You will not have my son!" Chiun said, taking a careful step forward.

And a voice at once mature and not returned, "You are too late. I own him now."

And though the lines of her white face were twisted and constricted into an unpleasant rictus, the Master of Sinanju saw that the face before him— her four arms waving, two holding the torn ends of the limp yellow scarf—was a face he knew well.

She was older. But there was no mistaking those brown eyes.

Freya, daughter of Remo and Jilda of Lakluun.

And behind her a great monster of clay in the shape of Kali the Devourer.

Every iota of energy called for a death blow. But to kill the demon Kali was to extinguish the life of Remo's only daughter.

His gleaming nails retreating into the sleeves of his kimono, the Master of Sinanju made his face severe. "Congratulations, unclean one. You have selected a host I dare not kill."

"Begone, old man," said the voice that was Freya, but held an echo of age-old evil.

Chiun's eyes went to Remo, standing off to one side, dark eyes stunned, face wavering between conflicting emotions. He was seeing and not seeing at the same time.

Chiun addressed the avatar of Kali. "I cannot kill you, it is true. But that does not mean I cannot subdue you, or cast you out of the innocent host you control."

Freya stood up. Her four arms extended outward, like the hands of a mad clock. She was a young woman, Chiun saw. No longer a child but not quite a woman yet.

"Go while you still stand upright," she hissed.

Retreating a step, he intoned, "I go. But I take with me my son."

"Go, but leave my father, who I knew would come, but not so soon."

"I will not leave without Remo," Chiun insisted.

"You should ask my father if this pleases him or displeases him," Freya-Kali suggested, her eyes and lips as venomous as her words.

Chiun turned.

Remo still stood off in the shadows, his eyes mere glints in the hollows of his skull. His face was a thing that couldn't be read.

"My son. Speak to me...."

The words issued, wrapped in quiet pain. "Chiun. It's Freya."

"No. Not Freya who speaks to you. But the spirit of Kali."

"Bull!" Remo spit, snapping to anger. "I don't believe it. Not to Freya. Nobody does that to my daughter."

"Believe. For it is true."

Remo took two halting steps forward. He raised pleading, helpless hands while his eyes turned to avoid the four-armed thing that dominated the room.

"Chiun, I don't understand any of this. Help me."

"There is nothing I can do," the Master of Sinanju said sadly. "I cannot slay this thing with two souls, one innocent, one wicked. For to slay the wicked would bring death to the innocent. She is of your blood and still but a child. Therefore she is inviolate. We must retreat to a place of safety."

Remo made fists of stubbornness. "I'm not going anywhere. Not without my daughter."

And the voice of Freya-Kali intoned coldly. *"You will remain, flesh of my borrowed flesh. The other must go."*

Chiun regarded Remo without emotion. "Remo, you must make an exceedingly difficult choice. To come with me means safety. To remain is peril beyond anything you can imagine."

Remo's dark eyes flicked to the stunted, four-armed creature draped in yellow silks. "She won't hurt me. She's my daughter," he said.

"She is a thing with four arms and terrible lusts. In her mind you are the lover of her past. She seeks to mate with you. To dance the Tandava."

"I don't know what you're talking about," Remo said hotly.

"The Tandava is the dance that will end the universe and all who dwell in it. You. Me. And your hostage daughter."

"Crap. Look, stop trying to confuse me. I have to stay. I have to work this out."

"Remo..." Chiun began.

"You have your answer," Kali hissed through painted yellow lips. *"Now take your life to a safe place and forget all you have seen and heard. For while you dare not lay a hand on my innocent flesh, I can slay you with a glare."*

Chiun hesitated. Turning to Remo, he bowed once, very carefully. "I leave."

Remo hesitated. "Maybe that's the way to go," he said uncertainly. "Maybe we can work this out."

Chiun's voice skittered close to fear. "Do not

succumb to her charms, my son. Above all do not succumb to her charms.''

"For Christ's sake, Chiun. She's my daughter.''

"She is your enemy. And she has you in a thrall even I cannot break.'' And with those sad words, the Master of Sinanju walked backward out of the room, not turning his back on his foe, nor taking his eyes from her hypnotically waving arms.

Once in the corridor, he moved swiftly. Racing to the niche, he prepared himself as before and slipped back into the main chamber. It was easier this time. His silks did not snag.

No sooner had his sandals touched the black flooring than as if touched by magic, they cleared.

And below him the Master of Sinanju saw the reason for the constant purl and mutter of the waters below.

Eyes looked back up at him with dull, hungry expectation.

And as if touched by an invisible hammer, the suddenly transparent floor shattered like glass, and the Master of Sinanju was precipitated into the bitterest waters he ever knew....

43

Sandy Heckman was talking to the captain of the *Hareng Saur* with the assistance of her pocket French dictionary.

"Either you speak the worst, most mangled French imaginable or you aren't French-Canadian," she accused.

"Up yars" the captain said at last.

"A Newfie! You're a Newfie!"

"I have nathing to say," the captain said. "What has begun cannat be stapped naw."

"In that case consider yourself a prisoner of war."

"I cansider myself a hastage to environmental pharisees," the captain spat.

"Consider yourself that, too," said Sandy, who led the search of the ship.

On the upper decks they found what appeared to be a bustling factory ship busily converting fresh-caught fish into fillets and blocks designed to be frozen and made into fish sticks. Sandy remembered that the creation of the frozen-fish-stick market in the early fifties had begun the pillage of the North Atlantic of cod and haddock—a market Canadian companies had soon dominated.

When she reached the lower decks, she forgot all about fish sticks.

The door was marked Torpedo Room in English and French. Inside they found two types of torpedoes, explosive and the bullet-headed fish chasers. There were compressed-air tubes to blow them out and recover them again.

The torpedo crew looked at them with blank amazement, then surrendered sullenly at the point of M-16s.

The captain was dragged into the torpedo room and a choice of spilling his guts or being sent through the slime line where fish were gutted en masse on a conveyor belt.

He elected to spill the guts he could most afford to spill. "We call them Truffle Hounds, for the way they send the fish where we want them to go," he said, pointing to three torpedoes sitting in cradles.

"Is this a Quebec operation?" Sandy demanded.

"Da I sound like a damn frag to ya?"

"Not exactly," Sandy admitted. "Who gives you your orders?"

"The cammadare."

"You mean 'commodore'?"

"That is what I have said, cammadare," he said stiffly.

"Canadian navy?"

"Na. Fisheries Minister Gilbert Houghton, who is the bright lad who gathered up all us poor, out-of-work fisherman and gave us back our birthright, which is to fish. That is all we were doing, fishing."

"What about the sunken fishing boats and their lost crews?"

The captain looked as guilty as a lobsterman caught holding someone else's trap. "We were just fallawing arders in this little scrum."

"Scrum? Is that a fish?"

"Na, a scrum is what you call a set-to. We been scrumming with Yank fishermen since before Confederation."

"Well, you can tell it to a UN high commission, or whoever is going to hang your sorry behinds from a rusty yardarm."

"I request palitical asylum!"

"For what?"

"Are ya daft, woman? So I can get back to fishing as soon as passible. For I don't much care if I fish for pharisees or federals. Just so lang as I can fish. It's all I know."

"You fisherman won't be satisfied until you've landed the last pilchard in Paradise."

"Not even then," the captain of the *Hareng Saur* said solemnly.

44

The crystalline shattering sounds penetrated to the room where Remo stood looking with dull, questioning eyes at his daughter.

It had been a long time, almost ten years, Remo realized with a start. The little girl he knew so briefly had changed. Her baby fat was almost gone. Her brilliant eyes were the only link to the innocent face he remembered. But they held a different light now.

Then came the crashing. Remo turned. "What's that?" he asked worriedly.

"The old man has been thwarted. He is angry and is taking his anger out on my temple. It does not matter. He will break some things, then he will depart, never to trouble us again."

"You sure?"

"I am Mistress Kali."

"Jilda said she was Mistress Kali."

"I allowed her to think she was. For to manipulate my supplicants I needed a surrogate. I bent her to my will, made her think the thoughts I wished her to think and only those thoughts. She made an excellent domina, for in dominating, she had submitted her will to my own."

"She's dead," Remo said hollowly.

"She no longer matters, any more than a puppet

matters. Any more than our temporary, mortal flesh matters."

"She was your mother! What's wrong with you?"

"I have achieved the thing I have planned for these long years. Do you not remember, Remo, the last time we met?"

"Sure. It was in Sinanju. You were a little girl then."

"No, you fool! Do not address my host. Speak to Mistress Kali, who has yearned for you for aeons."

A hand reached up to touch Remo's face. Remo recoiled.

"Red One, remember me with your ageless soul, not with your mortal mind.... Separated, we have been drawn together again. Apart, we will rejoin. Two, we shall fuse into one...."

"Get away from me! I don't want to talk to you. I want to talk to Freya."

"I am she and she is me. We are one. Soon you will be one with Shiva, who is my consort...."

"I'm not Shiva."

"You do not remember the last time, in Arabia? We danced the Tandava but were thwarted. You slew my last host."

Remo frowned. His memories of that time were vague. He had put most of them out of his mind....

"I will not make the mistake I made then," Kali went on. *"We inhabit temples of mere meat and bone. It is time to step out of them. To step free into our true bodies...."'* Her yellow-nailed hands began to wave and gesture provocatively before his hurt eyes. *"When you possess four arms as do I, our lovemaking will be exquisite...."*

Her hands touched his chest and crept up to his throat. They felt cold. Alien. Inhuman.

In that moment Remo let out a bellow of fear and confusion.

And somewhere in that scream of pure pain, he heard the Master of Sinanju call out his name.

CHIUN, REIGNING MASTER of Sinanju, floated in warm water, his face a tight web of wrinkles.

About him the waters roiled.

The flat-headed body of Gilbert Houghton was the center of a boiling of tiny, voracious needle-toothed fish. They nipped and ripped at his dead flesh. In death his arms flopped with such abandon as to seem alive.

Nearby, in the pool that was fast turning pink and then scarlet with blood, the scheming Copt, Anwar Anwar-Sadat was likewise being denuded of all flesh.

Attacked from all sides, his separated head bobbed and rolled, the face turning ceilingward and back again in mad denial of its fate.

And as the feeding frenzy grew to a boil, the Master of Sinanju lifted his long-nailed fingers to spear and flay any and all of the meat-eating fish who dared approach.

But as many nails as he possessed, there were still more fish. And in the room of doom existed only walls and no floor.

Opening his bitter mouth, he called out his pupil's name.

REMO MOVED into reverse before the yellow talons found his throat.

A screech trailed after him as he went down the narrow corridor, a human blur, but he blocked it out.

Coming to the niche, he saw a vertical slice of

bubbling red water and saw the Master of Sinanju floating, surrounded by arrowing bone white fish like tiny attack dogs snapping at anything they could.

Without slowing, Remo hit the niche with raised fists. Brick shattered and tumbled.

Remo dived through the rubble and into the water as the reverberant thunder of collapsing stone and mortar filled the building. Only then did he remember the Master of Sinanju's warning of a keystone. By then it was too late.

"Hang on, Little Father!"

Striking the water cleanly, Remo came up with two fistfuls of squirming fish. He squeezed. The fish extruded their innards from both ends. Dropping them, he grabbed two more.

Immediately, living fish attacked the helpless dead.

Chiun switched tactics and followed suit.

Together they squeezed, impaled, kicked and stunned any fish that dared approach with bared needle teeth.

Hungry as they were, the fish got the message. The survivors concentrated on the bodies of Canadian Minister of Fisheries Gilbert Houghton and UN Secretary-General Anwar Anwar-Sadat, which fast became floating lengths of raw, red bone that continued to be pecked at even as the voracious fish nipped and stripped them of cartilage.

"Piranha," said Remo.

"I would not eat a fish that eats me," Chiun said dismissively.

Then, still treading water, they looked at the niche. It was a tumble of broken stones. Settling dust made a film on the agitated water.

"Freya…" Remo whispered. "Don't tell me I've killed you.…"

IT TOOK TWO HOURS but they carefully heaved stone and brick until they uncovered the brick chamber in which Freya, daughter of Remo, had reached out to work the will of Kali, goddess of death.

A motionless fall of golden hair spilled out from under a tumble of rock.

Remo froze.

Beside him Chiun said, "Kali's final trap, my son. Even in victory, she has handed you bitter defeat."

Remo reached down and heaved up a stone. It went tumbling away. He threw off another. The air was choked with disturbed mortar dust.

When he exposed the body of his daughter, he gently turned it over. Placing one ear to her heart, he listened, his eyes squeezed almost shut. The tears starting. The pain only beginning.

Yet he heard a beat.

Parting her mouth, he wiped off the ghastly yellow lipstick and blew in an urgent breath. The chest inflated, then fell. Remo blew another breath. He got the same result.

"You can't die on me," Remo said, his voice twisting and churning. "You can't. I won't let you."

"The spirit of Kali has abandoned her," Chiun intoned. "Accept that blessing and mourn."

"Like hell," Remo snarled. "I'm not giving up. I'm not giving up. Come on, baby. Breathe. I can hear your heart beating. Breathe for Daddy. Breathe and I'll take you away from all this. Open your eyes and I'll take you to a safe place where no one will ever harm you. I swear. I swear I will."

And in his arms, his daughter gave a sharp little

gasp. Dusty air was drawn into her open mouth and nostrils.

"Remo!" Chiun squeaked. "Look! She struggles. Her brave lungs crave air!"

"I see, I see," Remo said, bringing her pale face up to his.

Silently, grimly, he performed mouth-to-mouth resuscitation until he had breathed life back into the body of his only daughter. Her eyelids fluttered briefly, showing butterfly glimpses of the most beautiful eyes Remo had ever seen.

She murmured a soft "Daddy..."

"I'm here, baby."

Then she drifted off into recuperative sleep.

Without a word Remo Williams carried his Freya out of the building, over a path of broken stone where red bone floated and piranha darted for the last scraps of food.

He said nothing. Trailing after, the Master of Sinanju was a silent ghost.

The RCMP car still waited for them. Remo dragged the Mountie from the trunk and placed Freya in the back seat.

Then he went back in for the body of Jilda of Lakluun while the Master of Sinanju stood guard, removing it from its protecting shelf.

No word passed between them all the way to the airport. None needed to. Both knew their destination.

There was a little trouble getting the sleeping Freya onto the Air Canada flight. Eventually airport security ran out of functioning Mounties, and the plane was cleared to depart.

IN THE SONORAN DESERT near Yuma, Arizona, Sunny Joe Roam, Chief of the Sun On Jo tribe, raced to meet the flight carrying his son, Remo. He got a flat and was in the middle of changing it when a Jeep Cherokee came roaring up the dusty trail and screeched to a halt.

He wasn't surprised to see his son, Remo, and the Master of Sinanju in the front seat. He stood up, all seven feet of lanky, sunburned rawhide.

"Howdy," he said in his taciturn way.

"Hail, cousin of my blood," said Chiun.

"Sorry I couldn't meet you at the airport. You can see the reason why."

"Got a favor to ask," said Remo, stepping out.

"Last time you asked me to do you a favor, you dumped off your no-account son."

"How's he doing?" Remo asked.

"He can ride, rope and chase white girls, but so far he isn't fit for much else. Still hurting in his soul, I reckon."

Remo got out and opened the back door. Out came a girl with the sunniest hair Sunny Joe Roam had ever seen.

"Well, this is his little sister," said Remo.

Sunny Joe took off his Stetson and wiped his rugged brow of sweat and surprise.

"You're a regular Johnny Appleseed in your way, aren't you, Remo?"

"I need to hide her," Remo said anxiously.

"For how long?"

"Don't know."

Sunny Joe hesitated.

Chiun spoke up, his voice grave. "She has endured things best left unsaid."

Sunny Joe looked at the girl with the deep brown eyes and at Remo. "Tell you what," he said at last,

"I'm getting along in my years. You fix that flat for me and it's a deal."

They shook hands on it.

And while Remo changed the flat, Sunny Joe bent over his granddaughter. "What's your name, golden hair?"

She looked up at him with growing wonder. "Freya."

"What the heck kind of name is that?"

"Her mother named her," said Remo.

"Where is she?"

"Wrapped in a sheet in the trunk."

"Well, I guess we're about to have us a family reunion and a funeral all in one."

Turning to Chiun, Sunny Joe asked, "Should I be asking what all this is about?"

His eye going to Remo, busy at the tire, Chiun said quietly, "No. Do not ask. Do not ask ever."

THE BURIAL WAS SIMPLE. Words were spoken over a sandy grave in the shadow of Red Ghost Butte, and it was done. No marker was erected. No tears shed. There was too much shock for tears. Tears would come later. The sun went down on a profound silence of their souls, making the candelabra cactus cast long, streaky shadows of surrender.

After it was over, Remo went out into the red sandstone desert alone, and everyone understood they were not to follow.

THREE DAYS LATER, Remo returned, his face burned redder than Chiun had ever seen it.

Freya was letting her older brother, Winner, show her how to Indian-wrestle. Winner was burned red, and his hair was a paler, sun-faded version of Freya's golden locks. Otherwise they looked nothing alike.

"He's only half trying," Remo said to Chiun.

Chiun nodded.

A moment later Freya had Winner on his back and cursing the open sky.

Remo cracked a grin that was half amusement and half satisfaction. "I knew they'd get along."

"Only you, Remo Williams, would sire a son even a slip of a girl can best," Chiun sniffed.

"Maybe I had a daughter that just can't be beat. Looks to me like there's more Sun On Jo blood in her than him."

Chiun made a disapproving face, but his hazel eyes shone with veiled pride.

"Any sign of Kali while I was away?"

"No. The demon's spirit has found another vessel, from there to torment us another hour in a distant day."

"Been in touch with Smith?"

Chiun nodded. "The godless Canadians have sued for peace."

Remo looked away from the sight of Freya bending Winner's thumb out of joint. Winner howled. His ostrich-skin boot heels were beating the desert floor in agony.

"How'd that happen?"

"I informed Emperor Smith of the fates of the Copt and his fishmongering Canadian confederate. Smith informed the Eagle Throne, and the President shared this with the Lord of Canada. This was sufficient to chill Canadian lusts for war and fish. The seas are quiet once more now that good fishermen are not being hectored into greed."

"Good. I plan on staying here a little while and catching up on my kids."

"And I will dwell on my errors, which have wounded you deeply, my son," Chiun said dispiritedly.

"I buried the past out in the desert, Chiun. It's behind me. Forget about it. I loved Jilda a long time ago, but it wasn't supposed to be. Our lives didn't fit together. That's why she must have taken Freya to Canada. She thought it would be safer there and we'd probably never cross paths."

A warm desert breeze caught the wispy beard at the Master of Sinanju's chin. He nodded. "We will speak of this no more, then," he whispered.

And Remo went off to disentangle his children before one of them got his cocky bones bent into pretzels.